WAYNE STINNETT

RISING MOON

A JESSE MCDERMITT NOVEL

◆—◆—◆

Caribbean Adventure Series

Volume 19

2020

Copyright © 2020
Published by DOWN ISLAND PRESS, LLC, 2020
Beaufort, SC

Copyright © 2020 by Wayne Stinnett

Library of Congress cataloging-in-publication Data
    Stinnett, Wayne
    Rising Moon/Wayne Stinnett
    p. cm. - (A Jesse McDermitt novel)

ISBN: 978-1-7356231-0-8 (print)

Cover photograph by John P Rossignol
Graphics by Wicked Good Book Covers
Edited by The Write Touch
Final Proofreading by Donna Rich
Interior Design by Ampersand Book Designs

Dedicated to CeeCee James and Dawn Lee McKenna, two authors I greatly admire. Not just for their works, but for the endurance and fortitude they exhibit every day.

"I am not afraid of storms, for I am learning how to sail my ship."

–Louisa May Alcott

If you'd like to receive my newsletter, please sign up on my website:

WWW.WAYNESTINNETT.COM.

Every two weeks, I'll bring you insights into my private life and writing habits, with updates on what I'm working on, special deals I hear about, and new books by other authors that I'm reading.

The Charity Styles Caribbean Thriller Series

Merciless Charity
Ruthless Charity
Reckless Charity
Enduring Charity
Vigilant Charity

The Jesse McDermitt Caribbean Adventure Series

Fallen Out	*Rising Storm*
Fallen Palm	*Rising Fury*
Fallen Hunter	*Rising Force*
Fallen Pride	*Rising Charity*
Fallen Mangrove	*Rising Water*
Fallen King	*Rising Spirit*
Fallen Honor	*Rising Thunder*
Fallen Tide	*Rising Warrior*
Fallen Angel	*Rising Moon*
Fallen Hero	*Rising Tide*

THE GASPAR'S REVENGE SHIP'S STORE IS OPEN.

There, you can purchase all kinds of swag related to my books. You can find it at

WWW.GASPARS-REVENGE.COM

MAPS

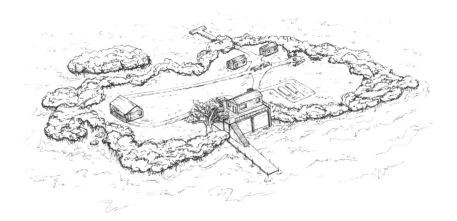

Jesse's Island

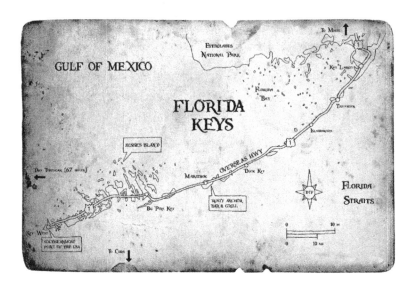

The Florida Keys

CHAPTER ONE

November 2020

The screen door slammed behind her as Cobie rushed down the steps of her mom's mobile home. She took them two at a time, then sprinted to her little car. She was almost late for work and needed to make a stop on the way there.

Her mother's trailer, like many others in the park, had seen better days. But it had weathered two big hurricanes in Cobie's lifetime, both passing close enough to the small island of Grassy Key to cause a lot of damage. Their trailer had survived, though, one of the few still remaining in the Florida Keys.

In 2005, Hurricane Wilma had passed fifty miles to the north. Cobie was just a toddler then. The storm was a Cat-3, spinning crazily out over the warm waters of the Gulf of Mexico. It pushed winds from the northwest and piled water up against the Gulf side of the low-lying key. Wind-driven waves had lapped at the trailer door and they'd lost their porch awning. But the trailer had held fast with a dozen hurricane straps attached to anchors her father had labored to drive into the limestone bedrock by hand.

The hurricane had come just five months before her daddy was killed in a car crash.

He was coming home late from a bar down on Big Pine Key, where he played on a pool team. Witnesses said he was driving fast and erratically, almost hitting another car head-on. He'd swerved and then overcorrected, hitting the barricade and flying over it into the ocean. They found his car days later, his body still inside. Everyone thought her father had been drunk, but Momma swore that he didn't drink. Later, the autopsy showed she was right. He'd had a heart attack, but the cause of death was drowning.

She remembered how scared she'd been during the storm, but little of the details of her father's accident. Momma hadn't shared that information with her until she was much older.

Three years ago, Hurricane Irma had made landfall just down island, on Cudjoe Key. It was a big one, a Category 4 storm, sending powerful winds and torrential rain through their neighborhood, which was thirty-five miles away. The trailer park itself was on the Gulf side of the Overseas Highway and the wind had been mostly from the south, so the park was slightly sheltered from the wind by the raised roadbed. The ocean side flooded, and some waves even crested the highway, flooding the park. The wind blew boats and cars around, some crashing into neighbors' trailers.

They hadn't evacuated for either storm. The first, because Daddy was a Conch and stubborn about such things. Momma would have taken them away before Irma, but they had nowhere to go and no money to get there.

"What time do you get off work?" Cobie's mom called from the door.

Donna Murphy was an attractive woman in her late thirties. She was lean and short in stature, like Cobie. They often wore each other's clothes. Her hair, also like Cobie's, was the color of wheat, streaked with lighter colors from the sun. Her face was beginning to show lines, mostly from worry about Cobie and their future. Hard times seemed to follow Donna like a dark cloud.

"Three," Cobie yelled back, as she yanked open the car's door. "A bunch of us are going to Cable Park after."

Cobie stepped back, dodging most of the heat that came boiling out of her car. Though it was only a few days until Thanksgiving, it was still ridiculously hot, and her blue car seemed to absorb it.

Cobie got in, leaned across the seat, and rolled down the passenger-side window before winding down her own. The old Fiesta lacked a lot of the things some of her friends' cars had, like electric windows and air conditioning, but it ran forever on ten dollars' of gas, didn't cost much to buy, and started. Most of the time.

A typical Keys car.

Her mom approached and leaned on the doorframe. She instantly jumped back, rubbing her forearm. "The park closes at sunset, Cobie."

"That'll give me almost three hours to try out my new board," Cobie responded. "You working today?"

"This afternoon, in the Gift Shop."

"Tell Manny and the gang I said hi," Cobie offered, turning the key with a silent prayer. The little blue car started. "I really gotta run, Mom. I'm late and I have to stop at Ty's and pick up my new board. He just texted me and said I could pick it up this afternoon." She bounced in her seat and clapped her hands. "But I can't wait to see it and try it out."

"Don't forget," Donna said, as Cobie shifted to reverse, "your Uncle Rob and Gina are arriving this evening. They should be here by eight o'clock."

How could she forget? Her mom had told her every day for two weeks that her uncle, a musician, was driving his RV down with his girlfriend for a few weeks and staying at a nearby campground through Thanksgiving weekend.

"I'll be home before then," Cobie said, backing out into the street.

She waved at her mom and drove off. Her job at Kmart was just a ten-minute drive and she had fifteen to get there. If Ty was home, she'd stop on the way. He'd texted her that her board was ready, so why wait till after work?

Cobie and her friends knew one another's schedules. There were only a handful of kids her age on Grassy

Key—most of her friends lived in Marathon, as did Ty. He was older and a little odd, but because he made wakeboards and surfboards, he was within her circle of friends.

Traffic was light when she turned south on Overseas Highway, toward town. She saw a friend riding the opposite way on the bike path and honked the anemic-sounding horn. Trish waved and Cobie waved back.

A few minutes later, she turned onto a street on the ocean side, made a quick right and then another left and saw Ty's van in his driveway. There was another car parked behind it, so she just pulled over under a gumbo limbo tree at the edge of an empty lot next door. She would only be there for a minute.

Ty had a little shop behind his house on the corner where he made custom boards; wakeboards mostly, but he also made kiteboards, even surfboards. You'd have to go way up the coast to surf, unless there was a storm out on the Gulf Stream. Whatever kind of board anyone wanted, Ty was the guy.

Cobie didn't recognize the Nissan parked behind Ty's old VW van, but it was new and not from the area. Having grown up on Grassy Key, she knew every car on the island and could always spot a friend in a long line of tourists' cars. The black GT-R sportscar with dark windows stuck out. But Cobie knew that people came from all up and down the Keys to get one of Ty's boards, so a strange car didn't seem unusual to her.

Ty was rarely in his house, except to eat or sleep. His shop was air-conditioned and he had plenty of work to keep him out there from sunrise to well past sunset. He had a stereo system in his shop, as well as a refrigerator. Though she and most of her friends were still in high school, Ty allowed them to sneak a beer from the fridge once in a while. He was older, almost thirty. He even smoked weed with one or two, but Cobie never tried it or the beer.

Knowing he was most likely in the shop, Cobie went around the side of the house, following the well-worn path. As she approached the shop's door, she could hear the voices of Ty and another man coming from inside, but not what they were saying.

Without knocking, she turned the knob and walked in. Ty and the other man looked up from Ty's small desk. Cobie didn't recognize him.

On the desk was the digital scale Ty used to mix epoxies, resins, and powders. A pile of blueish-white powder sat on the scale.

"Hey, Ty," Cobie said, smiling brightly. She closed the door behind her. "Making a new resin or something?"

"I thought I told you to lock the door," the other guy said, rising from his seat at Ty's desk.

"It's okay," Ty said, also rising. "She's cool."

The stranger went past Cobie, staring at her body, and locked the door. He was medium height, dressed too nice for the Keys, and had dark eyes and black hair, slicked back.

"Cool?" the man said, looking her over again. "I'd say hot."

Cobie ignored him and turned to Ty. "What's going on?"

"You picked a bad time for a visit," the man said. He moved in front of her, letting his eyes roam once more, stopping for a moment at the square neckline of her tank top.

Cobie was used to boys looking at her chest. But they mostly just stole a glance, or a stealthy peek. This guy gave her the creeps, staring at her boobs.

"What's your name?" the man asked, removing her sunglasses, and tossing them on a table.

"Hey!" she exclaimed. "Those were expensive."

A corner of his mouth went up, not a smile or a grin, but more of a sneer. If he drove the high-priced sports-car out front, Cobie was sure he could easily afford to replace the sunglasses.

"I asked your name."

Cobie looked from him to Ty, who now wore a worried expression.

"Cobie Murphy," she replied, then looked back at her friend. "What's going on here, Ty? Is my board ready?"

"You shouldn't have come till this afternoon," was his only reply.

The stranger grabbed her wrist and jerked her toward a chair, pushing her down onto it. Before she could protest, he grabbed a piece of rope from Ty's workbench and pulled her arms tightly behind her back.

Cobie screamed.

"Cover her mouth!" the stranger ordered Ty, as he tightened the knots on her wrists.

Cobie screamed again and the guy hit her. The punch to the back of her head made her groggy.

"You don't have to do this," Ty said. "She won't—"

"Shut up," the stranger growled. "Since you don't have money, I'll take this as payment. She can work off your debt for my supplier."

Ty reluctantly took a roll of tape from a shelf and tore off a strip. The guy behind her pulled Cobie's head up by her hair and held her in place with one hand under her chin.

Cobie's eyes were having a hard time focusing. Then she saw Ty coming toward her with the tape.

"No, Ty," she squealed, struggling in the other man's grasp.

In Ty's eyes, she could see pity, as if he truly were sorry that she'd chosen to come early to pick up her board. But she also saw a little of what was most prominent in the other man's eyes—lust.

The tape went over her mouth, and Ty mashed it in place. Cobie squirmed on the chair, but the man held her firmly as she began to cry.

The stranger let her go and started rummaging through the different cans and bottles of epoxies and solvents on the shelf.

Cobie started to stand; to try to make a run for the door, but the man wheeled and hit her in the stomach with his fist. She doubled over, unable to breathe, then he pushed her back onto the chair.

"Top shelf," Ty said. "The brown bottle."

The man grabbed the bottle and a towel. He poured some of the contents onto the towel and squeezed it in his fist a few times.

Cobie started to struggle again as the man put the chloroform-soaked cloth over her face.

The last thing Cobie heard, before passing out, was the man telling Ty to get rid of her car.

CHAPTER TWO

December 2020

I t looked kinda weird to me—out of place. I cocked my head, staring at it, then took a sip of Costa Rica's finest from a chipped Force Recon mug and studied it some more.

Definitely out of place.

There'd never been a Christmas tree in this house. In fact, I hadn't had one since my first wife left me.

I'd been deployed the day after we put the tree up in our living room in base housing. We'd spent all evening decorating it with our daughter Eve's help. When my FAST team received orders the next morning, we didn't have time or permission to make even a quick phone call. It was my third combat deployment in six years— the fourth deployment overall, because I did a two-year billet as a drill instructor at Parris Island during that time, and Sandy and I rarely saw one another.

Eve turned six just a few days after Sandy left on Christmas day, and Kim was just a baby then. I returned from Panama to find an empty house, save for a dried-up brown tree, lying on the floor in the living room.

A single ornament had lain in pieces beside it. I remember recognizing the remnants of that blue and red glass ball from Sandy's and my first Christmas together. It'd been a gift from the company gunny, Owen "Tank" Tankersley. The significance hadn't been lost on me then.

Sandy blamed the Corps for our failed marriage.

"Do you like it?" Savannah asked, turning, and smiling brightly.

"Yeah," I replied, deep-sixing my thoughts, and smiling back. "Looks real...Christmassy."

She came closer to me and slipped her arms around my waist. I stared down into twin azure pools, clear and bright—deep enough to dive into. I often thought it was Savannah's eyes that had first attracted me to her so long ago.

"When was the last time you had a Christmas tree in this house?"

"Well...this one's the first."

She frowned. "When was the last time you put up a tree anywhere?"

I kissed her forehead. "Kim was in diapers."

Her eyes widened. "Now, Jesse, she's thirty-one. You mean to tell me that you haven't had a Christmas tree in all those years?"

12

"Not until today," I replied, taking another sip from my mug. "Unless you count the fake ones the clerks put up in HQ, when I was still in the Corps."

"That's a crying shame," she said, turning back to the tree with another ornament in hand. "Do you at least have something personal to decorate it with?"

My mind returned to the broken blue and red ball. It'd had the Marine Corps emblem on it with my and Sandy's names around the top and the date, October 23, 1983 around the bottom. That was the day terrorists killed 220 of my fellow Marines in Beirut, along with twenty-one others.

Tank, then a gunnery sergeant, had given one of the ornaments to each of his NCOs in tribute to those who would not see Christmas that year, or ever again. The fact that the ball had been broken, but all the pieces lay in one tiny area on the floor several feet away from the tree, had told me that Sandy had placed it there and stepped on it.

She and I had been married less than a month when I was deployed to Lebanon for the second time that year. Our wedding was rushed, in the middle of our scheduled rotation, because Eve was on her way. It was on that second deployment to Beirut when the bombing occurred.

I made it home that Christmas and for the birth of our first child. But part of me, even to this day, had been left behind in the rubble of the Marine barracks.

On what would have been our seventh Christmas together, Sandy left, taking our girls, Eve and Kim.

I was in a jungle in Panama.

"No," I replied, snapping the memory from my mind. "I'm afraid I don't have any decorations for it. But I think there's still time to order one."

Savannah turned and smiled. "Order one? Who in the world orders just one Christmas tree ornament three days before Christmas?" She cocked her head a moment, looking at me curiously. "Wait, forget I asked that. You. That's who." I grinned at her and she turned back to the tree. "But I doubt you could get it in time."

"We'll see about that," I replied, pulling my phone out. "Gotta make a call."

Out of habit, I stepped outside to the corner of the deck. It used to be the only place on the island where you might get one bar of signal strength. And that was only if you held your tongue in your cheek in exactly the right position. With the new cell tower on Big Pine, though, we could now get a signal anywhere on my island.

I pulled up the number and stabbed the *Call* button.

"Master Guns," I said, when Tank answered. "You're still coming down, right?"

I'd talked to him just a few months earlier. Tank called me every October 23rd without fail. He probably called all his NCOs that were there.

During that last call, he'd expressed a desire to visit the Keys and I'd told him to come down any time he liked. When Savannah overheard that he wasn't planning anything for Christmas—she had been listening to my end of the conversation while we watched the sun go down—she insisted that we invite him to spend it with us on the island.

Tank had served in the Corps longer than just about anyone. He'd enlisted during Vietnam at the age of seventeen and was finally forced by an act of Congress to retire two years ago. He'd served fifty-one years.

"Lookin' forward to it, Gunny," he boomed back.

After five decades in the Corps, Tank didn't usually speak or talk. He boomed and roared.

"You got no idea how much it made my day when you invited me. But didn't we just confirm this a couple of days ago?"

"I know." I felt foolish for asking what I was about to ask. "Do you remember the Christmas of '83?"

He didn't respond right away but when he did, his voice was much more subdued. "That's one I can never forget, Jesse. Why?"

"You had Christmas tree ornaments made for a bunch of the company non-coms. I remember you got a lot more of them than we had NCOs."

"I was a dumbass gunny then," he said with a chuckle. "Ordered them off the wrong roster and still had to get a dozen more than I thought I needed. They only sold them in boxes of twenty."

I remember how devastated he'd felt ordering Christmas ornaments for some of the guys who didn't come back. The fact that he had to buy even more than that at least made my question a little easier.

I wouldn't be asking for a dead man's ornament.

"Do you still have them?"

"I do," he said solemnly. "I hang a different one every year. But you probably mean the extras that didn't have names on them, right?"

"Yes. I don't suppose you hung onto those too, did you?"

"I did." He paused a moment, then said, "Been wondering when you'd want a new one. They've got the date on 'em, but no name. I know a guy here in Jacksonville. If you want, I'll have your name on it when I bring it."

"Yeah," I said, looking back through the door. "That'd be nice, Tank. Just put Jesse and Savannah on it—double November and ends with Alpha Hotel."

"Got it. Will do," he said. "Oh, and one thing."

"What's that, Tank?"

"It's taken you a while to get another one, son. Don't break it like you did the first."

I chuckled and we ended the call.

Tank had gone with me when I went home that day to find my family gone and my house empty. A moving van does not escape scrutiny in base housing communities, so word spread quickly among the wives and other Marines in the neighborhood.

But Tank was one of only three people deployed with us who knew that Sandy had left me. Just before we took off from Panama, the battalion CO, back at Lejeune, had informed our company CO, who in turn told the sergeant major. I was on the list for gunny at the time, and the sergeant major and Tank didn't tell *me* she was gone until we were wheels down at Cherry Point.

When I looked back into the house, Savannah had her back to me. She was wearing shorts and a lightweight, blue, sleeveless blouse. Stretching high on bare feet to reach the top of the tree, she extended one leg behind her for balance, like a ballet dancer. Her blouse rode up, showing a smooth, tanned, lower back—the muscles along her spine as tight as any ballerina's.

I had a sudden realization—Tank hadn't been talking about the glass ornament when he warned me not to break the new one. He was talking about my upcoming marriage.

"Who were you talking to?" Savannah asked as I came back in.

When I first met her, she'd been on the verge of kicking my ass up one side and down the other for scaring her sister, Charlotte. I'd warned her sister about sex slavers abducting a woman and her two teenage daughters just a few weeks before that. Charlotte had thought I was making it up. I remembered that Savannah had called me *bud* then, and it wasn't meant in a nice way.

But by that time, it was already too late. Her long, tanned legs, blond hair kissed by the sun, and those big blue eyes had already worked their magic on me.

It seemed like yesterday. She was twenty-nine then, visiting the Keys with her sister after breaking up with her husband, still full of youth and raw energy. The last two decades had done little to diminish either of those traits. She was easily the most beautiful and passionate woman I'd ever known.

"That was Tank," I replied. "Leave a spot in the middle for me, okay?"

"The middle of the tree?"

"Yeah," I replied. "Special delivery memorial Christmas tree ornament from Tank Tankersley."

"I'm looking forward to finally meeting him," she said. "You talk about him so. How long did you say he served?"

"Fifty-one years—from LBJ to the Donald."

Her head tilted up as she counted on her fingers. "That's ten presidents! Why so long?"

That was a good question. After Sandy left me, the Corps filled the gap as my family. I was promoted to gunnery sergeant six months later and threw everything I had into my job. Not long after, I was deployed as part of the Marine Security Detachment aboard the *USS Independence*, last of the conventionally powered supercarriers. All of the larger naval warships had a contingent of Marines aboard for security. The other Marines in the MSD had been together a while. I was the new guy, but I wasn't going to be with them long. I had a lot to keep me occupied as the *Independence* was deployed to the Persian Gulf during the runup of Desert

Shield. I would spend the next four months mostly on my own in the desert.

A couple of years later, I tried marriage again, a bartender named Kristina Butcher, who was four years older than me. That had been a huge mistake, which I quickly corrected. A month after divorcing Kristina, I'd found myself in the Mog. Somalia was a nightmare, but I remember thinking it a reprieve. I'd married one other time, but Alex had been murdered on our wedding night by arms smugglers.

Not the greatest track record, I know.

I guess the emptiness had been the same for Tank after he and his wife divorced. From the age of seventeen, the Corps had been his only family until he met Jolene. Their marriage didn't last as long as my first one. I figured he had done what I had—adopted the Corps as his only family. But he'd just never moved on from there.

And the Corps was in no hurry to see him leave. Having the Medal of Honor around his neck meant Tank had a home forever. Or so he thought. Having an MOH recipient on active duty was good PR for recruiters. But even Chesty Puller couldn't stop the march of time.

"I guess he just never had any reason to leave," I said. "U.S. Code says you can't serve beyond the end of the month of your sixty-eighth birthday. Otherwise, he'd probably still be in the Corps."

"I'd think after that long, he'd have a hard time re-adjusting."

I nodded. "Not really readjusting. He probably doesn't remember much about his life before the Corps. I'm sure it was tougher than most."

"There," she said, stepping back. "It's not my best. The trees we put up on *Sea Biscuit* were smaller, so I don't have as many decorations as I'd like to have for such a big tree."

She turned and hugged me. "Thanks for getting it for me."

She'd chosen the spot in front of the big double window that faces south; the direction someone would come, if someone were inclined to visit. I'd never had many visitors to my island, but over the last few months, we'd had quite a few friends stop by. I had to admit, the new drapes, pulled back with a sash, went equally well with the rough-hewn interior wall boards and the tree.

"We can hit the Kmart if you want," I offered. "Pick up some more ornaments."

"They're probably all picked over," she said, turning back to the tree and moving one ornament to a different spot on the same branch. "I bet they don't have anything left but those tacky elf-on-a-shelf ornaments."

"Oh, no," I said, clutching at a strand of imaginary pearls around my neck. "Not *those* hideous things."

She turned and put her hands on her hips, staring at me. "So, are you going to tell me what this memorial ornament is?"

My grin disappeared. "Tank was the company gunny when I was in Beirut in '83. I was one of his squad leaders. That first Christmas after the bombing, he had some glass balls custom made for all the NCOs, commemorating the date of the attack."

"I remember you telling me how hard he took that."

"We all did," I said. "I was lucky, I guess. My squad was on mounted patrol that morning, miles from the barracks."

I turned toward the sound of a dozen feet coming up the back steps, eight of them with claws.

Finn came through the open door first, followed by Woden, then Jimmy and Florence. The dogs proceeded to their rug in the middle of the room and sat, looking at the tree.

I pointed at each dog in turn. "There will be no drinking of the tree water. No peeing on any tree inside the house. And no roughhousing around it. Do I make myself clear?"

They both looked at the tree, then at Savannah, and finally back at me before lying down with their big heads on their equally big paws.

"It looks beautiful, Mom," Florence said.

Our daughter was home for two weeks from UF and was staying in Kim and Marty's little house on the north side of the island. They weren't there very often; both being sworn officers with Florida Fish and Wildlife. They worked out of Everglades City on the southwest coast.

Jimmy looked around the room. "You've sure done a lot for the old place, Savannah."

"Hey," I said, indignantly, "I did most of the work."

"Thank you, Jimmy," Savannah said, then turned and kissed me on the cheek. "And you worked very hard on it, Jesse."

Florence helped herself to the coffee pot. "It's bigger than we ever had on *Sea Biscuit.*"

"Go big or go home," Jimmy said. "That's what Jesse told me when we were picking it out."

Savannah had subtly hinted at wanting a tree for a week and I'd pretended not to pick up on it. Then I'd surprised her with a nine-footer strapped to the Grady's Bimini top.

"I remember when I was a kid, my dad said that a Christmas tree should be as tall as the room," I offered in defense.

My phone chirped and vibrated in my pocket. When I looked at it, I didn't recognize the number, but it was local.

"McDermitt," I said, after stabbing the *Accept* button.

"Hi, Jesse," a man's voice said. "You might not remember me—we met at the Rusty Anchor a few years back. This is Manny Martinez."

"I remember," I said. "The Grassy Key Resort guy, right?"

"Yeah. Look, I know you're probably busy with Christmas right around the corner, but I was wondering if I could meet with you? Maybe over lunch or something?"

"What's this about?" I asked, heading to the table next to my recliner, where there was a notepad and pencil.

"Did you hear about the girl that went missing just before Thanksgiving?"

"Yes, I did. I haven't heard much recently, though."

"Her name's Cobie Murphy," Manny said.

I scrawled the name on the pad.

"Her mother works at the resort," he continued. "Her name's Donna and you're right, there hasn't been any movement on her case since about a week after she disappeared. A search was conducted by volunteers over the long weekend, but the only thing that was turned up was her car, abandoned at the Kmart where she worked. The cops are convinced she just took off, like so many do. Donna and I are convinced that's not what happened. She thinks Cobie's still alive, but even if she's not, there's just no closure."

He was right. It happened a lot in the Keys, it seemed. Paradise to an adult is boring to a teenager and sometimes they ran off for the bright lights and action of cities like Miami or LA.

Marathon, like most of the small towns up and down the Keys, didn't have its own police force. That was left to the Monroe County Sheriff's Office, which was stretched thin. The county included much of southwest Florida, from Everglades City south and a good portion of the Glades itself, not to mention all of the Keys.

"And you want me to look into it?" I asked.

"I figured with your background in Homeland Security and owning a security business up island…"

"Hang on a sec," I said, and turned to Jimmy. "Do we have any charters coming up?"

"No, man," Jimmy replied. "Nothing till after the first of the year. But remember? You're dropping me off at the Anchor tomorrow, so I can stay with Naomi for Christmas. And you're supposed to pick your friend up at the airport early in the afternoon."

I put the phone back to my ear. "How about lunch at the Rusty Anchor tomorrow, Manny? Say, about eleven hundred? I have to pick up an old friend at the airport at twelve-thirty."

He agreed and we ended the call.

"What was that all about?" Savannah asked.

"That was Manny Martinez," I said. "The owner of Grassy Key Resort. Remember that girl that disappeared a month ago?"

"I saw her a couple days before it happened," Florence said. "I'd met her at a friend's birthday party over the summer and ran into her again the week I was home for Thanksgiving. From what I've heard, the police seem to think she ran away. I didn't get to know her all that well, we just talked a little, but she didn't seem like the type to me."

"They never do," I said. "Until they actually do it. Anyway, her mother works for Manny and he asked me to look into it."

"It was like five weeks ago," Jimmy said, looking down and shaking his head. "I, and most of the guides, helped with the search. But you know what they say when someone's been gone more than forty-eight hours, man."

I did. The first day was search and rescue. The second day was searching beyond hope.

After that, it was a body recovery operation.

CHAPTER THREE

At 1045 the following morning, Jimmy and I idled up the canal in my old Grady-White center console. Passing between my sailboat and Savannah's trawler, I looked to the right. *Island Hopper's* red wings and fuselage gleamed in the late morning sun at the top of the boat ramp. It'd been a couple of weeks since she'd stretched those wings. I made a mental note to take Tank up and show him around.

Coming back to the Rusty Anchor always felt a little bit like I was returning home. Sure, there had been a few physical changes—the canal was dredged, sea walls and docks rebuilt, and the bar was renovated after Hurricane Irma. But the feel of the place was the same as it was when Rusty had first brought me there, a week after we returned from Okinawa.

Rusty and I had met on a Greyhound bus on our way to boot camp. We'd been in the same platoon at Parris Island, then served together for most of three years after graduating. By then, he and I were closer than brothers.

We'd had two weeks leave after Oki, and we'd both stayed at Mam and Pap's house in Fort Myers for a week, paddling and fishing the Ten Thousand Islands. Then we'd driven on down to the Keys in Rusty's Camaro to spend another week with his parents in Marathon. We'd spent our days free diving and spearfishing. And spent a couple of nights down in Key West, hitting on tourist girls.

"You're not gonna tie up under *Salty Dog's* bowsprit?" Jimmy asked.

"Less distance for Tank to walk," I said.

"He have trouble getting around, man?"

"Not sure," I replied. "I haven't seen him in a long time. But he's likely to have some luggage."

"How long's he staying?" Jimmy asked, as we neared the turning basin at the end of the canal and he made ready to step over to Rusty's big barge.

I brought the Grady alongside and reversed the engine, spinning the wheel to bring the stern closer. "Through New Year's Day," I said. "But I told him to get an open-ended ticket, in case we get rolling on tuna."

As we bumped the barge's fenders, Jimmy stepped over with the bow line in hand and I killed the engine. "If he's up to it," he said, "maybe he'd like to ride along for the tournament up in Palm Beach the week after that."

"I mentioned it to him," I replied, looping the stern line around a deck cleat on the barge. "We'll see. You staying with Naomi tonight?"

He grinned up at me as he knelt and tied off the bow line. "You won't see me again until at least Friday, man."

Together, we walked toward the bar. Even though it was still an hour before noon, there were a good half-dozen vehicles in the parking lot, most of them familiar to me. But I noticed an expensive-looking black sports-car with dark-tinted windows that I didn't recognize. It looked very out of place among the pickups and Keys cars—inexpensive beaters, commonly driven by locals.

"Catch you later," Jimmy said, turning toward the lot.

"Call me if you need me to pick you up," I offered. "I think Savannah's planning a run into town tomorrow and we'll be here for Rusty's Christmas party."

"I will," he said. "But we can take Rusty's old boat if we need to."

I waved and turned, opening the door to the dimly lit interior of the Rusty Anchor Bar and Grill, then removed my sunglasses and looked around.

Though there were windows all along the side facing the canal, they were covered with louvered hurricane shutters to block the sun and still allow a breeze to pass through. Not that it mattered anymore—Rusty had installed central air a while back.

"Hey, Jesse," Amy Huggins said from behind the bar.

"Hey, right back," I said. "Is Rusty around?"

"He just stepped out to the walk-in for a case of beer," she replied. "Coffee?"

"Yeah, thanks."

29

I moved to my usual spot at the far end of the bar, surveying the room again and nodding at a few people I knew. They were mostly fishing guides waiting on afternoon clients.

The only person I didn't recognize looked like a fisherman and he was sitting with one of the guides. Maybe he drove the flashy sportscar out front.

"Here you go," Amy said, sliding a mug in front of me. "How's Flo like the Jeep?"

Amy was in her late thirties. She and her late husband had built a house on No Name Key, where she now lived alone with their son. Dan Huggins had been killed in Ecuador. Just before the start of the school year, she sold me her Jeep Wrangler to give to Florence.

"She loves it," I said. "And it's perfect for getting her back home and to the beach."

"Are y'all ready for Christmas?"

I shrugged. Getting ready for Christmas had never been a real high priority since Sandy and the girls left. "I suppose. Savannah says we need more decorations for the tree."

Voices outside drew my attention—an argument.

Then I heard the door of the walk-in cooler slam shut out behind the bar. I was already on my feet when I saw Rusty through the window. His heavy footfalls on the deck resonated immediacy.

"What the hell's going on here?" he shouted.

I moved quickly toward the back door, as did a couple of the unoccupied guides. That's just the way things worked. Mess with a local and five more would stand up.

Pushing the door open, I saw Rusty confronting two men. One was a guy I'd seen around town a few times, usually drunk or high on something. The other man looked Latino, with dark skin and black hair, slicked back.

"Get lost, Boomer," the Hispanic man said to Rusty. "You don't want none of this."

"This is my place," Rusty growled. "I ain't having no drug selling here."

The other guy took off, running toward the dinghy dock, leaving his friend to face Rusty's wrath.

I moved quickly across the deck and stepped down to the grass just as the man pulled a switchblade knife from his pocket, flicking it open with an ugly sound.

"You want some of me, old man?" he asked, a malevolent light dancing in his dark eyes.

As fast as the knife had appeared in the man's hand, a Beretta 9mm appeared in Rusty's. I drew my Sig and leveled it at the man as I strode toward them.

"The real question is," Rusty said, grinning at the man, "what kind of *cabrón* would bring a knife to a gunfight?"

"Drop the knife," I said, coming up beside my friend. "Do it now and nobody gets hurt."

His fierce eyes cut from Rusty to me and back again. He had only one chance of getting out of this situation unhurt and he knew it. He dropped the switchblade like it was a hot coal.

"Leave and don't ever come back," Rusty said. "If I ever see you again, I won't even ask if you got a new *cuchillo*. I'll just shoot you dead and dump your body in the Gulf Stream. Nobody worth a shit will miss you. *Comprendo?*"

He glared at Rusty for a moment. "Oh, you will see me again. Of that, you can be sure."

Without another word, the man turned and headed toward the parking lot.

"Who was that?" I asked, sliding my Sig back into its holster at my back.

"I don't know," Rusty replied. "I've seen him around a few times and suspected he was a dealer. But this time I caught him in the act."

I turned toward the sound of a high-performance engine roaring to life in the parking lot. The black Nissan sportscar I'd seen there earlier roared out of the lot, spraying gravel.

"How do these people even find your place?" I asked rhetorically.

Out by the highway, Rusty didn't have a sign or anything indicating there was a restaurant and bar. Just an old mailbox, leaning slightly. You couldn't see the place from the highway, just the crushed shell driveway disappearing into the overhanging tropical foliage. It looked like one of thousands of private driveways.

"The price of advertising, I guess," Rusty said. "Sid does a great job of filling the place up, but a lot of them are tourists and…that type. You come to town to pick up Tank?"

"Yeah," I replied, as we reentered the bar. "His plane lands at twelve forty-five. But I'm meeting Manny Martinez here for lunch."

"Speak of the devil," Rusty said, as Manny and a woman I'd seen around stepped through the front door. "Y'all grab a seat anywhere. Amy'll get your order. I gotta get back to stocking the bar."

I motioned Manny toward a corner table.

"We saw what happened out back," he said, as he and the woman sat down. "What was that all about?"

"Somebody selling drugs," I replied. "Rusty doesn't much care for that going on in his place."

"Thanks for seeing us, Jesse."

"Manny said you were the right guy," the woman offered. "I'm Donna Murphy, Mister McDermitt."

"Just call me Jesse," I said, as Amy arrived with menus.

"I'll have whatever's fresh, please," I told her. "Rufus knows how I like it. And a glass of ice water."

Donna Murphy nodded, not even looking at the menu. "Same for me."

"Me, too," Manny added.

"Three blackened hogfish sandwiches coming up," Amy said, gathering the menus, then heading out the back door to the outdoor kitchen.

"You're Cobie's mom?" I asked Donna, though I already knew.

"Yes," she replied.

"I'm sorry about what happened."

She nodded, fidgeting somewhat.

"Is there something wrong?" I asked. "I mean aside from the obvious."

"I'll be straight with you," she said.

"I appreciate people who are."

Amy returned with a pitcher of water and three glasses, leaving them on the table.

"Cobie and I live in a trailer near the resort. We don't have much, and I don't know how I can afford to hire a private detective."

"First off," I said, "I'm not a PI. I'm part-owner in a security firm up in Key Largo and I own a charter business. Secondly, if there's some way I can help, I will. I don't need your money."

"That's what Manny told me you'd say."

"So, tell me what happened," I said. "I'm afraid I only know what's been reported on the radio. I don't have a TV."

"It was the Friday before Thanksgiving," she said. "Cobie had to work at the Kmart that morning. She was supposed to start at nine and left the house about a quarter till. She was planning to stop on the way and pick up a new custom board, then go to Cable Park after work."

"Custom board?"

"A wakeboard," she explained. "They usually ride them towed behind a boat, but the park has towers with cables that pull you from end to end."

"She never made it to work?" I asked.

"Her car was found there," Donna said. "But her co-workers never saw her go inside."

"And the police didn't find anything in the car? Prints or something?"

"No," she replied, her eyes beginning to well up a little. "The cops think she met someone there and left with them."

"What about the store she bought the board from?"

"It wasn't a store," she replied. "A friend of hers, who lives near the airport. He makes custom boards and stuff. His name's Ty Sampson."

"And the police talked to him?"

"Yes," Donna replied, wiping the corners of her eyes with a tissue from her purse. "Sorry. He told them that he'd texted her that morning, telling her she could pick the board up in the afternoon and he didn't get home until two."

"So, why do you think she went there before work?"

"She said she was going to. Just before she left the house."

"The police cleared the guy?" I asked.

"Yeah. He showed them his phone and the texts between him and Cobie. They said he had an alibi. He was in Miami picking up fiberglass."

"In Miami?" I asked. "Seems odd with all the fiberglass shops around here."

"The cops asked him that, too," she said. "He told them he gets it cheaper from a place up there. Cheap enough to warrant the drive."

"Did the police check Kmart's security cameras?"

"Where her car was parked wasn't on the footage," Manny said. "They require employees to park way out by the highway."

"And there's been no sign of her since? No calls or texts, or Facebook posts or Twitter?"

"No calls or texts," she replied. "She doesn't use Facebook or Twitter. They use Snapchat these days. But no, there's been no trace of her anywhere since she disappeared. When I called her that afternoon—my brother and his girlfriend were coming in that night—my call went straight to voicemail."

"And there's been no activity on her phone since? What about credit cards or debit cards?"

"No, nothing."

Almost five weeks ago, I thought. Most cops would tell you that the odds were that the girl was dead.

Donna must have read it in my expression. "She's not dead. I'd know—a mother would know, right?"

I glanced over at Manny. He'd mentioned needing "closure" on the phone. I couldn't read anything in his eyes, but I got the feeling that he wanted me to find Cobie's body or find out what happened to it, so Donna could accept the fact.

"Do you have the name of the investigating officer?" I asked.

"Detective Andersen," she said. "Clark Andersen."

"That's spelled with an E, not an O," Manny offered.

"Do you have a recent picture of Cobie?" I asked.

Donna opened her purse and took out a snapshot. "I printed a bunch of these from a picture I took of her last month, when she bought her first car." She handed it to me. "The car isn't much, but she loved it and was proud that she'd saved up and paid for it herself."

I looked at the photo. It showed a pretty, blond-haired teen standing beside a blue Ford Fiesta, smiling proudly. She wore cutoff jeans and a tank top. The car was small and the top of her head barely cleared the roof.

"Pretty girl," I said. "How tall is she?"

"Five-two," Donna replied. "And just over a hundred pounds."

"This is a hard question to ask," I said. "But has she ever been gone without your knowledge before?"

Donna shook her head. "No. Cobie's a good kid, Jesse. And I'm not saying that because she's mine. She's athletic and considers drugs and alcohol to be poison to her body. She even does volunteer work at the turtle hospital."

I glanced at Manny, who nodded agreement. "I've known Cobie since she was a baby, Jesse. She wouldn't go off without telling Donna. Zero chance of that."

"I've met Detective Andersen a couple of times," I said, putting the photo in my shirt pocket. "First thing I'm going to do is go over the Kmart video myself. Then I want to pay a visit to this Ty character and get a feel for him."

Donna told me where the guy lived and how to get to there. It was only a couple of miles away.

"After that," I said, thinking out loud, "I'll dig through all of Andersen's notes and photographs and see if there's anything there he didn't tell you about."

Donna's eyes signaled bewilderment. "What would he not tell me?"

"I doubt he'd withhold anything," I replied. "But another set of eyes might see something he missed."

"I asked him for the case file," Donna said. "He wouldn't show me."

"Oh, I don't intend on *asking* to see anything," I said with a grin.

"Then how—" Donna started to say, as Rufus arrived with a big tray.

"Cap'n Jesse," he said, with a big toothy grin. "I and I were just thinkin' 'bout yuh dis mornin'."

"Good thoughts, I hope."

"Aye, mon," Rufus said, passing plates around the table.

His eyes fell on Donna and he frowned. "Do not fret, Miss Donna. Little Cobie will return. Cap'n Jesse see to dat."

CHAPTER FOUR

After lunch and more questions, I went out to the parking lot with Manny and Donna to say goodbye.

"How did that waiter know my name?" Donna asked.

I turned to her. "You've never met Rufus before?"

"I'd remember if I had," she replied.

"He's Rusty's chef," I told her. "He's lived here for twenty years but doesn't go much of anywhere. I don't even think he has a car."

"He brings fish by the resort every week," Manny said, opening the passenger door to his car. "Maybe that's how he knows you."

"I've never met him. And how does he know Cobie?"

"Rufus is an odd sort," I said. "He stays to himself for the most part and often speaks in riddles."

Secretly, I wished he hadn't said anything to Donna about her daughter. I couldn't guarantee her I'd find the girl. Not after five weeks.

Donna got in and leaned over the console to open the door on the driver's side for Manny.

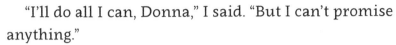

"I'll do all I can, Donna," I said. "But I can't promise anything."

She smiled and nodded. "Thanks, Jesse."

We bid each other goodbye, then I walked over to where The Beast sat in the shade of a buttonwood tree.

My truck had started out as a Keys car and still looked the part. I'd bought it about the day I first arrived in the Keys, so it was sort of a part of me now. Pushed back under the trees, the old '73 International Travelall appeared to be an abandoned wreck, with faded light blue paint, a roof and hood almost completely covered with surface rust, and reddish-brown streaks down the sides. But if you looked closer, you'd see that the patina was sealed with clearcoat and the tires were newer and over-sized.

I got in and started the engine. The sound of the big diesel gave away The Beast's true colors. She was a wolf in sheep's clothes—only the body panels and frame were original. The interior, drivetrain, and suspension were all modern. My late wife, Alex, had dubbed it The Beast and the name just stuck.

Five minutes after pulling out of the shadowy, crushed shell driveway, I was at the airport. It was still a good fifteen minutes before Tank's plane would arrive, so I took my phone out and made a call.

"Livingston and McDermitt Security," Chyrel said.

"It's Jesse. Are you busy?"

Chyrel Koshinski was always busy. But she was a multi-tasker and relished any challenge. I explained what I wanted her to do and she said she'd call me as soon as she had anything.

After ending the call, I went inside to escape the heat. It wasn't summertime hot, but it was the Keys. The sky was clear and the temperature was probably in the mid-eighties, a little hotter than usual for just before Christmas.

Looking out the window, I spotted the Super King Air on approach. The sleek-looking Beechcraft twin turbo arrived just about every day, flying out of Daytona Beach. If I didn't have *Island Hopper*, a King Air would be at the top of my list. Well, that, or an old DC-3. Or any Grumman flying boat.

I remembered a guy in Key West who owned a Grumman Widgeon. He did some charter work and treasure hunting and was once a pretty big deal in the antiquities business. About twelve years ago, he'd helped me unload a bunch of emeralds Amy Huggins's late husband had brought back from South America.

I disliked asking favors, but if anyone knew of a flying boat for sale, it'd be Buck Reilly. Ray Floyd, his long-time friend and business partner, was also an airframe and powerplant mechanic. He worked on *Island Hopper*, taking care of things that were beyond my ability.

As the King Air came back along the taxiway, I pulled up Buck's number and stabbed the *Call* button.

"Last Resort Charter and Salvage," Buck answered.

"It's Jesse McDermitt."

There was a pause for a few seconds, as if he was going through a Rolodex in his mind.

"Find any bright, shiny things lately?" he asked.

"Not really my thing," I said. "I wondered if I could pick your brain about an airplane?"

"What plane and where?"

"Not any specific plane," I replied, watching the shiny King Air turn toward the FBO. "I'm thinking of upgrading. You remember my little Beaver?"

"Great little puddle jumper," he said. "I know a lot of people who'd be glad to take it off your hands."

"Maybe upgrade was the wrong word," I told him. "'Add to' might be better. Do you know of any Grummans for sale? Flying boats, specifically."

"I might," he replied. "That's a very small community. Any preference on size?"

"My Beaver and your Widgeon are comparable in range and passengers. I'm looking for something with greater range and room."

"I'll check with a few people and see what's out there. Do you care about what condition it's in?"

"Airworthy would be a plus," I said with a chuckle. "But dismantled and on a trailer would work if it's all there. Or fully restored. I just don't want to have to hunt for a specific wingnut on a strut."

"I can get back to you at this number?"

"Yeah," I replied.

"Give me a couple of days," Buck said. "I'll call you after Christmas."

There was a click and when I looked at my phone, the call had ended.

I stood by the door, admiring the King Air as it taxied into position. There were usually only a handful of people on these shuttle flights from Miami or Daytona. Tank was the first to deplane, a single small bag in his hand.

Though it had been fifteen years since he'd helped me and Deuce overturn a Marine's dishonorable discharge, he looked exactly the same. Well, except for the beard. He was sporting a neatly trimmed—and completely gray—goatee.

Tank strode confidently across the tarmac. He wasn't an overly large man—about six feet tall with a slim build—but there was a presence about him that commanded respect. To look at him, you'd never guess he was seventy years old.

"How the hell are you?" he asked, as I opened the door for him.

"Right as rain, Master Guns," I replied. "Are you ever going to grow old?"

"Maybe after I die," he said with a hearty handshake. "But to be honest, I'm feeling the years a little these days."

"That's not your only bag, is it?"

"Nah, I had to check my sea bag."

We went over to the small carousel, which was already turning as others filed in from the plane.

"How was the flight?" I asked.

"This last leg was great. I flew American Airlines out of Wilmington and had to change planes in Charlotte. Both were cramped." He glanced around the small terminal. "I figured Thurman would be here with you," he said, lifting a full sea bag easily to his shoulder.

"He's working," I said. "But we have to go there to take my boat out to the island."

"Someone's gotta work," he said with a grin. "My pension ain't gonna pay for itself. What've you been doing in *your* retirement?"

"Hah," I scoffed. "I keep busy. I doubt I'm ever going to fully retire."

"Looks like you've taken pretty good care of yourself."

"Thanks," I said, as we reached The Beast and I opened the back door. "This is me."

"I take that back," he said, looking over the truck. "Apparently, charter fishing doesn't pay quite so well."

I laughed and tossed his carryon in the back. "Around here, nobody owns expensive cars. The fenders will rust off before you make the last payment."

We got in and I started the engine as he looked around at the interior of The Beast.

"This thing's a good forty years old on the outside," he noted. "But I see you've made some upgrades on the inside, and I don't think these thirteen-letter shit spreaders ever came with a diesel engine."

I laughed at his reference to International having its roots in the farm tractor industry.

"Bought it the day I arrived here," I said. "Some friends did the restoration and installed a new engine. It gets me around."

"How far's Thurman's bar?" he asked. "They didn't serve anything on the plane and I'm as dry as a powder house."

It'd been years since I'd last walked into a bunker at an ammo dump, but I remembered the feeling of the air inside—absolutely devoid of even a single molecule of moisture. It was something that flashed back into my mind quite easily from my days as a range coach.

"Just a few minutes," I said. "But if you don't mind, I have a stop I'd like to make first."

"Oh?"

"I'm investigating the disappearance of a young woman."

"That what you do these days? You're a PI?"

"Not exactly," I replied, putting the truck in gear. "Though I do have a license. You remember Deuce Livingston, right?"

"Yeah, Russ Livingston's kid. You and he came up to Lejeune, what, fifteen years ago?"

"He and I own a security agency, but it's more him than me. I just put the money up to get things going."

"So, who's the low-life you need to shake up? He got a name?"

I grinned over at him. "Who said it was a man or that I was going to shake anyone up?"

"Young girl disappears—it's always a man. A PI is called in after the cops don't get anywhere but there's a suspect. So, the punk-ass turd-fondler needs to be made uncomfortable."

I just stared at him a moment.

He shrugged. "Been watching a lot of *Law and Order*."

It couldn't be helped. I laughed deep from my gut. I'd forgotten how straight to the point and pragmatic Master Gunnery Sergeant Owen Tankersley was. Or was it all Marines? Had my attitude dulled?

"Yeah, he's got a name—Ty Sampson. The guy's been cleared by the police. I just want to stop and see if there's anything he might remember now. She disappeared a month ago."

A few minutes later, I pulled into a driveway behind a Volkswagen van and shut off the engine. We got out and walked to the front door.

"Let me do the talking, okay?"

Tank nodded and I knocked on the door. After a moment I knocked again. Then I remembered that Donna had told me over lunch that the guy had a work-shop behind the house.

"Let's try out back," I said. "That's where he works."

The two of us walked around the house to the right. There wasn't much grass in the yard and none at all in a very visible trail around that side.

"First day of winter was two days ago," Tank said. "Almost as hot here as in the Sandbox."

"Not really," I said, noticing a sheen of sweat drops on Tank's forehead. "It's the humidity here. Over there it was a dry heat."

"Dry heat, humid heat—hot's just hot and it ain't supposed to be hot at Christmastime."

"Welcome to the Conch Republic," I said.

Rounding the back corner, I saw a building about fifteen feet wide and twice as long, with double doors at one end, a man-door at the front and a box air conditioner hanging from a window beside it.

The AC was chugging.

I knocked on the door, leaning over to look through the window above the rattling air conditioner. I couldn't see much, just some shelves with supplies.

There was the sound of movement inside, as if someone had set something down. Then I heard footsteps and the door opened.

"Can I help you?" a young man asked.

He looked to be in his twenties or early thirties, longish hair, and a scraggly little beard. He was dressed in long pants and a long-sleeved shirt, typical for anyone who worked with fiberglass.

I handed him a business card from my pocket. "My name's Jesse McDermitt," I said, as he glanced at the card. "We're looking into the disappearance of a friend of yours, Cobie Murphy. That is, if you're Ty Sampson?"

His pupils dilated slightly, but he stepped back and waved a hand toward the inside. "Yeah, I'm Ty. Come on in out of the heat. I'm glad to see Cobie's mom finally hired someone. The cops here are a joke." He glanced at the card again, then at Tank, and finally back to me. "You're from up in Key Largo?"

It wouldn't hurt to let him think what he wanted. Deuce's office was there and that's what it said on the card. I'd never seen this guy around, but Marathon was a big, growing city.

I nodded. "I understand she was supposed to stop here after work to pick up a new wakeboard."

"Yeah," he said, plopping down in a swivel chair by a desk. "Everyone at the park misses her."

"The Cable Park?"

"Yeah. There's about ten of us who are regulars. Most ride my boards."

He motioned toward a stool set up next to a work bench.

I remained standing.

"I'd just finished her board the day before," he said. "She'd paid in advance and I texted her the next morning to tell her she could pick it up when I got back from Miami, later that afternoon."

That wasn't exactly the way Donna said it, I thought. He was mixing his alibi and message.

Donna Murphy had told me that Cobie had received a text the morning she disappeared telling her she could pick up her board in the afternoon, but she never mentioned the text saying he wasn't there or where he'd be. Detective Andersen had told her that Ty had a Miami alibi.

"Do you remember what time you got back?" I asked, looking around the shop.

The place was messy but appeared to be organized. A mess would be expected in a shop that worked with fiberglass.

Ty looked up, thinking. "I'm pretty sure it was around noon," he said. "I left early that morning, before sunrise. The sun was coming up when I hit traffic in Key Largo. My business there only took a half hour—picking up some special glass mat and carbon fiber material. So, yeah, no later than twelve-thirty."

"Was that when you told her she could pick up the board?"

"No, I'm fairly sure I just told her after twelve, just in case. And she had to work that day and didn't get off until three, anyway."

"How well did you know Cobie?" I asked, wondering how he knew her work schedule.

"Not real well," he said. "Some of the local kids hang out here sometimes, and I'm a regular at the Cable Park. That's where I met her, I think."

Leaning over, I looked at a board he was apparently working on. I didn't know a thing about wakeboarding, but I surfed every once in a while, and any boat owner could tell you a thing or two about fiberglass.

"Nice work," I said, without looking up. "You use a polyresin, right?"

"Yeah, man. It's lighter than epoxy."

I turned and faced him again. "Did you call or text Cobie after she didn't show up to get her board that afternoon?"

Again, his pupils flared slightly larger.

"I don't think so," he replied. "I guess she was too busy after work."

Donna had told me about how excited Cobie had been to try out her new board, and even though the park closed at sunset, which was about 1800, she would've had at least a couple of hours at the park. If she'd conveyed her excitement to her mother, her friends were sure to know.

"When *did* you call?" I asked.

Ty glanced over at Tank, who had his back turned, examining a bunch of bottles and cans on a shelf. "Be careful there, man. Some of those solvents are dangerous."

Tank looked back at him with what could only be described as a smirk but said nothing. He'd carried three wounded Marines, one after another, through a minefield in Vietnam, with walking wounded following him, stepping in his footsteps. And he'd risked his life many times since then.

When Ty looked back at me, he fidgeted in his chair a little, much like Donna had, worried that she couldn't afford to hire an investigator.

"I didn't," he said. "I found out she was missing the next day, when the cops came here asking the same questions."

I bet they didn't ask that one, I thought. Ty Sampson was lying or hiding something.

I pretended to examine the board on the work bench again and tried another question that they might not have asked. "Can I see Cobie's board?"

"Her board?"

"Yes," I said. "Is it as smoothly faired as this one?"

I turned to look at him again.

Bingo! Another question the cops didn't ask. I could see it in his expression.

"It's not here anymore," he replied. Now his eyes were darting from one of mine to the other, trying to maintain eye contact, but wanting to look away.

"You gave it to her mother?" I asked. "Or did the police take it?"

"I...I sold it," he said.

I could sense Tank tensing up. He had strong notions of what's right and what's wrong. "You sold something the girl already paid you for?" he growled, his eyes cold and unsympathetic.

"It's been a tough year, man," he practically whined. "I, uh, really need to get back to work. A customer's picking that board up in a couple of hours."

I glanced down at the workbench again. The board would need a final coat of resin, which would take twenty-four hours to fully cure.

"We won't keep you," I said, smiling at him. "Thanks for the help."

Tank turned as I did and led the way through the door. Neither of us spoke until we were around the corner of the house. Then I pulled my phone out and called Chyrel, holding a finger up to Tank.

"Chyrel," I said. "Get a fix on my cell location and check for any outgoing calls from a nearby phone."

She recognized the urgency in my tone. "On it, Jesse."

"You can do that?" Tank asked.

"I can't," I replied. "But she can."

"No active calls within several hundred yards, Jesse." Chyrel said.

"Watch this location," I told her as we reached The Beast. "Let me know the first call that's placed from a phone within a hundred feet."

"Will do," she replied and ended the call.

I put my phone in my pocket and started the engine.

"I meant the technology," Tank said. "I know dumb grunts like us couldn't do something like that."

"It's a big new world," I said with a grin. "All full of bright, shiny things."

"By the way, that guy was lying."

I backed out of the driveway and headed toward the Overseas Highway. "Yeah, I know."

"Did you know he has a bottle of chloroform on the shelf?"

CHAPTER FIVE

On the way back to the Rusty Anchor, Gavriel called. Someone had made a cell phone call from within a hundred feet of the side of Ty Swanson's house. The house was situated on a corner lot with a wooded lot next door. Behind Ty's was a canal and the house across the canal was way farther than a hundred feet. I put her on speaker.

"It has to be a prepaid phone," Gavriel said in Miami.

"That's a start," I said. "You got the numbers, right?"

"Yeah, and I'll track each one and see who they came in contact with and who they call or text."

"I don't suppose you can listen in or read the texts."

She laughed. "Yeah, if given enough time and advance notice."

I thought about it for a moment. It was against the law and she and I both knew it. "For now, just keep track of the numbers either for those phones call or spends longer than a few minutes close to Ty, except maybe they aren't all burner phones."

"Will do," Chyrel said. "I just emailed you the case file from Marathon Police Department concerning the missing girl. It includes the video surveillance footage from the parking lot, which is good. Most stores only hang onto security footage for a month."

"Good work," I said, turning into the shadowed driveway to the Anchor. "I'm almost to *Salty Dog*. I can access it there."

When I ended the call, Tank asked, "Who was that?"

"Her name's Chyrel Koshinski," I replied. "She works for Deuce and used to be a computer analyst with the CIA."

"And she can tell when two cell phones are close together or call one another?"

I put the truck in reverse and backed it in under the buttonwood again. "That, and a lot more. She's hacked into the FBI computers to get information for us, and even accessed the Kremlin once, just for fun."

"The world's changing," Tank said, as we climbed out of the truck.

"Just leave your gear," I said. "We'll grab Rusty and a few beers and head down to the boat. I have a laptop on board."

"Thurman's part of your crew, too?"

"No," I replied. "But he knows just about everyone between Key West and Miami, so he's always good to have around. And those he doesn't know, his wife does."

I pulled the door open and allowed Tank to walk in first. We paused at the door, removing sunglasses, and allowing our eyes to adjust from the bright sunlight.

"Tank!" Rusty called from behind the bar. He moved quickly around it and came toward us, with a big grin. "Man, I haven't seen you in forever."

Rusty was a hugger, but for whatever reason, he extended a hand to Tank, who shook it.

"Fifteen years," Tank said. "Good to see you again."

"Come on up to the bar," Rusty said. "Sid!" he called back to the little office. "Get out here."

The place was nearly empty, most of the guides now out on the water with clients.

Sidney stepped out of the office and smiled at us. "This must be the famous Tank," she said, coming around the bar.

"Tank," Rusty said, "this here's my wife, Sidney."

"My friends all just call me Sid," she said, wrapping Tank in an embrace like an anaconda. "I hope you will, as well."

Tank stepped back and looked at the two of them. Rusty wore flip flops, which he did most of the time. And Sid wore four-inch heels, as she usually did. Even flat-footed, she was a good five or six inches taller than Rusty. She stood an even six feet tall and she was taller than me in those heels.

"Pleasure's mine, ma'am," Tank said nervously.

"I need to go out to the *Dog* and fire up the laptop," I told Rusty. "How about putting a few cold ones in a cooler and joining us?" I leaned in closer. "I have a lead on Cobie's disappearance."

"Y'all go," Sid said, shooing us with both hands. "I'll bring it out."

The three of us went out the back door and headed toward the far end of the dock.

"You own all this, Thurman?" Tank asked, looking around.

"Been in my family for over a century," he replied. "Four generations of Thurmans have lived here. It's my job to see that all this doesn't slide off into the Atlantic."

"How much land?"

"Forty acres total," Rusty replied. "But most is mangrove marsh. Only about a fourth of the dry property is developed. I leave that jungle you drove through as a buffer against the traffic noise."

We reached the *Dog* and I went up the dock-mounted steps to the side deck. "Come aboard."

I unlocked the companionway hatch and slid it open, then reached inside and unlatched the small double doors.

"This is more like it," Tank said, stepping down into the cockpit. "Is this how we get out to your place?"

"No," I replied, starting down the steps. "It'd take the rest of the day to get there on *Salty Dog*. I have a small powerboat at the other end of the dock. Come on down."

The AC was on but set at 80°—low enough to keep the humidity down, but not cost a fortune for electricity. I lowered the thermostat and switched on the lights at the navigation station.

"Sorry for all the delays, Tank," I offered. "This just came up this morning and I need to check a few things before we head to the Contents."

"That's what you call your island?"

"No, the Contents were named that long before I arrived," I said, opening the laptop and switching it on. "It's a group of islands about an hour northwest of here. Mine doesn't even have a name."

The computer booted up and connected to the Wi-Fi router, which in turn connected to a satellite way up in space. I opened my email server, then opened Chyrel's email. There were two links, both to files on Deuce's network. I clicked on the one labeled Kmart and sat down.

"This is a clip from the security camera in Kmart's parking lot," I said. "Hopefully, it's not long."

It wasn't. Once it started playing, the timer showed it was less than four minutes of footage. Someone had clipped it from the original. A few seconds after the start, I saw a car headed south on US-1 that looked like the one in the picture Cobie was standing beside.

I stopped the video and backed it up, then pulled the picture out of my pocket and leaned it against the side of the screen.

Rusty and Tank leaned in closer, looking at the picture.

"That's Cobie Murphy," I said, for Tank's benefit. "Her car's a blue Ford Fiesta."

"I just bought one," Tank said, drawing curious looks from me and Rusty. "It was for my grand-niece's graduation from high school."

I clicked the play button and the car again entered the picture, crossing from right to left, then disappearing at the nine-second mark.

"It's the same car," Tank said. "A Ford Fiesta."

"Why didn't she just turn in at Mickey D's?" Rusty asked.

"Good question," I said. "She's young. Maybe nervous about turning left across three lanes, and there's a median in front of the entrance she used, so maybe she's more comfortable going to the light at Sombrero. She should reappear down here at the bottom left of the screen."

A few seconds ticked off on the timer, as well as on the time and date stamp in the upper right corner of the security video.

"Nope," Rusty said, pointing. "She did a U-turn."

Sure enough, the same car reentered the screen from the upper left, slowed, then turned into the lot at its center. I was sure it was the car from Donna's picture and the time stamp in the upper corner showed that it was 0923. The forensics guys would have watched hours of footage and that was the only car matching Cobie's they'd seen, hence the four-minute clip.

Donna had said Cobie was supposed to be at work at 0900 and had left at 0845. She was late for work and it had taken over half an hour to drive less than ten miles. With only two lights, that'd rarely take more than ten or fifteen minutes.

The blue Fiesta immediately turned left upon entering the parking lot, following the row of spaces that faced US-1. Then it disappeared from the picture.

"Can't see much from that," Rusty commented.

"That's what Donna said," I replied. "Maybe Chyrel can—"

"Wait!" Rusty said, leaning in closer as the clip ended. "Back it up to when her car disappears."

I did, and he pointed. "That black car that turned in right behind her and followed her? I swear that's the same car that guy was driving this morning. The drug dealer we ran off!"

I couldn't see the car clearly, not enough to be sure of the make and model, but it did look like the Nissan sportscar.

"Back it up to the beginning," Tank said, his voice an octave lower.

There was a rap on the hull and Sid called out, "Coming aboard."

A moment later, she stepped down into the upper salon, where she opened a cooler and passed a beer to each of us.

"Red Stripe?" Tank asked, trying to twist the cap off.

"Here," Rusty said, pulling a bottle opener from his pocket, and uncapping the bottle for him.

I started the video from the beginning. Three seconds after Cobie's car entered the screen, Tank pointed. "There it is. The same black car that followed her in."

"You think that drug dealer kidnapped her?" Rusty asked.

Sid looked at Rusty. "What drug dealer?"

"Me and Jesse had to run some punk off this morning," he replied.

"Jesse and I," she corrected him.

"There's no way to be sure it's the same car," I said, trying to make the connection in my mind and thinking out loud. "I half-expected to see a VW bus pull in behind her."

"What do you mean?" Sid asked.

"Do either of you know Ty Sampson?" I asked.

Sid shook her head.

"Heard the name," Rusty said. "Fiberglass guy. But I don't know anything more about him than that."

"He made a custom wakeboard for Cobie," I said. "Tank and I just talked to him and he was...evasive at best."

"Is that a new word for *liar*?" Tank asked.

Rusty drained his beer and opened another. "What'd he say?"

I told him and Sid about the series of events as Donna had related them, then what Sampson had told me and Tank. Then I told them the part about him not calling when Cobie didn't show up to pick up the board that afternoon, and that he'd told us he'd sold her board.

Rusty shook his head. "Sounds to me like he knew she'd *never* be picking it up."

"What's the other link in the email?" Tank asked.

I reduced the video clip and clicked on the second link Chyrel had sent me. It opened a file folder, which held more folders. I clicked on one labeled "Crime Scene Photos," and it revealed forty-eight photographs. I started with the first one and progressed through each, just getting a feel for what the photographer was looking at.

"I'm sure glad your girl is on our side," Tank said. "Isn't it illegal for you to even have this stuff?"

"It's a thin line between legal and illegal," Rusty said. "Sometimes ya gotta step over it. Like, it's against the law to jaywalk, but if you see a kid in the middle of a busy street, you'll run out there and get them."

"If I find anything the police overlooked," I explained, starting back at the beginning of the photos, "I'll get hold of the lead detective and steer him in a conversation so *he* can discover it himself."

I stopped on an image of the driver's side of Cobie's car. Something about it had seemed off on the first pass. I suddenly realized what it was.

"Take a look at this," I said, picking up the photo and holding it beside the image on the screen. In the snapshot, Cobie was standing beside the car and the door was closed. In the crime scene shot, the door was open.

"The seat's been moved," Tank said. "She's a short round—barely taller than a car I leaned my arm on. Look at the picture. You can see the headrest is forward of the door pillar." He pointed at the screen. "In that one, the seat's pushed all the way back."

I stood and paced the upper salon, thinking.

"Cobie's five-two," I said, turning to Tank. "How tall would you guess Sampson to be?"

"A bit shorter'n me," he replied. "Five-nine or -ten, maybe."

"Do you think one of the officers might have moved the seat?" Sid asked.

"I don't think so," I said. "I'm not a cop or forensics tech, but I think if I were going to take pictures of a crime scene, it would be to preserve information before the forensics team started tearing it apart for clues."

"That would be logical," Tank said. "Do you have any former law enforcement officers on your payroll?"

"No LEOs on the *payroll*," I said, pulling my phone out. "But I have one in the family. Two, actually."

"Hey, Dad," Kim said, answering her phone. I could hear an outboard burbling in the background.

"Hey, kiddo. I have a question for you. Are you busy?"

"Just patrolling with Marty. What's up?"

"Tough job," I said with a chuckle.

"Somebody's gotta do it."

"This is a cop question," I began. "If a car is found abandoned and foul play is believed to be involved, would pictures be taken before anything was disturbed?"

"Yes," she said. "Preliminary photos of a crime scene keeps everything as it was for further study. Then more pictures as the forensics guys process evidence, and finally, photos of any items removed, each in a sealed evidence bag. What's going on?"

How to word it so I wasn't lying?

"I'm looking into the disappearance of that girl just before Thanksgiving. Cobie Murphy is her name. Anyway, I came across a picture showing that the driver's seat of her car had been moved."

"You came across a picture?"

"It's a crime scene photo I saw. I was just wondering if I should bring it to the attention of the police."

"Uh-huh," she said slowly, doubt dripping from her words. "To answer your question, no, the seat wouldn't be moved until forensics is finished. The crime scene photographer is normally on the forensics team. As to the unasked question—yes, you should let the police know."

"Great," I said. "Thanks, that's a lot of help."

"Dad, you're not with the government anymore. Cops, even private detectives, have to play by the rules."

"I'm just poking around," I said. "Gotta go. Bye."

I ended the call before she could ask anything else. She and Eve have both been bugging me to retire and just fish.

Sitting at the desk again, I clicked on the file labeled "Crime Scene Notes." There weren't a lot of them. I saw nothing about the driver's seat being pushed back.

Another file was labeled "Phone Records," and I opened it. She texted a whole lot more than she called. Scrolling to the morning of her disappearance, I looked for a phone call to a local landline.

"What are you looking for?" Tank asked.

I turned to Rusty, the all-knowing keeper of Middle Keys knowledge and scuttlebutt. "Donna said Cobie was a good kid—a great kid. She worked hard, was athletic, didn't do drugs or drink. Does that jibe with what you know of her?"

"The same," he replied. "Smart as a whip, as fast as the wind, and she has a good heart. Remember? She volunteered to help serve food after Irma."

"If Cobie had to be at work at zero-nine-hundred and knew she was going to be late, what would she do?"

His eyes cut to the screen and the two images frozen there; her phone records for the morning of Friday, November 20th and the time-stamped video showing she was twenty-three minutes late for work.

"If she was going to be a *minute* late," Rusty said, "I'd put my bottom dollar on her calling her boss."

We spent another ten minutes looking over the rest of the information in the folder, but nothing else jumped out at me. There just wasn't a lot there, and nothing more had been added since December 8th, over two weeks ago.

Finally, I closed the laptop. Then I drained my beer and turned to Tank. "We can head up to the island now."

"You sure?" he asked. "This is getting interesting."

"Nothing more I can do," I said. "I need to contact the lead detective on the case and see if I can't get him to stumble on these clues without telling him I saw his files."

"Does it matter that much if he knows? You're running out in the street to save a kid, right?"

"The rules of engagement are different off the battlefield," I said. "If and when it goes to trial, the evidence would be tainted if the defense learned it came from a computer hacker."

He stared at me a moment—that hard, blank stare I remembered from my youth, inscrutable and wise at the same time. But there was something else there. Was it fear?

"Improvise, adapt, and overcome," Tank said. "You've made the transition well, Gunny. Yeah, a little fresh air always gets my brain ticking again."

"Who's the lead?" Rusty asked, as Sid led the way up the companionway ladder.

"Clark Andersen," I replied. "You know him?"

"Yeah. Good fisherman. His parents used to run a bait shop down on Summerland. Or was it Ramrod? Anyway, he's always been a straight shooter, that I know."

I locked up the *Dog* and we said our goodbyes to Rusty and Sid.

"Let's get your stuff from the truck," I said, as we walked toward the turning basin and dinghy dock. "My boat's down here."

Once we had Tank's gear aboard, I started the Suzuki outboard and untied the lines. A few minutes later, we were out of the canal and I told Tank to hang on.

I pushed the throttle nearly to the wide-open position and the nimble little boat sprang up onto the step and accelerated. I pulled back to about halfway—enough to maintain twenty knots and not have to shout over the engine, then trimmed the boat for the rough chop.

We skirted East Sister Rock, putting the waves to our stern, and throttled up a little more.

Tank stared at the house on East Sister. "That what your place looks like?"

"Not hardly," I said, turning toward the Seven Mile Bridge. "Mine's just a pile of timber and steel that I built myself."

"That's good." He leaned back against the post. "That place is a little ostentatious."

"Ostentatious?"

"Means a vulgar display, designed to impress. I'm not impressed."

I grinned over at him as we passed under the bridge. "I know what it means. I just didn't know that you did."

He looked over at me and nodded. "A man can learn new things, son. I been doing a lot of reading."

CHAPTER SIX

The little Grady didn't need to follow channels. At least not the deep ones. On plane, she'd skim across anything deeper than two feet. I knew where those shallow banks were located, even without having to resort to the little chart plotter mounted to the console. I'd made this run thousands of times.

The ride took less than an hour, as I pointed out the different landmarks along the way. Finally, I weaved through several cuts, entered the deep water of Harbor Channel, and turned west toward my island.

"How far is this from the nearest road?" Tank asked, as I pulled the throttles back and turned into the channel I'd dug to my house.

"Over four miles," I replied. "Straight behind us on Big Pine Key."

"No neighbors for four miles?" he said, moving to the bow and freeing a coiled line from the rail, which was tied to a bow cleat.

"Actually, my nearest neighbor is just over a mile away," I said, pointing up the channel to Mac Travis's island. "On that island."

I reversed and turned the wheel toward the dock, then killed the engine. Tank stepped over with the bow line and I grabbed the stern line and did likewise.

He looked around. "Still, from a strategic standpoint, this is excellent."

A clicking of claws announced the arrival of Finn and Woden. The dogs stopped a few feet away and sat. There was a stranger with me, and they were on alert until I told them it was okay. Normally, they'd be frantically dancing on my toes.

"Tank, meet Finn and Woden," I said, as he looked at the two large canines.

"Finn's the Lab, right?"

"Good guess," Savannah said from the top of the steps.

Tank looked up and smiled as she started down. "Not really a guess, ma'am. Woden was the chief god of ancient Germanic tribes. Labs are water dogs from Canada. Both are named appropriately."

"Learned that from your recent reading?" I asked.

"I'm not a big fan of generic pet names, like Fido or Spot."

"You must be Tank," she said, reaching the bottom of the steps and striding toward us. "Please, just call me Savannah."

"A pleasure to meet you," he offered. "Jesse's told me all about you."

Savannah's eyes cut to me. "He has, huh?"

"In man talk," Tank said. "He told me he was getting married and I asked him if his rum locker was full."

She laughed as they shook hands, then we grabbed Tank's gear from the boat and headed up the steps.

"I thought you said you've lived here for fifteen years," he said when we reached the deck and he'd had a chance to see the whole island for the first time. "Everything looks brand new. How many people live here?"

"Most of it is new," Savannah said.

"Hurricane Irma passed right over here three years ago," I added. "It destroyed just about everything."

I pointed to the nearest building. "My first mate, a Navy guy named Jimmy Saunders, lives over there. At least he does when he's not at his girlfriend's. Besides being my crew on charters, he takes care of things here on the island."

Pointing north, I added, "My middle daughter and her husband live there, but they work up on the mainland, so they have a place up there, too. Our youngest is staying there for now. That last place is the bunkhouse. You have your pick of twelve racks."

"Jesse, no," Savannah said. "He can stay here, and we'll stay in the bunkhouse."

"Wouldn't hear of it, ma'...er...Savannah. I've lived most of my life in a squad bay. It'll be more comfortable for me than the Grand Hotel."

"Are you sure?" she asked, opening the door to our house.

"Absolutely," Tank replied, shrugging his seabag off his shoulder, and dropping it to the deck to accentuate his resolve.

"Well then, come in and rest," she said, moving toward the door. "I was just starting dinner and was getting worried."

"We found a lead in the Cobie Murphy case," I said. "Sorry it took so long."

We went inside and Tank asked if there was anything he could help with.

"No," she replied. "The steaks are marinating, and I just put the potatoes in the oven. There's nothing to do right now. I was going to cut up some vegetables for a salad."

Finn and Woden entered, then followed one another around the big rug a couple of times before lying down, both facing the tree.

Tank looked around. "Gotta hand it to you, Gunny. This is the way to live. He carried his small bag toward the tree and pointed to the center of it. "But you're missing something right here."

With great care, he opened his bag and reached inside, then extracted a small wooden box and opened it. After removing wads of tissue paper, he removed the blue and scarlet tree ornament. "May I?"

"Be honored," I said, my voice catching in my throat a little when I saw it.

It'd been over thirty-seven years, but the memory of that fateful day was as clear in my mind as ever. I no longer dwelled on it, and there were times when several days would pass without the names entering my consciousness. Tank being here, though, brought a flood of emotions.

Savannah stepped over beside him. "Jesse and Savannah," she read from the ball. "October 23, 1983. You do me a great honor, including my name with that date."

"You probably weren't much more than a girl," Tank said.

"I was twelve. And I remember watching it on the news."

"Hey, Dad," Florence said, coming through the open door.

Tank wheeled.

"Come in, Florence," I said. "I'd like you to meet someone."

"Did this pretty little girl call you *Dad*?" he asked.

Florence blushed.

"Tank, this is my youngest daughter, Florence. She's a freshman at University of Florida. Florence, meet Owen 'Tank' Tankersley, my mentor when I was in the Marines."

"Pleased to meet you, Mister Tankersley," she said, offering her hand.

"Whenever someone calls me that, I look around for my dad," Tank said. "Everyone has always just called me Tank. Even when I was a kid."

Florence glanced quickly at her mother, who nodded. Though she hadn't grown up in the Deep South, as Savannah had, she'd been taught all the social graces, as if she were a South Carolina debutante.

"Sweetie," Savannah said to Florence, "would you mind going down to the garden and picking some of that broccoli and a couple summer squash?"

"You have a garden?" Tank asked. "I'd like to see that."

"Follow me," Florence said, heading toward the door. Woden rose from his spot on the rug and trotted after her.

"It's an aquaculture garden," she said, as they walked across the deck. "Do you know what that is?"

Tank replied that he didn't, and Florence explained as they went down the back steps to the island's interior.

"You said you found out something?" Savannah asked.

I told her about my meeting with Manny and Donna, then our visit to the sketchy board builder's house, and the difference in their stories. Then I told her about the car seat being moved, and the black sportscar I'd seen at the Anchor and on the video.

"A flashy car like that ought to be easy to find," she said, breaking open a head of lettuce for a salad. Have Rusty put the word out on the coconut telegraph."

"Good idea," I said, pulling my phone out and writing a text message.

"Do you think the drug dealer and this Ty Sampson know one another?"

"They might," I said, looking out the window at my daughter showing Tank the garden. "Why?"

"What is it you call it? Target fixation? You're concentrating too much on just one thing. Step back and look at the big picture."

"What big picture? I really don't have much to go on yet."

"If the car seat was pushed back," she said, "then somebody else drove her car. How did that person leave Kmart? What if Cobie went to this Ty Sampson's house and the drug dealer in the sportscar was there? They might have abducted her together and one of them drove her car to Kmart."

I turned slowly and faced Savannah. "You know, that makes perfect sense. Now, how do I get this intel to the cops without telling them we hacked their computers?"

"Oh, that part's easy," she said, as she picked up a knife and started chopping celery. "Buy a cheap throwaway phone and call them."

I put a finger under her chin, tilted her face up toward mine, and kissed her. "You're a genius."

"Yes, I know," she replied, smiling. "In fact, I remember seeing some cheap cell phones at Old Wooden Bridge Marina the other day."

"I'll be back in twenty minutes," I said, heading for the door. "Come on, Finn."

"The potatoes will be ready in an hour," she said.

"The steaks won't take but fifteen minutes."

Outside, I went to the rail and yelled down at Tank. "I gotta run to the store. You wanna go?"

"You go ahead," he called back up, as he and Florence started up the steps. "Flo's going to show me the squad bay and I'm going to unpack."

"*Bleib bei* Florence," I said to Woden, commanding him to stay with her.

Finn followed me down the front steps and I quickly stepped aboard the Grady, started the Suzuki, and untied the lines. Finn jumped onto the forward casting deck as we idled toward Harbor Channel.

I resisted the urge to mash the throttle. The combination of the bow rising and the boat shooting forward would throw Finn to the deck. But we were soon on plane and headed toward the cuts near Mac's island.

Barely slowing, I snaked through the unmarked passages, then turned south. Ten minutes later, I passed under Old Wooden Bridge, which is now made of concrete and steel, then idled into the marina.

I was in and out in a matter of minutes, and back at my own dock just twenty-five minutes after leaving.

Pulling a knife from my pocket, I used it to slit the plastic open on the phone. It was the cheapest one they had, not that they had a large variety, but it only needed to make one call. While I waited for it to power up, I pulled out my iPhone and looked up the non-emergency number for the Monroe County Sheriff's Marathon sub-station. A woman answered.

"Could I speak with Detective Andersen?"

"Who's calling?" she asked

"Just tell him it's about the Cobie Murphy case," I said. "I'd rather stay anonymous."

"One moment, please."

There were a series of clicks.

They would try to pinpoint my location, but the phone I bought didn't have GPS. The best they'd be able to tell would be that I was pinging the cell tower on the north end of Big Pine Key, as were most of the residents of that island and No Name Key, as well.

"Detective Andersen," a man's voice finally said. "Who is this?"

"That's not important," I said. "Go through your pictures of Cobie Murphy's car again. Look closely at the one with the driver's door open and remember that Cobie is only five-two. Then watch the Kmart video again and look for a black car following Cobie's into the lot."

"Who is this?" he repeated. "And how did you see any of that?"

"I told you. That doesn't matter. Do you understand what I explained to you?"

"Check the picture of her car," he said. "And look at the security footage again. Yeah, I get it. Now who—"

I leaned over the gunwale and held the phone underwater for half a minute. When I pulled it out and looked, the screen was blank.

Finn stood on the dock, eyeing me curiously as I pried the phone apart with my knife, yanked the battery out, then wrenched the circuit board loose, tearing it out and breaking the wires.

Putting the pieces in my pocket, I stepped up over to the dock and went up to the deck to grill some steaks.

CHAPTER SEVEN

The phone on the nightstand started playing salsa music. Benito Moreno sat bolt upright, yanking a handgun from under his pillow. It was early afternoon. The girl beside him stirred as the music continued. They'd partied and had sex until they'd exhausted themselves at dawn.

"This better be important," he hissed, answering the phone.

"We might have trouble," a voice said.

Benito looked at the number on the screen, then recognized the voice. The new dealer down in the Middle Keys. He stood and padded naked into the bathroom. "What's this 'we' shit, *cabrón*?"

"Somebody's snooping around," Sampson said. "The mother hired a PI and he came by here asking questions."

"So?" Benito said, as he relieved his bladder. "You were already cleared by the cops. What did you tell him?"

"The same thing I told the cops," Sampson said. "But this guy was suspicious because I never called the girl about her board."

"What board?"

"The custom board I made for her that she came to pick up that day. I texted her to come by that afternoon, but she came early, and you know the rest. I never called when she didn't show up that afternoon."

Mierda estúpido, Benito thought. *The idiota should have followed through as if nothing ever happened.*

"I see," he said, waiting for more.

"I told him that I just figured she was busy that day, and then after the police questioned me the next morning, there wasn't any reason to call her."

"Who is this PI?"

There was a pause. Benito made his way back to the bed, waiting.

"He gave me his card," Sampson said. "Where is it? Ah, here. His name's Jesse McDermitt, with Livingston and McDermitt Security, in Key Largo."

"Text me the address," Benito said, scribbling the name on a notepad lying on the bedside table.

"What are you going to do?"

"I ain't doin' shit, *pendejo*. If he comes around again, tell him exactly the same thing. You don't know shit about where the *puta* is."

Benito ended the call and looked at the girl in his bed for a moment, a stirring in his loins. Her long, black hair was sprawled across the pillow, partially covering her face. Her dark brown skin contrasted to the white garter and nylons she still wore.

"Get up, *puta!*"

The girl stirred and then sat up. "Timezit?"

"What? You have a board meeting uptown you gotta get to?" he asked sarcastically. "Get your skanky ass outta my bed."

The girl—Benito couldn't even remember her name— came to her wits quickly.

"Did I do some—"

"I got shit to do!" Benito yelled. "Get dressed and get out."

The young woman started grabbing up her clothes, which were strewn all over the room.

Vanessa! Benito thought. *That's it.*

"*Espere*, Vanessa," he said, taking her arm as she tried to get past him. He turned her roughly to face him, then looked her up and down while pawing at her right breast. He bent and kissed her roughly, biting at her lower lip and tongue.

He pushed her back by the shoulders and let his eyes roam over her body again. "Hey. You were good. I'm just not what you'd call a morning person. Lookit. I want you at the Booby Trap tonight. If you do okay, then you can dance there this weekend, *si?*"

Her face brightened. At least, as much as a coke whore's face could, only a few hours after crashing.

"Really, Benny?"

"Yeah, you just show up there at nine and tell Marvin I sent you."

"*Gracias,*" she said. "Um…"

"Here," he said, opening a drawer on the side table.

He handed her a tiny plastic bag. It held about half a gram of pure Peruvian. "Go easy on this," he said. "It ain't been stepped on at all."

She snatched the little plastic bag from his hand and hurried into the bathroom.

Benito pulled some clothes from his closet. He could hear the girl talking in Spanish in the bathroom. She was gloating to one of his other girls about the promotion.

Once dressed, he went into the kitchen and set up the coffee maker for one cup of strong Cuban coffee.

While he waited for it to finish, he tapped out a small line of coke on the table and snorted it with a platinum tube. Pinching his nose, he tilted his head up and sniffed, drawing the expensive, uncut cocaine deeper into his sinus passages.

The effect was immediate. His eyes went wide, pupils as big as the iris as the drug reached his brain, firing every synapse at once.

He went back to the bedroom, his libido charged to the limit, and checked the bathroom. Vanessa had left.

"*Mierda,*" he muttered.

Just as well, he then thought. With a nose full of this shit, he'd end up spending the rest of the day screwing her and he really did have things to do. Like call his Peruvian connection and get more.

Benito Moreno was a *Balsero*. He'd come to Miami as a child of five, just after the rioting in Havana and the outlying areas. His family had left Cuba in a flotilla of makeshift rafts. They'd stolen away from the coast at sunset—forty-some rafts attempting the crossing together. Benito and his family were on two of them.

The rafts were little more than two big truck inner-tubes, held together with a net, and strapped to a pair of wooden doors. Each could hold only a few people, and the only power they had was a single handmade wooden oar, fashioned using part of a street sign.

Just before dawn on the first day, as the flotilla was entering the Florida Current, a powerful squall blew up out of the southeast. Wave action in the Florida Straits was rough on a good day, but within minutes, waves up to fifteen feet were tossing the makeshift rafts around like so many Styrofoam cups.

By daybreak, there were only eighteen rafts in sight, and four of those were empty. One of the vacant rafts had been that of Benito's mother and two older brothers. Benito, his little sister, and their father pressed on with the other *Balseros*, but he could tell, even at that young age, that his father's spirit had been broken.

His sister died before they reached land three days later, her little brain cooked by the relentless tropical sun. His father took Benito to a cousin's house in Miami, then used the only money he had to buy a bottle of rum and a gun, which, after drinking the liquor, he used to blow his brains out. Of a family of six, Benito Moreno was the only one still alive just four days after leaving Cuba.

Little Benito, the orphaned Cuban boy, had not only survived, but in the next twenty-five years, he'd thrived. With his family gone, he didn't care whether he lived or died, and a young man who couldn't be threatened was a dangerous thing in Miami.

Benito picked up his phone and made a call to his supplier, across the state on the west coast. The man answered quickly.

"This is Benito," he said. "That shit was off the hook last night, *compadre*! Can we do it again?"

"Do what again?" the man growled.

Benito didn't like dealing directly with his supplier, but the man insisted that was the only way he did things. From the top, to the top. No middleman. He said go-betweens were careless with his product and money.

"Ten times the weight," Benito said. "Same price as last night?"

"That was a sample. Ten times the weight will be fifteen times the price per unit."

"*Que carajo!*"

"You heard me," the man bellowed. "I gotta drive across the state with it."

Benito did the calculation in his head. Even at a fifty percent higher price, he'd clean up. And it would only take a day or two through his club contacts. Still, he had to put his hands on a quarter million dollars first. But at a hundred bucks per gram, cut to a still-potent forty percent purity, ten kilos would bring in well over two million.

"Okay," Benito said. "Same place and time tomorrow night?"

"Same place," the supplier said. "I'll let you know in the morning what time I'll be there. Bring the girl."

"Vanessa?"

"She the little dark-haired one in white?"

"*Si*, I can have her there."

"I'll see that she gets home." the man said with a sadistic growl.

Benito ended the call and went back to the kitchen for his coffee. He didn't like the big swamp ape. But he was the only one who could supply such pure Peruvian flake. And if he wanted the *puta* for the night, or permanently, he didn't care.

CHAPTER EIGHT

A fter dinner, the four of us went out to the firepit and I started a driftwood fire.

"Why did you stay in the Marines so long?" Florence asked, after learning Tank had spent nearly his whole life in the Corps.

"There were a lot of reasons," he replied. "I enlisted when I was younger than you. I could've taken a partial retirement in '87, not long after I met your dad. Or in '97, with a full pension. But I felt a need to stay, to look after my troops, help shape them and motivate them."

"You motivated the hell out of me," I said, then took a pull from my beer. "That first time in Beirut, when you stood up on that parapet and aimed down at the leader of the group banging on the embassy gate..."

"Did they have guns?" Florence asked.

I laughed. "Yeah, they sure did. Mostly antique hunting rifles. Tank was in his dress blues—he was a gunny then—and he was aiming an M240 with one hand, holding a bandolier of ammo in the other. He shouted down at them in Arabic, 'Go away now or be the first martyr.'"

"What's an M240?"

"It's a crew-served machine gun," I replied. "It weighs about twenty-five pounds, unloaded."

"You kinda stood out, too," Tank said with a chuckle.

"How so, Dad?"

"He was a corporal then, at the end of his first enlistment," Tank replied. "Your dad stood up right beside me on that wall."

Florence's eyes went wide.

"The group below us didn't know what the blue ribbon on the top of Tank's rack meant," I explained to Florence. "But every single man on that rooftop knew the Medal of Honor. I stood up next to Tank because it was the right thing to do. Immediately, every Marine there rose and exposed themselves. All of us aiming at the leader of the group. What was it the guy said, Tank?"

"Said he was sorry. That he'd made a mistake. Hey, what's with the weird-colored flames?"

"It's driftwood," Savannah replied. "It absorbs sea water and when it dries out, the salt and other minerals remain. Festive, isn't it?"

"Yeah," Tank said, stretching his legs out and staring into the red and green flames. "I really appreciate you having me as your guest for the holidays."

"You don't have any family?" Florence asked innocently.

"No," Tank replied, a bit of melancholy in his voice. "I had two older brothers. One was killed in Vietnam and the other died of a stroke a few years back. I never had any kids, so it's just me."

"We're glad to have you," Savannah said, just as my phone chirped.

I pulled it out and checked the screen. "It's Chyrel," I said, standing. "I need to take this."

Pushing the *Accept* button, I strolled toward the tree line on the eastern shore.

"Hey, Chyrel," I said. "What's up?"

"I just emailed you a list of numbers and names," she said. "The burner phone Ty Sampson called in Miami made a call within minutes of the time you had me watching. About the same time, another phone awfully close by the burner made a call. The unknown burner and the other phone remained close together for several minutes. It belongs to a woman named Vanessa Ramos. She's been arrested twice for prostitution."

"How's that help?"

"It doesn't, in and of itself," Chyrel said. "The number she called belongs to another woman, Pilar Fuentes, also a known prostitute."

"Okay, but hookers are a dime a dozen in Miami. Who did the Miami unknown call?"

"The burner called a number in the 239 area code a few minutes after Sampson called it."

"That's Fort Myers," I said.

"In this case, the call was placed to a cell phone that pinged a tower on Marco Island."

"No name to go with that one?"

"No," she replied. "But it was a GPS phone and at the time of the call, it was moving at highway speed near Goodland. That phone then made two more calls, also to unregistered numbers, one in North Miami and the other in Fort Lauderdale."

"Monitor the Marco Island number, as well as the one in Miami that called it. Whoever that guy is, he was the first person Sampson called after I shook him up. If any of those three talk again, will you record the call for me?"

"You only gotta ask," she replied. "And buy me a cheeseburger next time you're up this way."

"Deal," I said and ended the call.

"What was that all about?" Savannah asked, as I sat back down beside her at the fire.

"Not real sure yet," I replied. "But I don't believe in coincidences."

"What's that supposed to mean?" Tank asked.

I sat forward with my elbows on my knees. "Remember when we were at Sampson's workshop and I had Chyrel watch for an outgoing call from nearby?"

"Yeah. And I asked you about that technology."

"Most phones have GPS software built in," I said. "Even most burner phones. I made sure to buy one that didn't when I went down to the store earlier. Chyrel can enter a phone number into a computer program and it will track that number's physical location and identify other phones that it spends more than a few minutes in close proximity with. It was designed to identify bad guys by matching the burner phone in one pocket with the reg-istered phone in the other. But we found that it worked on identifying cohorts too. When it finds one close, it tracks that phone as well, and does the same to it while also recording the phone numbers of any incoming or outgoing calls that anyone in this network of people makes. Chyrel says that it can conceivably track and record the connections of up to a million people."

"Six degrees of Kevin Bacon," Tank said with a grin.

"Something like that," I said. "Anyway, Sampson called someone in Miami's Upper East Side—an area known for adult nightclubs and prostitution. It was a burner phone and whoever it was, they were with a prostitute by the name of Vanessa Ramos, whose phone *is* regis-tered. Within minutes of the call from Sampson, Ramos called another known prostitute and whoever she was with called another burner near Marco Island, over on the west coast. Then later, the unknown phone near Marco made more calls to other burners in Miami and Fort Lauderdale."

Tank also sat forward, nodding his head. "That's what you wanted, when you told your girl to watch his phone, huh?"

"Pretty much," I replied. "I was hoping for names, though. But all these unregistered phones is a good in-dication of illegal activity."

"And you knew if you shook him up a little, he'd make a call to some cohort?"

"Yeah, but there's no way to know who it was or who the person on the west coast was." Savannah and I shared a glance. "At least, not yet."

Tank raised his bushy eyebrows questioningly. "So, what's the coincidence?"

"The Blancs?" Savannah asked, putting all the clues together.

I nodded at her and turned back to Tank. "The Blanc family is probably the biggest cocaine and methamphetamine importer in South Florida."

"I thought they were all arrested," Savannah said.

"Only one of them is serving any serious time. I haven't talked to Bill in over a month, but last time we spoke, he told me that Marley Blanc had suffered a heart attack and died while in custody, and her daughter, Kurt, was sent to prison for five years."

"Wait," Tank said. "A daughter named Kurt?"

"These aren't your run-of-the-mill denizens of the swamp," I told him. "None of them work, except one, who is a state senator, and they're always high on something. I learned that Kurt is actually short for Courtney, which in their backwoods lingo was pronounced Curtnee. She shortened it to Kurt with a K. Within a week of arriving at Raiford, Kurt tried to kill a guard and is now looking at life. They didn't have enough to hold the others without bail, and they were released. Marley's husband, Willy Quick, disappeared into the swamp and hasn't been seen since."

"And this Bill you talked to?" Tank asked. "He's another person on your team?"

"Bill Binkowski," I said. "He's FBI and we worked together with Homeland Security a few times, but he's retired now. This all happened last summer."

"What was this Kurt character arrested for?"

"She took a shot at me and Kim, my middle daughter. Kim and her husband are Fish and Wildlife officers. A few days later, we managed to get most of the family in one place at one time—a place that later turned out to be the burial ground of a serial killer who was Kurt's grandfather."

"I'm hearing banjo music," Tank said.

"I have a friend over in that area who thinks the same thing," I said. "He says their family tree doesn't have a lot of forks. They bring in most of the drugs that flow into Miami. But the cops have never been able to catch them."

"How come?"

"They use a combination of Cigarette boats and airboats to move the drugs to a location deep in the Everglades, where the drugs are then moved by truck to the east coast. The police have never been able to pin anything on them, mostly because the leader's brother was a state senator who knows whose pockets to grease."

"And this Willy Quick is the leader?"

"His wife was," I replied. "They figure her heart attack was brought on by decades of drug abuse. Meth monsters aren't in the best of health. Kurt was next in line, but she's in prison. Bill thinks Quick is running the show now."

"And here I thought you were living in a quaint tropical paradise down here," Tank said. "Sounds a lot more like the Mog."

In a way, he was right. The drug problem in south Florida was massive. Tons of cocaine, meth, pot, and other controlled substances came into the area by sea every day. There were kidnappings in the street, where young women were snatched up, forced to take drugs until they were addicted, then sold into prostitution.

Florida's coastline was more than a fourth of the combined 5,000 miles of oceanfront in the lower forty-eight states. Each day, thousands of boats and ships came and went. It was impossible to track them all, let alone search them.

The cartel kingpins were bigger than the mafia dons, wielded more power, and were ten times as ruthless. A lot like the warlords of Somalia were back in the day.

"What's the next step?" Savannah asked.

"Sampson was scared," I replied. "I could see it in his eyes when I asked some questions the cops hadn't. Questions he didn't have good answers for. The first thing he did after we left was to call someone in Miami. And the first thing that guy did was call someone over on the west coast. Chyrel is going to record the call next time any of them talk to one another."

"The kid in the street idea?" Tank asked, referring to the illegal wiretap I'd requested.

"It's a means to an end," I said. "The cops can't use it, but I can."

"You think Cobie's over there? With the Blancs?" Savannah asked, noticeably shuddering.

"I don't know," I replied. "But the guy with the burner phone in Miami is likely a drug dealer and the Blancs are importers. It's just a possible first step."

We talked a while longer, then Florence said she was tired and was going to bed.

As soon as we heard the door to Kim and Marty's house close, Savannah looked at me over the dancing fire. "Are you going to Miami?"

"Tomorrow's Christmas Eve," I said. "I think we have plenty to keep us busy here. I'm taking Tank flying tomorrow, to show him around."

CHAPTER NINE

We woke early. It was still dark as I gazed out the window to the bunkhouse on the north side. Both it and Florence's temporary home were dark. I switched on the low-power LED lights in the living room. That way, Tank would know we were up when he looked over.

Then I let the dogs out.

As I was pouring my coffee, I saw Tank pass the window and motioned him to come in. When he did, I expected the dogs to be right behind him, but they weren't.

"Did you see the dogs?" I asked.

"Waited for them to pass by," he said. "You sleep late in your old age."

There'd been no light in the bunkhouse because Tank had already left it. I guess retirement to him didn't include sleeping in.

"They didn't notice you?" I asked, as I poured another mug and handed it to him.

"The day I can't slip past a couple of guard dogs, just bury me, because I'm already dead."

I shouldn't have been surprised, considering who Tank was, but I was impressed, nonetheless. Every morning, the dogs went down the back steps and split up, circling the island. Finn had been doing it for years and now the two of them worked together.

"You should teach them vertical recon," Tank said, as Savannah came out of the bedroom.

She came straight to the coffee pot. "What, pray tell, is vertical recon?"

"The tendency for predators on the ground to hunt for prey on the ground," I replied. "Tank was on the catwalk around the fish tanks when the dogs went out and they didn't see him."

"I'll have breakfast ready in just—"

"Please," Tank interrupted, raising a hand, palm out. "Let me do that. You just sit back and relax. I insist."

I'd had dinner at Tank's house a few times. He was great with meat on a grill, but I had no idea how he was with eggs on a stove.

"Aw, that's very sweet," she said. "You'll find everything in the refrigerator and the iron skillet is in the cabinet to the right of the stove."

Then she turned to me. "What time are you boys leaving?"

"First light," I replied.

"Drop me and Flo off at the Rusty Anchor," she said. "We're going shopping."

"On Christmas Eve?" I asked. "It'll be a madhouse."

"You get a thrill out of beating bad guys," she said. "We get ours out of beating other shoppers to the punch."

Tank laughed. "Yeah, I can see how you two get along."

An hour later, with the sun just peeking over the horizon, the four of us went down the stairs to the dock area below the house.

"Holy shit!" Tank exclaimed when I switched on the lights. Then he spun around on the steps and looked up at Savannah and Florence in horror. "I am so sorry, ma'am."

"Don't be," Savannah said. "It's the same reaction most people have when they see what's under the house."

Tank continued down the steps, his eyes moving back and forth over *Gaspar's Revenge* and *El Cazador*. Then he noticed the smaller boats in the other half of the dock space.

"I was wondering where your little boat disappeared to when you got back last night."

"Let's take *Knot L-8*," Florence said. "There's room for four."

Tank let out a low whistle as he reached the bottom and saw the name on the stern of my homemade wooden speedboat. "Knot-L-eight, *Not Late*, very catchy. Is she as fast as the name implies?"

"I built her myself, with help from some friends," I said, as I took the keys from the box at the bottom of the steps.

I stepped into the little boat's forward cockpit and settled into the helm seat. After inserting the key and turning it, I pushed the starter button for the port engine, which fired instantly and settled into a low rumble.

"That thing sounds like a motorcycle," Tank said.

Pushing another button, the aft deck started to slowly open on hydraulic rams. Then I started the starboard engine.

Tank looked down into the engine bay. "Two Harley engines? You gotta be kidding me."

"V-twin engines, yeah," I said. "But they're custom built by a company called S&S. They're bigger and have a lot more power than just about any motorcycle."

I pushed the button to close the engine bay, then clicked the key fob to open the outer doors. "Climb aboard."

"You take the front," Tank said to Savannah. "I'll sit back here with Florence, if that's okay."

Florence smiled. "Do you like fast cars, Mister Tank?"

"What man doesn't?"

"Then you're in for a real treat this morning," she said, as she untied the lines before stepping aboard.

I put the boat in gear and idled forward until we were clear of the big doors, and then I clicked the fob to close them again. The dogs were sitting on the end of the short pier, watching as we passed.

"We'll be back in a few hours," I said to them. "*Bewachen!*"

Both dogs rose, heads up and on a swivel. After a moment, Woden turned and trotted toward the foot of the pier, splitting up from Finn to better guard the island.

"They speak German?" Tank asked, as we idled down the short channel.

I looked back and Florence grinned. "No," she said. "They *speak* dog. But they understand a few German words."

Tank laughed. "How'd they learn German?"

Savannah turned around in her seat. "Woden was trained for protection duty and learned certain commands in German. Finn figured out what they meant just from watching him."

"That's just like a Lab," Tank said. "My folks always had one or two and they learned from each other, one generation to the next."

I turned left into Harbor Channel and slowly brought *Knot L-8* up on plane. I continued accelerating until she reached thirty knots. When we got to the cuts just south of Mac's island, I veered out of the deep channel and weaved through the narrow passes, the boat responding effortlessly. Once in deep water again, I opened the throttles and turned south toward the Seven Mile Bridge.

We reached fifty knots in the sleek, barrel-backed wooden boat and made it to the Anchor in half the time it would take in the Grady.

"That's an incredible boat," Tank said, as we tied her off to the barge at the end of Rusty's canal.

"We'll be back here about two," Savannah said. "But I'll call you. Do you think you'll be gone that long?"

"Probably not," I replied. "If I don't hear from you before we land, we'll just hang out with Rusty for a while."

I gave them both a hug, then Tank and I headed toward the end of the dock as the girls turned toward the parking lot and Florence's Wrangler.

"Nice family," Tank said, as we walked along the dock.

"Thanks," I replied. "Fortunately, Florence got her mom's looks *and* brains."

"I don't know. I see a good bit of you in that girl." He stopped and looked across the canal toward Savannah's boat, *Sea Biscuit*. "Whoa! Is that what I think it is? Looks like an old Grand Banks."

"It is," I said. "That's Savannah's boat." I patted *Salty Dog's* gunwale. "And this is my ketch."

"Is that right? How many boats do you own?"

"You've seen them all but one. I have a long-range, all steel, pilothouse trawler, too. It's down in Central America right now."

"Why there?"

"It's a long story," I replied. "Just call it a strategic location."

"I always wanted to own one of those old trawlers," he said. "So, where is it we're flying?"

"Figured I'd show you the whole picture," I replied, as we neared *Island Hopper*. "We'll follow the Keys up to Biscayne Bay, then cut across the Everglades to Cape Sable, and fly out to Fort Jefferson before coming back here—about four hundred miles."

I looked at my watch. It was almost 0900. "We should be back shortly after noon, unless we stop for lunch somewhere."

While I removed the tiedowns and inspected the plane, Tank was busy on his phone.

"Those places you mentioned?" he said, as I opened the engine cowling. "We'll be flying over part of Miami, huh?"

I wiped the dipstick and put it back in. "Yeah. The Upper East side."

"Once a Devil Dog, always a Devil Dog," he said with a chuckle, from under the starboard wing. "You got your teeth in something and can't let it go. How precise is Chyrel's computer at locating a cell phone?"

I grinned over at him. "She can tell our two phones apart this close together."

"Is that right?" he asked, as I closed the cowling.

"Now comes the hard part," I said.

"Hard part?"

I wiped my hands with a rag and pointed with my chin toward the boats docked along both sides of the canal. "Waking up the whole neighborhood. Climb in."

"Ya know something," Tank began, as he stepped up onto the float and opened the door, "I've flown in all kinds of military aircraft and dozens of commercial aircraft, but this is my first time in a civilian plane. Just how old is this thing?"

I climbed into the pilot's seat. "Not as old as you," I replied. "But close. She first reached for the sky in 1953."

After strapping in, I turned on the battery and went through my preflight check list. Finally, I yelled out the window, "Clear prop!"

With the magnetos off, I hit the starter and counted revolutions. Radial engines will get a bit of oil settled in the combustion chamber of the lower cylinders and you have to "walk the prop" to clear it. In the old days, before electric starters, it was literally that—someone on the ground walking the prop through four revolutions.

When I turned the mags on, the big Pratt & Whitney caught, stumbled, belched blue-gray smoke, coughed a couple of times, and then settled into the familiar, smooth rumble that only a radial engine can produce. I put on my headphones and pointed to another pair by Tank's knee.

After a minute to let her warm up and, having seen more than one head pop out of a hatch, I advanced the throttle slightly to get her rolling, then stepped on the right rudder pedal to turn her toward the boat ramp.

I pulled the throttle back to idle as *Island Hopper* bounced, rocked, and rolled down the ramp and into the water. On land, she was about as ungainly as an albatross. Floating was a little better, but not much. In the air, however, it was a whole different story.

I raised the wheels and made the requisite radio calls to alert air traffic in the area, then turned into the southeast wind and advanced the throttle to full.

The engine roared in defiance as *Island Hopper* gathered speed and the floats climbed up on top of the water. In the distance of a football field, we were airborne.

Tank's voice came over my headset. "What got you into this kind of work?"

Glancing over at him, I replied, "It's not really what I do. I mostly just take people out fishing or diving."

I leveled off just below two thousand feet. We'd fly low and slow, following the highway toward the mainland, while staying about half a mile out over the water.

"And that's how you ended up working for Homeland Security? Taking people fishing?"

"I never really worked for *them* either," I said. "Deuce Livingston did—he headed a team of counterterrorist operatives, tasked with protecting South Florida. I sometimes provided covert travel for him and his men. The only reason my name's on the sign at his office is because I helped fund the startup."

"And yet, here we are. Flying to Miami in a seventy-year-old plane, to take a look at a drug smuggler's house."

I shrugged. "Would you rather have gone shopping with Savannah and Florence?"

"Ha-ha, no," he replied. "That's another thing I've been meaning to ask you. Why do you call your daughter Florence, while everyone else calls her Flo?"

"Savannah's last name is Richmond," I said. "Her parents were Jackson and Madison Richmond, and Savannah had a sister named Charlotte, but she died a few years back."

"Ah, now I get it. All southern city names."

I thought about it a moment. Savannah's college friend in Belize called her Savvy. Hell, even my name was shortened from the name I was given at birth—Jesiah. Was I too formal with my own family?

We continued to follow the Keys as they arced toward the mainland. I pointed out a few things of interest along the way and Tank asked a lot of questions about my plane and the areas we flew over. As we neared Biscayne Bay, I dropped our altitude to just a thousand feet and stayed well out over the Atlantic. That low and that far east, we weren't a danger to flights out of Homestead Air Reserve Base.

I put my phone in its cradle, secured to the dash. It was easy to see from both seats. I entered the GPS coordinates for the location the burner phone in Miami had been when Sampson called it.

Before leaving the island, I'd texted Chyrel to see if it was still there and she'd replied that it was, and she'd let me know if the phone moved. So far, she hadn't, so I assumed whoever Sampson had called was still in the same place.

"What exactly are we going to be looking for?" Tank asked, comparing the moving map image on the phone's screen to what he was seeing through the windshield.

"I have no idea," I replied. "I just want to get a look at where this guy lives."

"This has to cost quite a bit in gas," Tank said. "Just to look at where someone lives who may or may not be involved in the girl's disappearance."

"Need is a relative thing these days," I said with a grin. "It borders on desire. When my grandfather died, he left me enough that I wouldn't have to worry too much. Friends and I uncovered some treasure over the years, and a portion of that went into the kitty. These days, if I feel like doing something, I just do it."

"Is that right? So, why are you still busting your ass to take people fishing and hunting down crooks?"

"I like being on the water," I replied. "As for why I hunt down crooks, probably for the *real* reason you stayed in the Corps until they had to kick you out, yelling and screaming."

"You think you know my real reasons now?"

"Oh, the reason you gave Florence was true," I said. "But the underlying rationale behind your staying was because you were damned good at what you did—motivating Marines."

He looked over at me for a moment. "You do this just because you're good at it?"

There was more to it than that and he wasn't going to let me off the hook. "I don't like bullies," I said. "Never did. I don't like people who hurt others for financial gain."

"Like that warlord who was shielding himself with the boy."

He said it as a statement, not a question. And he was right. But it went back a lot further than that fateful day outside Mogadishu. It went back to my childhood, growing up in Fort Myers.

I was an only child being raised by my grandparents. I met another kid shortly after I went to live with Mam and Pap, a Calusa Indian who was also an only child. It was the late sixties, and he was kind of smallish then. Other kids picked on him because of his skin color and I didn't like that. I guess since Billy Rainwater and I didn't have any siblings, it was natural that we became friends, allies, blood brothers, and later, fellow Marines. I was bigger than most kids my age and nobody picked on Billy when I was around.

But on that one day in the Mog, I'd pulled the trigger to end a man's life, knowing full well that I'd most likely scuttled my career in doing so.

I'd been a Marine for fourteen years, three weeks, and two days, and just over three years as a gunnery sergeant, with the goal of reaching sergeant major one day. Over the next six years, I was passed over for promotion to first sergeant twice, because of what happened in the Mog.

The writing was on the wall. The times were changing, and the battlefield had become a political chessboard.

So, I quietly retired.

CHAPTER TEN

Benito's phone woke him again after a long night of business and pleasure. It was only eleven o'clock, but when he saw the number on the screen, he forgot about being tired or pissed.

The blonde next to him mumbled something as he rolled out of bed and answered the phone.

"I wasn't expecting to hear from you until later," Benito said.

"Change of plans," the voice on the other end growled over the sound of the wind. It sounded like he was driving with the windows down. "I'll be at the club in an hour. You ready to do business?"

"I'll be there," Benito said.

"Be sure to bring the girl."

The wind noise stopped, and Benito looked at the screen. The call had ended.

"Get up," he said to the blonde.

She was a new dancer at one of the clubs he scouted talent for. She'd just moved down from Boston, and still needed a lot of work. She looked a lot better than she performed in the sack, and for a dancer, the looks were the important part. Anything else could be learned.

"What's going on?" she asked drowsily.

"I have to go," he said, heading to his closet. "I got business to attend to, and that means you have to go."

He dressed quickly in white linen pants and a blue guayabera shirt, and when he came back to the room, the blond girl had already left.

He picked up his phone, found Vanessa's number and hit the *Call* button. She picked up on the fourth ring.

"*Hola*," she whispered drowsily.

"It's Benito. The schedule has moved up. The client will be arriving in an hour and we are meeting him at Uno."

"In an hour?" she said, sounding slightly more energized.

"Yeah. Dress for success, *chica*. And you probably should bring an overnight bag."

"Who is this guy, Benny?"

"He's my supplier, baby. So, you gotta treat him really good. There's an extra thousand if he's happy."

"I will," Vanessa said eagerly. "Do you want me to meet you there? My roommate has the car."

"I'll send an Uber," Benito said, as he pulled up the app. "It should be there in fifteen minutes to bring you here. Be ready."

He ended the call and went back into the closet. Benito thought the blonde was better looking than Vanessa; taller, with a more robust body. But the little dark-haired *puta* was far more energetic *off* the dance floor. Jasmin would learn; she was still young, awkward, and shy. Maybe he would bring both of them home one night, so the *pequeña cubana salvaje* could show her how it was done.

Benito knelt beside the floor safe. It had a biometric lock and opened simply by placing a hand on a hand-shaped outline on the top. He pulled a small overnight bag from a stack of them beside the safe and began removing bundles of hundred-dollar bills from inside.

He counted out twenty-five bundles, placing them on the floor, then counted them again as he put them in the bag. When he stood and picked it up, it was heavy, but not conspicuously so, weighing less than ten pounds.

Benito closed the safe and carried the bag to the living room, where he set it on the coffee table before going into the kitchen to make his usual cup of Cuban coffee. Just as the day before, and nearly every day before that, he tapped out a small line of coke on the dining room table and snorted it with his custom-engraved platinum coke tube. A snake wound its way around the side of the tube so that its head disappeared up his right nostril.

As had happened the day before, the rush was instantaneous when he tilted his head back and pinched his nose. He sniffed hard through the nostril with the candy in it.

"*Mierda!*" Benito cursed, stomping his feet, as he danced about the room. "Damn, that's good!"

While the coffeemaker surged and dripped, he decided to count the money a third time, so he opened the bag once more and placed each bundle on the table. Too bad Jasmin had already left. Benito liked to show off in front of his string of girls. They had to know that he was the *gran hombre* who could make them rich. But then, Vanessa was on her way.

He went back to the kitchen and poured a cup, then looked out the window of his little two-bedroom bungalow.

Homes in the Upper East Side started at half a million and Benito had bought the little house as a place to bring prospective dancers and models to "audition" for him. The second bedroom was a full photography studio, with lights and cameras, which impressed his new girls when they saw it.

A car stopped at the curb and the passenger door opened. Vanessa stepped out, wearing a skin-tight, pale yellow dress that barely covered her hips. It left little to the imagination. The contrast of yellow against her brown skin and black hair made her look oh-so-exotic.

She strode slowly and confidently toward the house, carrying a small overnight bag in her hand. The driver just sat in his car, watching. She saw Benito in the window and smiled.

He opened the door and waved her in. "I'm just about ready," he said, heading back toward the sofa in the living room. She followed and watched as he sat down and returned the money to the bag. He glanced at his watch. "We'll be early if we leave now."

"How early?" she asked, sitting close to him on the couch and rubbing him through his pants.

He let his dark eyes wander over her body. "Not early enough for that, *chica*." He then pulled his little bottle from his pocket. "But we have a few minutes."

He carefully tapped out two small lines on the table and offered her his tube. She greedily accepted it and bent over the table, pulling the hair behind her left ear. In a flash, one of the lines disappeared. Vanessa leaned back into the plush sofa, her hand going to her nose as she arched her back.

Benito's eyes locked on the gap between her thighs. As she leaned back, the dress rode up her hips, exposing matching yellow panties.

She handed him the tube and he quickly snorted the other line, his second in ten minutes. Vanessa looked at him with smoldering dark eyes. He sensed she was eager and ready. He was, too. But there wasn't enough time.

"We better go," he said, rising slowly while leering at her. "Or we will be *muy tarde*."

She rose and stood close to him. She wore stiletto heels, which elevated her tiny five-foot-one frame to make her appear much taller.

"Tomorrow, then," she said, a bright smile on her face. "After you watch me dance at Booby Trap?"

When Benito had stopped by the club after midnight, Marvin had told him that he'd definitely like Vanessa back for the weekend. She'd probably screwed him after her show. Benito didn't care. It was business.

"I wouldn't miss it for anything," he said, picking up the bag and gesturing toward the door.

The drive to Uno wasn't long—five minutes when traffic was light, ten when it wasn't. Benito guided his expensive black sportscar into the nearly empty lot next to one of Miami's best men's clubs. The place didn't open for another two hours, so he drove deep into the lot and parked against the side of the building near the back.

After he shut off the engine, he turned to Vanessa. "Now, when you meet this guy, be careful. He is *un gran hombre feo.*

"How ugly?"

"He is *muy viejo*, with long hair and beard," Benito said, "and he is *gigante*. He will be driving an old truck, but he is a rich and powerful *hombre, si?* You will be safe, and he will take you home tomorrow."

The two got out of the car. The heat hit Benito instantly. He started toward the back of the car but stopped as a beat-up old truck with big tires turned into the lot.

"Here he is," Benito said, looking at his watch. "And he is early. Remember, don't let him see that you think him ugly."

CHAPTER ELEVEN

Still south of Miami Beach, I switched from intercom to radio to contact Miami Approach. I would likely need clearance to transit their airspace.

"Miami Approach. Beaver, November one-three-eight-five. VFR advisory."

The response was immediate. "Beaver three-eight-five, go ahead with your request."

I gave them our location, heading, and altitude, so they could spot us on their radar, then requested flight following and transit over Miami's Upper East Side to look at property, then around the busy airport and across the state to Flamingo. The phone's location was right on the fringe of the busy international airport's airspace, but well out of the normal flight path of departing flights.

Approach gave me a squawk code, which I entered into the transponder as I repeated it back.

"Beaver three-eight-five, radar identified, fifteen hundred feet. Stay east of US-1 and maintain VFR."

I acknowledged and began our turn toward Miami Beach. Nine of the ten tallest buildings in the state were located in Miami. They were easy to spot. The tallest, Panorama Tower in Brickell, was almost half as tall as the altitude we were flying.

I throttled back to just above stall speed, almost paralleling Julia Tuttle Causeway a little to the south. I noticed the vector Approach gave me would put us right at the southern part of the Upper East Side.

As I neared the mainland, I started a slow turn to the north, making sure to stay slightly to the east of Biscayne Boulevard. The blue dot on my phone's screen was just ahead, slightly to the east of the busy thoroughfare. Off to the west, about a mile away, I could see I-95, where many of the cars in the left lane were passing us.

Tank looked at the phone's screen, then down at the landscape crawling past below *Island Hopper*. "Less than a mile," he said, craning his neck to find the location on the ground.

Just then, my phone chirped an incoming call. I glanced down at the screen and saw Chyrel's name, then clicked the *Accept* button. The phone's cradle was also a wired connection to the intercom system.

"I'm almost over the guy's location," I said, without preamble.

"He's on the move," she replied. "Northbound on US-1 from the location you have."

"There!" Tank said, unable to cover his excitement. "A black Nissan GT-R."

The car he was pointing at looked exactly like the one I'd seen the pusher driving at the Rusty Anchor and again later, on the security footage.

It was midmorning and traffic was light, but the car was stopped at an intersection. Sixty miles per hour was *Island Hopper's* stall speed. We couldn't go any slower.

"Thanks, Chyrel. Gotta go." I ended the call as I banked toward the right, increasing power slightly so we didn't fall out of the sky.

"There's a pair of binos under your seat," I told Tank.

"Don't be doing any of that pilot shit for a second," he said, as he unbuckled his harness and lifted himself off the seat enough to raise the bottom.

Once he was strapped back in, he looked out the windshield.

"Over there," I said, pointing at the black car now accelerating away from the stop light.

"Got him," Tank said.

I started a series of turns, bumping the speed up a little more as we flew out over the north end of Biscayne Bay. I couldn't go as slowly as the car, but I could zig-zag or do lazy circles to keep it in sight.

"He's turning west," Tank said. "It looks like two people in the car."

I glanced over, seeing the car turn onto NE 79th Street. In the opposite direction, it crossed the bay over to North Beach. He was probably headed to the interstate.

I continued to circle.

"He's stopping," Tank said. "Pulling into a place on the north side of that four-lane."

I came out of the circle just above the causeway and lined up with 79th Street. "Where'd he go?"

"Just ahead," Tank said. "I see him. He's parking beside a building with white stripes on the roof."

I saw a place about a mile ahead with a dark roof that had white sealant at the seams of the roll-on roofing material.

"It's a strip club," Tank said. "At least there's a sign showing a girl dancing on a pole. Know a place called Uno?"

"I've heard of it," I said. "You're right—it's a strip club. Take the yoke."

"I don't know how to fly a damned plane!"

"Just use the wheel to keep us level," I said, pointing at the artificial horizon indicator. "I have the pedals. I want to see this guy."

He handed me the binos and put his hands hesitantly on the wheel.

The Beaver is an amazingly easy and forgiving plane to fly. Unless he yanked on the yoke, we'd be all right.

I trained the glasses ahead and found the car, just as the doors opened. A man got out of the driver's side and a woman out of the passenger's. It was the same guy I'd seen at the Rusty Anchor. I was sure of it. He was dressed in white linen pants and a loose-fitting, light blue guayabera shirt. The woman had long, dark hair and wore a tight-fitting, exceptionally short, yellow dress. They were both dark skinned—probably Hispanic.

My cell phone chirped, just as a big 4x4 pulled in and parked next to the black sportscar. It was Chyrel calling again.

"I have eyes on the guy," I told her without a hello. "I'm certain his car is the one on the video and he's the same guy who was at the Rusty Anchor selling drugs."

The door to the truck opened and a large man with long hair and a beard got out. It was Willy Quick.

"You hung up before I could tell you that he's meeting the unknown guy from Marco Island."

"He's not unknown anymore," I said, as I handed the binos back to Tank, and took the wheel. "It's Willy Quick."

I banked to the right to get back out over the bay.

"The guy from last summer?" she asked. "I thought they arrested the whole Blanc clan?"

"Same guy," I said. "Only Kurt Blanc got any serious time."

"Looks like a drug deal or something," Tank said. "Both men and the woman are holding a bag of one kind or another."

As I turned, Tank lost sight of them until they reappeared on the other side of the aircraft. "The two men just exchanged bags," Tank said.

"The girl seem like a willing participant?" I asked.

"My guess is yeah," Tank replied. "The big guy's taking her around to the passenger side of the truck and she's being real...friendly, I'd say, with Miss Chyrel on the line."

"Gallantry in a situation like this isn't warranted," Chyrel said.

"Okay, she's gettin' all slutty with the ugly guy, then. The little guy is heading to the back door of the building. Looks like the girl is going with the guy in the truck."

"Can you read the tag number on the car?" Chyrel asked.

"Hang on," I said, turning to line up with the club again. "We're too far away."

When we were closer, Tank gave her the number and I could hear her fingers flying across her keyboard.

"Give me just a minute," she said. "There! His name is Benito Moreno. Thirty-one years old, Cuban national, feet dry at age five during the '94 *Balsero* crisis. He's got a lot of prior arrests, mostly drug-related, but only one conviction. That was when he was a teen. He was tried as an adult and did four years for involuntary manslaughter. What are you going to do, Jesse?"

"We don't have any idea what was in the bags they exchanged," I replied. "My guess is drugs and money. And my gut tells me to follow Quick."

Tank broke in. "The truck's going north on the main road now."

"I agree," Chyrel said. "I can find out a lot about Moreno and add that to the file you already have. Remember, Quick made two calls to burner phones in North Miami and Fort Lauderdale."

"He's a supply mule," Tank offered. "I bet we see close to the same scenario at those two places."

"You might be right," Chyrel said. "Quick is calling the same North Miami burner right now."

"Give me the location," I said, clearing the first way point from my phone. "It can't be far and if we're lucky, we might be able to ID more players."

Chyrel read the latitude and longitude numbers to me and I punched them into the phone. A blue dot appeared about three miles to the north.

"I'm going to fly on ahead, toward Haulover, at the north end of the bay," I said. "Is the phone located at a strip club like the first?"

"Good call," Chyrel replied. "Yes, it is. A place called Don's."

I pointed *Island Hopper's* nose toward the man-made inlet, where the barrier island was very narrow.

"They call that Haulover?" Tank asked, pointing to the inlet dead ahead.

"About a hundred and fifty years ago, way before the inlet was built, local sponge and turtle fishermen in this part of Biscayne Bay cut a trail through the narrow part of the island. It allowed them to carry small skiffs over to reach the fishing grounds to the north a lot faster than going way down to the end of the barrier island."

Minutes later, I flew *Island Hopper* directly over the blue dot, as Tank and I studied the place. Unlike the first one, this location was in a cluster of businesses with cars parked in close proximity to many of them. But few were parked around the club itself, which was on a corner. It had a large parking lot behind it and what looked like a couple of drive-throughs.

I started circling over the water treatment plant and out over the north end of Biscayne Bay. Tank watched the club and the highway, looking for Quick's big 4x4.

"There he is," he said, pointing.

Glancing over, I saw Quick approaching the light at the corner just before Don's. The cars in front of him started moving and he barely had to slow down. Just past the intersection, he turned into the entrance to the men's club. But instead of circling around the south side, he continued straight down what looked like a service drive on the north side of the club. We lost him for a second, but the truck finally emerged in the back of the lot and parked next to a red car.

"Is Quick side by side with the guy now, Chyrel?" I asked.

"Yes. Less than thirty feet apart."

"See if you can get the tag number of the red car," I said to Tank.

"We'll have to wait until he leaves," Tank said. "He's backed up against some bushes.

As we circled, Tank described what he was seeing through the binoculars. Two men got out of the car and Quick met them at the back of his truck, where they exchanged briefcases. It was over in seconds and the red car left first.

"He's pulling out," Tank said. "Get closer."

I turned and followed the car for a moment.

"Got it," Tank said. "Florida tag, KRP-J40. That's Kilo, Romeo, Papa, Juliet, four, zero. Or it might be an O at the end."

"It's a zero," Chyrel said. "Florida doesn't use the letter O on license plates."

"The truck's leaving," Tank said. "He's turning north on the main highway again."

"When you get the name, Chyrel, add it and anything else you can tell me about the person to the file for me to go over later. My bet is, Quick is heading to a strip club in Fort Lauderdale next."

"It's like you had one of my buds in your ear," she said.

I could picture her at her console, no less than five monitors in front of her. "He's telling the Lauderdale contact to meet him at a place called Le Bear at one o'clock," she said. "I'm checking...yes, it's a club all right, but the strippers are male and Quick is talking to a woman. Sending you the GPS numbers."

"A gay strip club?" I asked, not really meaning to say it out loud.

"What've I told you about being a Neanderthal, Jesse?" Chyrel scolded, garnering a chuckle from Tank. "It's a nightclub for *ladies*."

When I put the numbers into the phone, a blue dot appeared, less than a mile from the beach, and a good fifteen or twenty miles up the coast from our location. I banked right toward the northeast and headed out over the Atlantic.

So far, Miami Approach hadn't questioned my maneuvers. I hoped I was vague enough that the guy assumed we were looking at multiple properties, which we apparently were.

"He's turning west," Tank said.

"Probably heading toward the interstate. Chyrel, let me know if he doesn't go north on 95. We're going to have to kill about ten minutes, even flying slow."

When we were a mile out over the water, Chyrel told us that Quick was turning north on the interstate. "Jesse, the woman with him is the same woman with Moreno when Sampson called him yesterday—Vanessa Ramos."

"Maybe she's more than just a hooker," I said. "It could be that she's Moreno's partner."

I turned north until we reached a point just east of the target. Then I started a series of elongated figure eights, taking us up and down the coast, five miles to the north and south of the location.

A few minutes before the scheduled rendezvous, I checked with Chyrel, who said it looked like he was still five minutes away.

I turned due west, heading straight up the road the club was on, Oakland Park Boulevard.

I'd been thinking that Quick had a penchant for strip clubs, but this one being a club for women, maybe I was wrong. What else did they have in common?

Again, the parking lot was nearly empty, save for a few cars parked in front of adjoining businesses. There was a single car parked in front of Le Bear, a gray luxury sedan, maybe a Caddy or Chrysler.

I circled to the north, keeping within a mile of the club, so Tank could keep an eye on it while staying to the east of US-1. There were airports all up and down the coast, and some had seven miles of controlled airspace around them, which I needed to avoid.

"There he is," Tank said, as if voicing a cat's thoughts when it spied a mouse pop out of a hole.

"Chyrel, did Quick use his burner any more yesterday after the calls to Moreno and these other two?" I asked.

"None until he called Moreno today."

"My guess is he only had these three stops," Tank offered. "The bags and briefcases they're exchanging are small. None would hold more than ten kilos of coke."

"How do you know this?" I asked.

"I told you," he replied, lowering the binos and grinning. "I been doing a lot of reading."

"And a standard-sized briefcase can hold a million dollars in hundred dollar bills," Chyrel said. "That's about the price for that much coke. And *coincidentally*, a million in large bills would weigh about the same as ten kilos of coke."

"He just parked next to a gray Chrysler 300," Tank said. "It doesn't make sense. They're kinda out in the open there. Traffic is passing by no more than fifty feet away. These guys are bold."

"Now I get it!" I said. "During my first year at Lejeune, I worked as a bouncer at a club in Jacksonville. Every day, just before the place opened, a cash drop was made, so the club could make change for the patrons to put in the dancers' G-strings."

"Eww," Chyrel said, "talk about dirty money."

"Sorry, Chyrel. But I remember it always being a really intimidating guy who made the drops, and it was always in the open."

Tank laughed. "Remember that night at the Thunderbird? You blew through a month's pay—hang on. The guy's getting out of the truck, but there's nobody around. Wait! Someone just came out of the club, a blond woman wearing business clothes. She just opened the trunk of the 300. Okay, now the Quick guy is putting one briefcase in her trunk and taking another out."

"Exactly the way the cash drops went down," I said. "What's the girl doing?"

"Can't really see her well, but she's still in the truck. Quick just got back in and is backing out."

Tank read the tag number of the Chrysler to Chyrel. "She's going back inside, empty-handed."

"I need to know who Quick calls next, Chyrel."

"Will do," she replied.

"Lost him behind some buildings," Tank said. "He was headed west."

"I got him," Chyrel said. "He's getting back on the interstate, moving south."

"Headed home," I guessed. "I'm gonna let you go, Chyrel. I'll be busy with Miami Approach threading through these airspaces. If he deviates from a route back to the west coast, let me know."

"Roger that," Chyrel said. "I'll get to work on getting background info on all these people and add it to the file."

I thanked her and ended the call, then contacted Miami Approach again. They gave me a heading due west, between Fort Lauderdale International and the less-busy Fort Lauderdale Executive Airports, then handed me over to the Lauderdale tower until I was clear of their airspace.

Once we were out over the Glades, I contacted MIA again and canceled flight following.

"You think he's taking her back to Marco Island?" Tank asked, as we flew two thousand feet above the Everglades.

"It's Christmas and he's recently widowed," I said. "And he's got money to burn, I'd bet."

"Tell me more about this Blanc family."

"They live in the Glades, east of Marco Island and Everglades City," I replied. "They lie low for the most part. That is, when they're not actively bringing in drugs. From accounts I've heard, they supply a good deal of the cocaine and methamphetamine found on the streets from Miami to Orlando."

"I always envisioned big-time Miami smugglers as guys who drive fancy cars. Like on that show, *Miami Vice*."

"Not the Blancs," I said. "The house Willy lives in is old and looks abandoned—like it could fall down any minute. It sits about a mile off the highway, in the middle of the swamp."

"So, what do you suppose they do with the money?"

"The money?" I asked.

"If those three stops were deliveries of thirty kilos of coke, he's likely headed home with a half million dollars in profit. How often do you think he does that?"

"From what I've been told, at least once a week," I replied. "Probably more. You're right, the whole family—and there's like forty of them—couldn't burn through that much money if they tried. And they all seem to keep a low profile."

"And they been at this a while?"

"Since the '60s, I heard."

"They could be sitting on close to a billion dollars in cash."

That was mind-boggling, but not likely. "Did you ever watch *Breaking Bad*?" He nodded. "The scene in the storage unit with the pallet full of cash? If that'd been real money, it was probably less than five million bucks, even if it were all in hundreds. Imagine that pile of cash, times two hundred. I guess if it was stacked neatly and all in one-hundred-dollar bills, it'd probably fill a house."

"You got a ton of information," Tank said. "And it all started with that one phone call."

I shook my head sadly. "Just the tip of the iceberg, Tank. And we're not any closer to finding Cobie."

CHAPTER TWELVE

After leaving Benny at Uno, Vanessa rode north with the big brute, as he made similar exchanges at two more clubs, one run by a woman.

She'd learned the guy's name was Willy, but he didn't talk much, so she knew little else about him. Besides his name, all she'd learned was that his wife had recently died. She guessed that's why he wanted her company. Vanessa had no family, so Christmas was just another day.

After leaving the woman's club, they headed south, back toward Miami.

Vanessa had known johns like him before—lonely guys, who, after picking her up, had second thoughts. They acted the same way, quiet and nervous. She thought about the three bags behind the seat, each filled with money. How could anyone be sad with all that cash?

She turned in her seat and studied him. To say the man was big was an understatement. He sat, hunched behind the wheel of the big truck, his head almost banging into the roof, and even though the truck was huge, he took up half of the wide bench seat designed for three people.

Vanessa liked big men, but she'd never been with a man of Willy's proportions.

"Mind if I take my shoes off?" she asked. "Heels look good, but they're awful for riding in a car."

Willy looked over at her, pushed the hair away from his face, then glanced down at her feet. "Do what you like."

Reaching down, she slipped her heels off, then turned sideways in the seat and looked at him again.

"How tall are you?" she asked. "I'm five-one."

He looked over at her again, his eyes partially hidden behind the long, graying hair that she was sure hadn't been combed in a year.

"Six-eight," he said. "And before you ask—380 pounds."

"Wow," she said. "That's almost four of me."

"Scared?"

Vanessa smiled at him. He wasn't really all that ugly, just unkempt. He had dark, piercing eyes, and beneath his beard, she could tell he had a strong jawline. His shoulders were impossibly wide and he had arms as big as her thighs. She wondered decadently if the rest of his anatomy was proportionate.

"Not really," she said. "You look tough, but I like tough guys."

Vanessa had worked for Benny for nearly a year, though he barely knew her name. She often went with friends and clients of his, where no money ever changed hands. At least not with her. But Benny paid her well, and he'd promised her a thousand dollars for spending the night with Willy.

They were only a few miles down the interstate when he got into the lane for I-595 going west.

"I thought we were going back to Miami." she said.

"Naw," the big man growled. "I have a place just outside of town where I usually lay low the night after a delivery."

"Do you have any blow?"

Willy reached under his seat, pulled out a tightly wrapped kilo and placed it on the seat between them. "Knock yourself out, baby. But we'll be at my safe house in fifteen minutes."

Vanessa eyed the brick hungrily. But she was worried that she might come across as a common coke whore if she tore into it. "I can wait till we get there."

After about fifteen miles, the truck slowed, and Willy turned off at the exit for US-27. They were farther from the city than Vanessa had ever been, with nothing around but water and swamp.

"Is it much longer?" Vanessa asked.

"No," he grunted.

A few miles down the road, he slowed the truck, then turned onto a side road. There was a rickety bridge over the canal that ran along the highway. From there the road turned to dirt. After a few minutes, he turned right onto another dirt road, which was in even worse condition. Before long, sawgrass and tree branches grew in so close they were slapping the sides and roof of the truck.

Willy turned left through an opening in the foliage. It wasn't a road at all, just an overgrown, elevated dike that divided the swamp. A few minutes later, they entered a stand of cypress trees, where a small shack sat perched on stilts over the water. A wobbly-looking foot bridge connected the shack to the high ground, where he finally stopped the truck and turned off the engine.

It was deathly quiet; the only sound was that of the truck's engine ticking as it cooled.

"Well, this is really well hidden," Vanessa said, as the man turned toward her in his seat.

Without warning, he grabbed her throat with a big left hand, pinning her hard against the seat as he squeezed.

She tried to cry out, but her windpipe was blocked. She struggled, grabbing at the man's big, hairy forearm, her nails digging into his flesh. It had no effect on him at all.

After just a few seconds, she felt light-headed and the dappled sunlight filtering through the trees began to fade.

Then everything went black.

CHAPTER THIRTEEN

Flying out over Big Cypress National Preserve, I explained to Tank how large the Glades were, stretching away to the south, and how much bigger it had once been, before men arrived with machines to dredge, levy, and drain the land.

Then, as we flew out over the coast, just south of Marco Island, I showed him what most of the Florida coast had once looked like—wild and untamed.

I turned toward the south, flying just off the broken coastline.

"The area below us is called Ten Thousand Islands," I said.

"This is where that Quick character lives?" he asked, looking out at the uninhabited landscape.

"Farther inland," I said. "But yeah, the Blanc family is all over this part of Florida."

"I don't see a single house or building anywhere. Just a boat way up there at that point."

"That's Cape Sable," I said. "One of my favorite places on Earth."

Just then, my phone chirped. It was Chyrel again.

"Quick stopped," she said, after I answered. "He's parked in the middle of nowhere, about seventeen miles west of the city and a few miles north of Alligator Alley. He hasn't moved for twenty minutes. Sorry, I was called away to do some research for Jack."

"No problem," I said. "Maybe he stopped for lunch."

"You don't take a hooker to lunch," Chyrel said. "My guess is he took her there to—"

"We get the picture," I said. "And you're probably right. We're over Cape Sable now."

"I'll text you the location, but as far as I can see, there's just nothing there. And I'll keep an eye on him and let you know when he leaves."

"Roger that," I said, then ended the call.

"She's a Bama girl, huh?"

"Yeah," I replied. "But don't let the down-home accent fool you. She's smarter than any two people I know."

"And Jack is another of your operatives?"

"You might say that," I replied. "Jack Armstrong is the CEO of Armstrong Research."

"What kind of research?"

"Primarily oceanographic," I said. "Oil exploration. But he has a few others like me who go out and fix things."

"Fix things, huh?"

"Dig around," I elaborated. "Solve problems."

"By gun, by sword, or by bare hand."

"If necessary," I replied. "But he prefers wits and technology."

As we skirted the cape, I pointed out the small town of Flamingo in the distance. "It's about eighty miles from Everglades City to the Keys, and Flamingo is the only settlement between them."

"It's beautiful," Tank said, in uncharacteristic reverence.

I banked right, to a heading of 240 degrees, and climbed to 2500 feet. From there, we could see the Keys stretching out to the horizon.

"Next stop's Fort Jefferson," I said. "At the *real* end of the Florida Keys."

"I thought Key West was the end."

"It is if you're in a car," I said. "Fort Jefferson is in the Dry Tortugas, about seventy miles west of Key West. A lot of people think the Florida Keys and Key West are synonymous, but it's just one island in a long archipelago that stretches from Biscayne Bay to the Dry Tortugas, about two hundred miles. The island of Key West is barely five miles long."

"Is that the Seven Mile Bridge?" he asked, pointing to the high arch.

"Yeah, and about halfway between here and there, do you see that dark blue finger of water extending into the shallows to the southwest? My island's at the far end of it."

"Is that right? And you got all of this for your backyard."

"See those islands to the west of mine? We call that the backcountry. In many places you can walk from one island to another and barely get your knees wet."

"What good is that?"

"Sight fishing," I said. "The water's as clear and flat as glass. It's the habitat of bonefish, pompano, permit, snook, redfish, tarpon...all kinds of gamefish are caught back in the shallows, where you need a special boat to get to."

"That low one under your house?" he asked. "The one with the platform over the engine?"

"Yeah, it's called a flats skiff. You raise the engine and stand on the platform with a long push-pole, while your partner or client stands on the foredeck with a fly rod."

"I'd like to try that," Tank said, wistfully. "I used to do some fly fishing up in Montana when I was a kid."

I looked over at him and suddenly saw an old man wearing a Tank suit—the same on the outside, but old and withered within. As a Marine master gunnery sergeant, he'd been a very imposing figure, a larger-than-life hero, who'd risked it all for his brothers several times over. There were more than a dozen men who came home from Vietnam alive, thanks to Tank. And hundreds, maybe thousands more, since then, who'd survived the horrors of armed conflict due to his guidance and the lessons those under him learned and passed on to younger Marines.

But now, looking at him beside me, I saw a withered version of the man he once was.

"Is something wrong, Tank?"

He looked over at me, a forlorn expression on his face.

"I'm dying, Jesse."

"What?"

"Stage four pancreatic cancer," he said. "It's almost impossible to catch early, because of where the pancreas is located. It's usually only found when it spreads to other parts of the body and almost always diagnosed as stage four. Mine has spread to my liver, abdominal walls, and lungs. The doctors say I have just a few months."

I was dumbstruck. "Months?"

"Maybe a year if I undergo treatment."

"I don't know what to say, Tank. What treatment?"

"There isn't anything you or anyone else can say or do, Gunny. The treatment only extends life a few more months and eases the pain somewhat. There's no cure. I'm just going to die and that's the end of it."

I suddenly realized why Tank had wanted to come. He was childless, had no family left after his brothers died, and he'd never remarried after his divorce. All he had left were his brothers-in-arms.

"Why me?" I asked. "Of all your friends over the years?"

He looked me in the eye. "That's easy. You stood up beside me on that wall in Beirut."

"Yeah, well, it scared the living shit out of me."

He laughed. "Me too. My legs still get wobbly when I think about it. Look, I don't want to burden you, Jesse. While I'm still able, I just want to enjoy being alive, with someone who has a real zest for life. Maybe do some things I've never done before. I just thought you ought to know."

"Things like fly fishing for bonefish?"

He nodded. "That *was* what drew me to this place at first. But now, I think I'd be happier if you'd let me help find this girl and punish whoever took her."

"We'll do both," I said, staring through the windshield with sweaty eyeballs. "And a bunch of other stuff, too."

CHAPTER FOURTEEN

W e flew low and slow over Fort Jefferson. It was already getting close to the time Savannah said she'd be back from shopping. But that hardly mattered now.

There were a few boats at the fort's dock, and I could see a couple of people in the interior courtyard, and several more lying on the sand on the narrow strip that joined Garden Key to Bush Key.

A dark-haired woman, bare from the waist up, stood and waved, so I waggled the wings back at her.

"Everyone's so friendly down here," Tank said with a grin.

The flag at the fort hung limp, and the channel between Garden Key, where the fort was located, and Loggerhead Key to the west, had only a light chop. I circled to the north and lined up with the channel, reducing power as I lowered the flaps.

"We're landing?" Tank asked.

"You can't come to the Keys and not see the fort," I said. "While Captain Tony's and Sloppy Joe's might get a thousand tourists a day through their doors, Fort Jefferson has many days when the handful of park rangers are there alone."

"That sounds like the best job in the world. Do we have time? I thought you had to get back."

"I'll call Savannah on my satellite phone and let her know we'll be a little late."

Minutes later, we were idling toward the sandbar joining Garden Key and Bush Key to the east.

I could see the park ranger already heading our way on the path from the southeast corner of the fort. Private seaplanes had to have a special permit to visit the park. When the pontoons touched the sandy bottom, I killed the engine and pulled my flight bag out of a pouch behind my seat.

Tank spotted the ranger heading our way. "Kid looks a little hot under the collar. Are planes allowed to be here?"

I pulled my permit out and held it up. "With one of these, yeah."

Climbing down to the port pontoon, I waved the laminated permit at the ranger, then opened the storage compartment in the pontoon.

Inside was a bucket containing a small, ten-pound anchor and a hundred feet of line. I pulled it out and stepped down into the clear, knee-deep water.

"Good afternoon, sir," the ranger said, as Tank and I sloshed ashore.

"We won't be here long," I said, handing him my permit.

As he checked it over, I went back to the plane and easily pushed it off the beach a little to spin her around. Then, grabbing the rear crossmember, I dragged her back until I felt the pontoons touch the sand again. After that, I clipped the carabiner, attached to the bitter end of the anchor line, to an eyebolt in the sturdy crossmember between the pontoons and carried the bucket up onto the sandy beach. With all the line paid out, I pushed the flukes of the anchor into the powdery white sand, setting it deep. With no wind and little current to speak of, there was little chance *Island Hopper* would drift.

"Looks like everything's in order here, sir," the ranger said, handing the permit back to me. "Just a reminder: the park closes at sunset. That'll be at—"

"Seventeen-fifty," I interrupted. "Like I said, we'll only be here a short while."

He left and I turned to Tank. "Wanna see the fort?"

He looked off to the east, where the sandbar widened to become Bush Key. The little island was empty; the sunbathers were in the opposite direction. "Maybe later. I get the sense you want to talk, but don't know what to say."

We started walking then, crossing the sandbar to the north side of Bush, and heading away from the fort. Tank had always been good at reading his Marines' wants and needs, even when *they* didn't know what they wanted or needed. He'd dropped a MOAB right on my head. And he was right—I didn't know where to start.

"There's a lot of guys I could have gone to see," Tank said, walking barefoot with his hands behind his back. "I have to admit something to you here. I already knew a lot about how you've been spending these last twenty years since you left the Corps."

"What do you mean?"

"You cut a wide swath, Gunny. Always have. Stories of your exploits in and *out* of the Corps get around in certain circles. I know about the terrorist cell in Cuba who planned an attack in Miami."

We walked and I kept quiet, waiting. Only a handful of people knew about that. And if he knew that, he knew I'd lost my wife Alex in that same op.

"I know your determination to not leave a man behind," he continued. "And the extraordinary measures taken to bring him home. I know how and why you stuck your neck out for that Williams kid and then hunted down his murderer. By the way, his brother picked up master sergeant last month."

"Oohrah," I grunted. "Proud to know the man."

"I know about the treasure in the Bahamas," he said. "And the shootout there, I know all about the evildoers you've stopped, almost single-handedly; the sex traffickers, drug smugglers, terrorists, organ smugglers... Pretty much all of your adventures are known to a few. And I already knew about your inheritance. It's all these things and more that brought me here to have this talk with you today."

"I don't understand," I said. Not so much that he knew or how he learned these things, but I didn't see how any of that had to do with his being sick. "What's all that got to do with your... cancer?"

"Nothing," he replied, and kept walking, hands folded sedately at the small of his back.

He was in teacher mode. I'd been on the receiving end of a few folded-hands lessons before, and I'd seen a few field-grade officers receiving the same wise counsel. We walked on in silence for a while.

"Know how much the pension is for an E-9 over fifty years of service?"

"I know it's a hundred percent of base pay," I replied.

"I was a master gunny longer than most Marines serve—thirty-one years. During that time, my base salary almost tripled. I lived on base most of the time—ever since I was a gunny."

I remembered he'd moved from base housing to bachelor enlisted quarters after he and his wife split up. I'd lived in the BEQ for most of my career, also.

"That was what—'82?"

"Yeah, about then," he said. "I don't have a good memory for dates anymore. After that, I socked away ninety percent of my paycheck for thirty-six years."

"I still don't get how any of this involves me."

"It doesn't," Tank said. "Not directly, anyway. In no time at all, I'll be gone. I have no kids and over ten million dollars in investments."

I stopped in my tracks. "Whoa, Tank. I don't need or want—"

"And I wouldn't insult you by offering," he said, turning to face me. "You're doing something vital. I know all about your philanthropy, too—the funds you have set up to help others. And the occasional emerald you sell for your friend who works for Thurman."

"Wait a minute," I said, becoming flustered. "How can you possibly know this?"

He grinned, squinting up at me. "I told you. I've been reading."

I sat down in the sand and Tank sat beside me. I felt a light gust move the hair off my forehead as I stared out over the water. It was a long moment before he spoke again.

"I want you to administer my estate, Jesse. I want what I've earned and saved to go to good use. I want it to help others."

Of course, I thought. The man's been serving others for more than half a century.

"A legacy," I said softly.

"Yeah. A legacy. Will you do it for me, Gunny? Will you put what's mine with what's yours and continue doing what you do?"

I gazed out over the calm, azure Gulf waters for a moment, then nodded. "Yeah, Tank, I'm honored that you chose me."

"Good," he said firmly, rising with little effort. "Now, you better call that fiancée of yours. You don't want her thinking you got cold feet a week before the wedding."

"I have an idea," I said, rising from the sand. "Fishing isn't allowed here, but the Marquesas are right on the way back. A friend was there the other day and told me the water had warmed a little in the Gulf and the permit bite was exploding. Let's get out of here and stop there on the way back."

He glanced over at the old fort. "You said this was the biggest brick building in the Western Hemisphere?"

I nodded.

"Seems a shame to be all the way out here and not recon the place. Fish are everywhere. This fort is in just this one place. And we may be here just this one time. There's no guaranteed tomorrows for any of us."

He had a point. A particularly good point, considering what he'd told me. We shouldn't wait until things in our bucket lists had to be rushed. Like Travis McGee, we should take our retirement in little chunks and enjoy looking around at something unusual.

"Let's recon the fortress," I said with a grin, as we started walking. "It was never actually finished as a fully functioning fort. And enemy ships could easily avoid her guns."

"When was it built?"

"Mid-1800s, the golden age of sail," I replied. "The fort was way before its time, sitting so far out here in the Gulf. The ships and men who manned it needed constant provisions; there was no natural fresh water or food here. Just a big cistern below ground for rainwater, but seawater eventually seeped in."

"Sounds like a FOB."

"Exactly, a forward operating base, strategic for guarding the shipping lanes into and out of the Gulf. Her guns were for defense, but her ironclads and frigates took the fight to the enemy."

I waved an arm slowly to the north as we got to the sand spit. "The outer harbor could hold dozens of naval ships anchored safely from storms inside a ring of small keys, shoals, and reefs. Guarded by a half dozen fast frigates."

"You were born a hundred years too late," Tank said, as we walked back to the plane.

"Hang on," I said. "I gotta get my satellite phone."

"Go ahead and make your call," he said, continuing toward the sand path to the fort. "I'm gonna go ahead and start the recon."

Splashing out to *Island Hopper*, I climbed into the pilot's seat and grabbed the phone. Then I stepped out onto the pontoon to have a clear line of sight to the southwestern sky.

Savannah answered on the first ring. "Where are you? Are you okay?"

"I'm sorry," I said. "Something came up and we'll be late getting back. You and Flo take the boat back to the island and we'll just fly straight back there."

"What's wrong? You sound almost… defeated."

"Tank's dying," I said.

"Oh, dear," Savannah sighed. "He told you?"

"As far as I know, I'm the only one he's told, and now I've told you."

"Of course, I won't breathe a word," she said, then paused. "What is it?"

"Cancer," I replied, watching my mentor stop to chat with the people on the beach. The dark-haired woman had put her top back on. "His doctor told him he's only got a few months."

"I'm so sorry, Jesse. I know how much you idolized him."

"He wants me to administer his estate," I blurted out. "That's why he came down here."

"You'll do it, of course," she said, as if no other option existed. "He picked the right man."

Tank waved at the two couples on the sand and continued toward the trail that ran along the mote surrounding the giant brick buttresses.

"We're at Fort Jefferson," I said. "He wants to look around."

"Don't worry about us," she said. "We'll see you when you get home."

"Thanks, babe."

"Oh, and Jesse?"

"Yes?"

"You just called your daughter Flo."

"I know," I said with a chuckle. "Tank pointed it out. It was that or I insist on her calling me Jesiah."

I ended the call and noticed I had a text message from Chyrel. I opened it immediately.

I figured you were out of cell range. Quick started moving again at 1200. He was there at least an hour. Headed west on 75 now.

I'd almost forgotten about Willy Quick, the drug dealers, and Ty Sampson. I wanted to have another word with the surfboard maker. And maybe Moreno, too. But tomorrow was Christmas.

CHAPTER FIFTEEN

When Vanessa woke, her head hurt and her mouth was dry. The last thing she remembered was Willy choking her. It was dark and she was lying on a smelly blanket. The pain in her head told her she wasn't dead.

She heard a whispered voice as she tried to raise her head. "I think she's waking up."

That's when she felt the metal shackle on her left ankle. The cold steel brought her quickly to her senses, and she sat up, looking around in the gathering darkness.

Two figures sat cross-legged on a bare wooden floor, watching her.

"Where am I?" she asked.

The one on the left shrugged.

"Somewhere in a swamp," the other said. It was a woman's voice, but her face was shadowed behind her hair.

The two were facing each other, sitting in the middle of an empty room, with several feet between them.

Vanessa could see that they both had chains on their ankles. Their chains trailed back to two corners of the room. She looked down at her own leg and followed another chain to a third corner. In the remaining corner lay a fourth chain, an unlocked shackle on the end.

Vanessa struggled to her feet, picked up the chain and tested it, pulling hard. It didn't budge.

"Don't waste your energy," the woman said.

Vanessa looked over and studied them both. The quiet one appeared to be a woman, also. "What is this place?"

"Hell," said the quiet one.

"Where's Willy? Did he bring you here, too?"

"Willy?" the first woman said, looking up sharply, her hair falling away from her face. "The monster who brought you here? You know his name?"

Her left eye was puffy and bruised, and both eyes seemed hollow and vacant. Vanessa's eyes darted to the inside of the woman's elbow, which was also bruised.

A junky.

"Willy Quick," Vanessa replied, moving cautiously toward the two women. "He's a coke importer from the west coast."

Vanessa reached the end of her chain before getting close to either of the women. Apparently, Willy didn't want them to come into physical contact.

"How do you know his name?" the first woman asked.

"He, uh...knows my boss," Vanessa said. "I was supposed to spend the night with him."

"Why?" the quiet one asked. She had tracks on her arm, too.

"It's what I do," Vanessa said. "And I make a thousand bucks a night."

"You're a prostitute?" the first woman asked.

"Escort, bitch."

She turned and followed the chain to the corner. It was connected to a large eyebolt sticking out of a heavy wooden post. She tried to twist the big metal ring, but it didn't move.

"I'm sorry," the woman said. "Do you know anything else about him? Anything that we might use to get out of here? We don't even know where *here* is."

Vanessa looked over at them coldly. Sure, she tooted a little blow sometimes, or smoked some weed. But she drew the line at needles.

"We're about twenty miles from the city," Vanessa said. "We drove on 75 for about fifteen minutes, then turned onto Highway 27, then a bunch of dirt backroads with no names."

"You were awake when he brought you here?"

"Yeah," Vanessa replied. "Then the asshole choked me out when we stopped at a rickety old shack. He might have driven on from there. I don't know. Do you know what time it was when he brought me in here? What time it is now?"

"You've been out for a while," the woman replied. "It was past noon when he brought you in and shot you up."

Vanessa looked at her arm and touched it. There was a brown speck and the area around it was tender.

"He gave me a—?"

"All three of us," the woman said. "Then he left."

"What is it? The shot?"

The woman only shrugged. "I've smoked weed a few times, but that's it. I don't know what it is, but it makes the rest less painful."

"The rest?" Vanessa asked, looking from one to the other.

"We don't even know what day it is."

"Christmas Eve," Vanessa said.

The quiet one covered her face and sobbed.

"The rest of what?" Vanessa asked again.

"Rape," the woman said, her head falling again.

"How long have you been here?" Vanessa asked, then sat on the floor facing the two.

"He grabbed me on December ninth," the woman replied. "Broad daylight in the parking lot of a toy store. I know because it was my niece's birthday the next day and I was shopping for something to get her." She nodded toward the other woman. "She's been here since before Thanksgiving."

Their clothes were in tatters, especially the quiet one's. She looked frail, like she hadn't eaten in weeks. She was probably a little younger than Vanessa. The one doing all the talking looked healthier and maybe a little older. Both were small, like her.

"What does he want with us?"

"He's sick!" the quiet one shouted.

"He comes every few days," the woman said, her eyes glazing over in the failing light. "Sometimes he only rapes one of us, sometimes two. If he's feeling really brutal, all three."

Vanessa looked over to the vacant corner and the empty chain.

"There's never four of us," the woman said, and nodded to the younger one. "She told me when he first brought me here."

Then the woman indicated the empty shackle. "That was Margo. She'd been here since Halloween night."

"What happened to her?"

"She's dead!" the younger one shouted. "Just like Jenny before her! You're in Jenny's place! But you're not Jenny." Her voice was shaky and on the verge of hysterics. She sobbed into her hands again. "And just like me when he brings another replacement."

"He came yesterday," the woman said. "He unlocked Margo and took her into the other room, like he always does. We could hear him grunting and her crying. When he finished with her, we heard a big splash and then a lot of thrashing beneath the house."

"He fed her to the alligators," the young girl said softly.

Vanessa shuddered. "What's your name?"

"Michelle," the older woman said. "Michelle Tate."

"I'm Vanessa Ramos." She turned to the girl, expecting her to speak.

Michelle said, "Her name's Cobie Murphy."

CHAPTER SIXTEEN

Christmas dawned with a heavy sea fog shrouding the island. The blanket of low clouds absorbed the usual sound of waves lapping at the shoreline or splashing through the mangrove roots.

Tank and I had returned just in time for Savannah's sundowners on the deck. She'd pretended not to know until Tank said that it was okay, that he knew I'd already told her.

"Told her what?" Flo had asked.

So, Tank had explained to Flo that he was dying. He seemed to be easier with telling it to her than he had been with me.

Flo didn't really know Tank, but I could tell she liked him. She took the bad news like she always did. Acceptance of the fact and empathy for the man.

I'd planned on flying *Island Hopper* back to the Anchor before noon, so we could help Rusty get things ready. He had a small get-together planned—a tradition he'd carried on from his father and grandfather before him—to serve an early Christmas dinner for family and close friends. Several dozen people usually attended, all exchanging simple gifts, sometimes handmade.

I'd spent weeks tying assorted flies for some of the guides, and Savannah and Flo had made over a dozen beautiful necklaces, bracelets, and anklets for the women who would be there. Each had all sorts of tiny shells strung together. They'd used a fine bit and small drill press to make the smallest of holes in each.

I hoped the fog would lift before noon. From the deck, nearly twenty feet above the water, I could see the trees ringing my island, as well as the tops of trees on other nearby islands. The treetops floating on a blanket of mist looked surreal, like a Dali painting.

Flying above the fog wouldn't be a problem, but there was no way I could take off or land in it.

Savannah came out with a Thermos and three more mugs. "What time are we going to Rusty and Sid's?"

"As soon as the fog lifts," I said, as she poured her mug and refilled mine.

"Ahoy, the house!" Tank's voice boomed from the mist.

When I stood and looked down, I couldn't see him. "Follow my voice," I called down. "The bottom of the stairs is twenty feet to my right."

"This shit's thicker than a private's grape."

"Good morning, Tank," Savannah called down, pouring another mug of coffee.

"Apologies, ma'am," he said, as his feet stomped up the steps in perfect, rhythmic cadence.

"I live with a Marine," she said when he reached the deck. "And I'm a boat captain from the South Carolina Lowcountry. I grew up within spitting distance of Parris Island and the Marine air station."

She offered him a mug, which he accepted. "Visibility's better up here," he said, taking a sip and looking around. "Mmm, you sure do make good java, Miss Savannah."

"It's a special blend Rusty gets," she offered. "From a little farm in Costa Rica called Hacienda la Minita."

He raised his mug as Flo appeared at the top of the steps with Finn and Woden. "Merry Christmas to all of you," he said. "And thanks for allowing me to be here with you."

"Merry Christmas," Flo said, hugging him. "Now, I need a coffee."

The four of us sat down. Woden sat on the deck next to Flo, as usual, and Finn curled up beside me, crossing his paws and laying his big head on them. After a moment, Woden rose and went to sit beside Tank, sniffing at him.

"What's with him?" Tank asked, as he reached down and rubbed the big dog's neck.

Woden leaned into him, turning his head up and making eye contact.

"I don't know," Savannah said. "He's not usually so affectionate with people he's just met."

I'd read somewhere that some dogs had been trained to detect cancer through scent. They weren't trained to smell it; a keen sense of smell is something they're all born with. Rather, they were trained to recognize the scent of a person with cancer and respond to it.

Could Woden tell Tank was sick? I wondered.

"What's the plan?" Tank asked, now rubbing the underside of Woden's throat, which the dog offered with no fear.

Savannah and I looked at one another, both of us a little bewildered by Woden's sudden change in attitude from that of the usual stoic guardian.

"We'll fly down to the Rusty Anchor when the fog lifts," I said. "Rusty's serving Christmas dinner for a bunch of locals and family."

"Turkey?"

"If that's what you prefer," Savannah said. "He does a few birds, and a lot of fish, crab and lobster."

"What time's David coming?" I asked Flo.

"He said he was planning to leave before noon," Flo replied. "He should be here around sixteen hundred." She grinned at me and Tank, then turned to Savannah. "That's four o'clock."

Tank and I both laughed.

"But Savannah brought your boat back here," Tank said. "If we fly down, and leave *Island Hopper* there, how do we get back?"

"Jimmy and Naomi are coming back here after dinner," Savannah said. "We'll all ride with them."

"Or borrow someone's boat," I said. "All the regulars will be there. It's like one big extended family."

"And David is?"

"My boyfriend," Flo replied. "He's going to stay with me a couple of days, then, after the wedding, I'm going up to stay at his parents' until we have to go back to Gainesville for school."

Tank looked at me and I shrugged imperceptibly. Flo had turned nineteen last July—a grown woman. She'd even gone with Savannah and me last month to cast her vote for president. We never talked politics, and none of us revealed who we'd voted for. That wasn't what mattered. Taking part and performing one's duty was the real issue.

Both Savannah and I believed that voting was more than just a right. It was each citizen's civic obligation. If Flo could be that adult, she could choose when and where she spent time with David.

The night before, after everyone had gone off to bed, Savannah and I had had a long talk about our upcoming wedding. We wanted to keep it small, just close friends and family.

Rusty was going to officiate and Flo would be Savannah's maid of honor. I hadn't yet asked anyone to stand with me. Everyone just assumed it would be Deuce.

"Tank, I'd like to ask you something," I said, pausing until he looked up at me. "Will you be my best man next week?"

He looked sharply at Savannah, then back at me. "You haven't asked anyone yet? It's six days away."

"No, I haven't. And I can't explain why. Will you do it?"

He grinned. "Doesn't seem like a tough job. I don't have to sacrifice a goat or anything, do I?"

"It would mean a lot to both of us," Savannah said, reaching across and putting her hand on his.

Flo did the same. "All three of us."

I put my hand on theirs and nodded at Tank.

"Sure," he said. "But you don't have to get all mushy about it."

The four of us laughed.

Finn raised his head and looked up at me, cocking it to the side.

"He said he would, sleepyhead," I told him.

His fat tail thumped on the deck.

I felt the hint of a breeze on the side of my face. "The fog will lift soon. We'd better get ready to go."

Savannah and Flo nodded, having felt it too. "It'll be gone in half an hour," Flo added.

"Oh, you're all meteorologists now, huh?"

"When you live on the sea, you learn these things," I said.

We split up to gather what we were bringing, and when I stepped back outside, ten minutes later, the fog was beginning to blow out to sea.

I slung my pack over one shoulder and hefted a small box under one arm as Savannah and I started down the back steps.

"You should let me carry something," she said when we reached the bottom.

"I got it," I replied. "You don't mean it, anyway."

"Do too," she said, punching me playfully on the arm. "You just keep me around as a pack animal."

She took my free right arm in her hands and leaned into me as we crossed the clearing toward the bunkhouses. "That's not the only thing."

To call the clearing a yard would be a misnomer. It was over an acre, with a fringe of mangroves all around the water's edge, a few palms, gumbo limbo, even a bay rum tree among them. The interior was mostly sand, with clumps of sea oats scattered about and paths between them. Beach morning glory vines reached for the sun, stretching out onto the sand from the edge of the mangroves. Here and there, gardenia and hibiscus grew, along with night-blooming and confederate jasmine. But mostly sand.

Behind and above the trees, the four small houses were on stilts, affording a view unparalleled. Altogether, the island was about two acres; plenty of room for everyone.

Tank was coming down the bunkhouse steps with a small satchel that looked heavy in his left hand.

"What's in the bag, Tank?" I asked.

He knew Rusty, but not well, having only served in the same unit with him for a few months. And he'd only met Deuce one other time since he was a kid. Outside of them, he'd only been introduced to a couple of people here. Nobody expected him to bring gifts.

"Challenge coins," he said. "Might be a Marine or two there. I remember Thurman being pretty impressed when I gave him one all those years ago. Thought he might like to have the rest. I like the idea of my coins being handed to Marines who visit a bar down here."

"Why's that?" Flo asked, joining us.

Tank and I looked at one another and shrugged. "Tun Tavern," he told her.

I nodded and added, "The Marine Corps was born there."

"The toughest branch of the military was created in a bar?" she asked.

"Where else?" I replied. "The Anchor's a lot like the taverns back before the revolution—a meeting place for locals to discuss matters of the day."

We loaded everything into the luggage compartment, and I held the door for Savannah and Flo to get in. The dogs jumped in after them and got into the aft-facing forward seats. Savannah and Flo reached across and buckled them both in.

"That's a pretty good trick," Tank said. "They must fly with you a good deal."

"They're great on trips," Savannah said.

"Mind getting the lines, Tank?" I asked, as I climbed into the copilot's side, then shifted over. "Leave the stern line looped over the pontoon cleat and be ready to throw it off when the engine catches."

"Right," he said, moving forward and untying the bow line.

I turned on the batteries and started my preflight.

Tank stepped onto the pontoon, holding the stern line. "You gonna do that thing with the prop?"

"Yeah," I replied. "I'll yell contact when I turn on the mag. But wait a second after that until the engine actually fires up. The prop wash won't be much, but it'll try to blow the door closed."

"Got it."

"Clear prop," I yelled and hit the starter button.

After four revolutions, I yelled, "Contact," and turned on the magnetos.

As always, the engine caught and belched smoke, and just as Tank flicked the line loosing us from the dock, it settled into a steady idle.

"That's pretty exciting," he yelled, before putting his headset on.

I opened the window to let the prop wash pull the smoke out of the cabin as we idled forward. Once clear of the dock, I turned toward the northwest and entered 1200 in the transponder, the standard VFR code for low altitude when no other squawk is assigned.

Reaching my downwind marker, a red and blue lobster trap float anchored in five feet of water, I turned upwind and we were soon airborne.

It was too early for commercial flights into Marathon Airport, but they do happen sometimes. Probably not on Christmas day, but staying well to the west of the airport and below the glide path would only take a few extra minutes and ensured we wouldn't get in the way of any incoming private aircraft.

I'd become adept at flying low and slow and kept *Island Hopper* just a little above the mangrove patches that dotted the backcountry. We skirted west of Big Torch Key and I picked up Niles Channel, dropping down to just fifty feet above the water. I pulled up as we approached the bridge between Ramrod and Summerland Keys, then banked to the left as we climbed to five hundred feet.

Less than fifteen minutes after boarding the plane, the pontoons were again in the water and we were idling toward Rusty's channel.

We had to wait a bit while a couple of locals pulled their boat out before we could use the ramp. Quite a few weekend anglers used Rusty's ramp and kept their boats on his concrete pad. Trailering a boat anywhere meant driving on the Overseas Highway with a thousand tourists hellbent on reaching Key Weird. And leaving a boat in the water meant monthly bottom cleanings and repainting every few years. What Rusty charged to store a boat was easily worth it to avoid either hassle.

Finally, the ramp was clear, and I lowered the landing gear. *Island Hopper's* engine roared as we rolled up out of the water onto the ramp. At the top, I angled toward my tiedown, then gunned the engine with my foot hard on the right pedal to get her turned around.

"Y'all go ahead," I told the others after I'd shut off the engine. "I need to fill the tanks."

The truth was, we were flying on just the forward tank the whole way from the island. Not that we were in danger of running out. The *Hopper* had five tanks—one in each wingtip and three in the belly. During the previous day's flight, I'd burned through the forward tank, then transferred fuel back into it from the smaller wing tanks before we'd even left Miami's airspace. Then I'd used up all of the aft and middle tanks flying to the Tortugas and home. What was left in the thirty-five-gallon forward tank would have kept us in the air for at least another hour, had it been necessary.

Tank hung around to help with the hose. I kept a five-hundred-gallon tank of aviation gas next to a small tool shed near my tiedown pad and it was more than half full. He pulled the hose over as I got my ladder out of the shed and climbed up to remove the port wing's cap.

"How much does she hold?" Tank asked, handing the nozzle up.

"A hundred-and-thirty-eight gallons," I replied. "With a twenty percent reserve, that's enough to fly about six hundred miles."

"That's a long way," he said.

"There's a forty-gallon collapsible fuel bladder in the shed there. It fits snugly between the aft seats and extends her range to over eight hundred miles."

"Is that right? You ever fly it that far?"

I handed the nozzle down after filling the tank. "Not quite," I replied. "The longest non-stop flight I've made in her was to Cozumel; a little over five hundred miles, going around the western tip of Cuba. I had the bladder installed during that one but didn't need much of it."

Carrying the ladder around to the other wing tip, we repeated the process, then filled the three big belly tanks. It took just under one hundred gallons.

I saw Manny approaching as we were putting the hose and ladder away. "Hey, Jesse," he said, nodding at the two of us.

"Hey, Manny," I said back. "Meet a friend of mine, Owen Tankersley. Tank, this is Manny Martinez. Manny's also a Nam Marine. He owns a little resort up island a ways."

Manny stopped short and looked at Tank. "I've heard of you, sir. Honored to meet you."

"Just Tank," he said, extending his hand. "Pleased to meet you."

The two shook hands, then exchanged the usual information about units they'd served with in country.

Then Manny turned toward me. "Have you found out anything about..." His eyes shifted from me to Tank.

"Yes, we did," I replied, as the three of us fell into step, walking toward the deck behind the bar. "Actually, a good bit. Mostly names of drug dealers, though. Nothing solid about Cobie's disappearance. But they're connected some way."

"Connected to drugs? How? Cobie wasn't into that. Not even grass."

We sat down at a table on the deck and I explained about meeting with Sampson and how I thought some of the questions I asked had shaken him up. Then I told him about the phone calls and how these people might be connected.

"I knew he wasn't telling all he knew," Manny said. "So, the first person he called after you left him was a Miami drug dealer?"

I nodded. "One who just happens to drive a car identical to the one on Kmart's security cam that pulled into the parking lot behind Cobie's."

"What? The police didn't say anything about that."

So, I told him about seeing the same car right there at the Anchor and that Rusty had recognized it from the security video. "But I don't think she was driving," I cautioned. "The seat was pushed back too far. The police are following up on that now."

"Do I want to know how you found that out?" Manny asked.

"I wouldn't tell you even if you asked."

"What's your involvement in this, Tank?"

"Just along for the ride," he replied. "But if there's any way I can help, I will."

"That's where I saw you headed yesterday?" Manny asked me, jerking a thumb toward the plane. "When you flew over Grassy Key?"

"Yeah," I replied, then explained about the three drug deals we watched and how they were connected to Sampson, including what I knew and suspected about the Blanc family and the fact that Willy Quick had a woman with him.

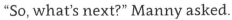

"So, what's next?" Manny asked.

It was the question I'd been hoping he wouldn't ask. It'd already been five weeks since Cobie disappeared. Any cop would say that if she didn't leave of her own accord, she was likely already dead.

And today was Christmas. As cold as it sounded, I wasn't doing anything today but enjoying life. Ridding the world of smug drugglers and killers could wait until tomorrow.

"I plan to lean on Sampson again tomorrow," I replied. "See if I can't make him rabbit and see where he runs."

Manny looked down at his hands, clasped together on the table. "I know it's Christmas and all, but..."

"There's little he can learn today," Tank stated calmly. "Jesse stirred up the hornet's nest good yesterday. Now, he's gotta give them all time to get back to the hive and compare notes before going at it again. They'll be lulled into a false sense of security. What's your tie to the girl?"

"Her mom works for me," Manny replied. "And her late father was a good friend. I've known Cobie since she was a baby. But it's a little beyond that. We're all family at the resort."

Rusty came out and joined us. "Hey, Manny. I didn't even see you come in."

"I just got here," Manny replied. "I saw Jesse's plane returning when I pulled in and went straight down to the ramp."

"Here," Tank said, lifting a box out of his bag and placing it in front of Rusty. "I want you to take care of these for me."

"What is it?" Rusty asked, sitting down in front of the box.

Tank looked at me for a second and seemed to come to a decision.

"I'm dying," he said flatly. "Maybe a couple months, maybe a year."

Before Rusty could say anything, Tank opened the box and took one of the coins out. It was wrapped in a plastic sleeve and had the gold chevrons of a master gunnery sergeant on the dark blue lower half and a pale blue banner above, with thirteen white stars depicting the Medal of Honor ribbon. Tank's name and the date of the action, January 31, 1970, arced across the top and bottom. I had one just like it in a shadow box in my bedroom. Typically, you'd always have your challenge coin with you, but that one meant a lot and besides, I had good reason to retire it to the box.

Tank handed the coin to Manny. "By stepping up to help others, you show great spirit and compassion, Marine. Never lose that. This coin means you drink free, whenever challenged, unless someone has a POTUS or SECNAV coin."

"Is this a challenge?" Rusty asked.

"Why not?" Tank replied, digging into his pocket as I dug into mine.

We both placed coins on the table with the seal of the President of the United States. Rusty produced one from the commanding general of the Second Marine Division in 1982, Al Gray, who later became Commandant of the Marine Corps. In most bars, in most places, Rusty would be drinking free, but not today. His only chance had been if I'd left home without my POTUS coin.

He pushed away from the table and opened the back door to yell inside. "Amy! Four glasses and the Pusser's red label."

He sat back down and looked at Tank. "Cancer?"

Tank nodded. "We all die sooner or later. I cheated the Reaper one too many times and now my hourglass is almost empty."

Amy Huggins came out carrying a silver tray. On it was a corked, nearly full bottle of fifteen-year-old Pusser's Royal Navy rum and four highball glasses. She saw the four coins on the table and silently placed the tray between them, not questioning why we were drinking before noon.

Amy was an Army widow and knew about such things.

Rusty stood, poured a shot into each glass, and passed them around. Then he lifted his high. We all stood.

"To the heroes of the Corps!"

We clinked our glasses together and tossed the rum. I could feel it burning down my throat and into my stomach, leaving a hint of island spices and caramel in my mouth.

We put our coins away and Amy took the tray back inside.

Nothing more was said about Tank's illness or the missing girl for the rest of the day. I introduced Tank to

Jimmy and Naomi, Rufus, and Dink and Ash, a couple of the guides who came early to help Rufus in the kitchen.

Sid assigned chores and in no time at all, the place was ready, and Jimmy was dispatched to open the gate at the driveway. It wasn't really a gate; just a length of half-inch anchor chain stretched between two posts. It didn't stop everyone from arriving early, as a good many came by boat and also pitched in.

I watched Tank throughout the day as we helped get things set up. He moved more slowly than I remembered, as if he were consciously pacing himself, squeezing every last drop out of each minute and taking time to talk to everyone he came in contact with.

As more people arrived, bringing gifts to place under the tree, he moved around the place, helping where he could and continuing to talk to people. I heard him introduce himself as Owen. That was it. The happy, smiling, old man moving about the place didn't look like a Tank.

Nobody there knew who he was, but he seemed to put a smile or grin on the face of each person he met. He was there and that meant he was part of the Rusty Anchor family, and everyone accepted that.

One of the guides, a guy named Jim Merlo, whom I knew to be a Marine during the latter part of the war in Afghanistan, arrived with his wife and two kids. Tank squatted down to say hi to the kids first, before introducing himself to the parents. Even from across the bar, I could see the look of recognition in Jim's eyes.

During the Second World War, Korea, and Vietnam, when recruits were moved through the receiving portals at Parris Island and San Diego at record paces, some parts of basic training were shortened or dropped. But not the classes on the history of the Corps, its leaders, and its heroes. It was such an integral part of becoming a Marine, and still essential today.

The legends were brought to life in the hearts of the recruits, creating that bond, that esprit de corps, that absolute knowledge that you were becoming a part of something much larger than yourself, and that in doing so, it became a part of you.

Tank was older, but his features were still recognizable from the photos in the history books and on barracks walls. There wasn't a Marine alive who didn't know the names Chesty Puller, John Ripley, Smedley Butler, John Basilone, or Tank Tankersley.

Jim recognized him immediately. I could see it in his body language as he practically snapped to attention to render a salute. In no time at all, word spread among the Rusty Anchor family, and soon everyone not only knew who Tank was, but what he'd done.

It's hard to hide a real-life hero, and in my book, none were more noble than the old man laughing and talking with my friends.

David arrived just in time for the feast, as did Deuce and Julie and Chyrel. Tank seemed a bit smitten with Chyrel and spent a good bit of time with her at Deuce and Julie's table. But she couldn't stay long and left an hour before we did.

Later that evening, Rusty and Sid walked with the seven of us down to his boat and we loaded our booty into it with the dogs.

The festivities would go on throughout the night. There were people on the deck, friends laughing and talking, all illuminated by tiki torches and table fires as the sun started slipping below the tree line. The bar lights were on, and through the windows I could see everyone having a good time. But we needed to get home. I wasn't a fan of dodging lobster trap buoys in the dark.

Tank sat on the gunwale and looked around the yard. I could see he was tired. "This is a fine place, Thurman," he said. "You're a very fortunate man to have so many in your life."

Rusty slipped his arm around his wife's waist. "Don't I know it, Master Guns." He looked over his shoulder at the crowd of people in his bar and on the deck. "Just one big, crazy family." When Jimmy started the outboard, Rusty tossed the bow line aboard as I got the stern line. "Y'all be careful and I'll see you tomorrow."

CHAPTER SEVENTEEN

The ride back up to my island took a lot longer than coming down. The water north of the Seven Mile Bridge was unusually calm and the low sun cast the islands around us in a soft, warm glow.

Jimmy didn't drive fast—not that he could have, with just a forty-horse pushing a boat with seven people and two large dogs. But he managed to find the sweet spot, just above planing speed, where he could slow the engine and stay on top of the water while keeping the noise level low enough for conversation.

"You're more than just friends down here," Tank said, leaning close to where Savannah and I sat in the rear seat. "I can see why you wanted to come here. Everyone is so open and friendly."

"It's called One Human Family," Savannah said. "The concept that, whether you believe in creationism or evolution, we really are all the same, all related in one way or other."

"Be nice if the whole world thought like that," Tank said. "It'd put people like me and Jesse out of a job. Which, by the way, I'd be highly in favor of."

The sun, now dark orange and enormous, was setting as we turned into Harbor Channel, painting the high, wispy clouds above my island in a pinkish-orange color.

I could see lights through the trees coming from Mac and Mel's place, and there were two boats I didn't recognize tied up to the lone post sticking out of waist-deep water on the east side.

"Did you have a good time, Mister Tank?" Flo asked, as Jimmy slowed the boat, approaching the pier.

"Yes, I did, Miss Flo. An exceptional time. I'd say one of the best of my life. It was nice to be included."

"Dad says the folks at Rusty Anchor are just like family and that extends to their friends, too. He's known most of them for years."

"David, would you mind staying up for a bit?" I asked, as Jimmy and I tied off the boat.

He handed me a boxful of gifts we'd received. "Sure, what's up?"

"It's work-related," I said, getting a disapproving look from my daughter.

I had an idea and wanted to see if it could work.

"Not a problem," he said.

"We can use the computer on the *Revenge*."

We carried everything up to the deck, where Jimmy and Naomi said goodnight. They were turning in; Jimmy was taking a friend out early in the morning to fish the backcountry.

I unlocked the door and pushed it open. "Got enough energy left to do some planning, Tank?"

He grinned and followed Savannah and Flo inside. "Is David part of your group, too?"

"He is," I replied.

"We'll be down in a minute," Savannah said. "I just want to arrange these under the tree and make some sundowners."

Flo carried a box to the tree. "I'll help you, Mom."

After I'd turned on the lights for the dock area, the three of us went down the steps to the *Revenge*.

I stepped over the low gunwale into the cockpit and opened the aft hatch to the salon, turning on the lights inside. "Come aboard."

When Tank entered, he whistled softly. "This is a yacht, not a fishing boat."

"Who says fishermen have to ride in a garbage scow?" I asked. "Get the laptop out, David, and get Chyrel on the horn."

"You don't think that Bama girl's got a life?" Tank asked.

"She does," I replied. "But she had to leave early to oversee a surveillance job a couple of Deuce's guys are on."

"Related to the missing girl?"

I shook my head. "He has two of his guys watching a warehouse in Panama."

"Pana—? Wait, you guys work internationally?"

"Armstrong Research is a worldwide organization," David said, getting the laptop out of the cabinet and taking a seat at the settee to boot it up.

Sitting beneath the house, the *Revenge's* modem connected wirelessly to another inside the house, which was hardwired to a satellite dish on the roof.

Tank and I sat on either side of him, watching. A moment later, a window opened and Chyrel's face appeared. She wasn't in the office.

"Where are you?" I asked.

"At home," she replied. "On the deck by the seawall. My neighbors are used to seeing me on the computer here late at night. They probably think I'm on a dating site or something."

Over her shoulder, the sky was painted dark red and amber. Swaying palms stood in silhouette at the point on the other side of her canal.

"I wanted you both to work on something together," I said. "I don't even know if it's doable, so it doesn't have to be right now. If it is, you can set up the groundwork now and work on it tomorrow."

"What's that, Boss?"

"Remember how you tracked that email to one of three farms up in the Shenandoah Valley that time?"

"Yeah," she replied. "Using the IP address from the sender. Nothing hard about that."

"Does it work both ways?" I asked. "If you knew the physical address of a person, could you get their IP address?"

"Maybe," David said. "If the user doesn't have it hidden or hasn't rebooted their modem recently."

"Still," Chyrel cautioned, "there could be quite a few IP addresses in a geographically small area. What were you thinking?"

"We have the phone numbers of Sampson, Quick, Moreno, and dozens of others."

"Thousands of others by now," Chyrel corrected me.

"The main players are all we're interested in. If you can pinpoint their location, is it possible to locate nearby wireless networks and access their computers?"

"O-o-oh, you're devious, Jesse," Chyrel said with a grin. "I like that in a man."

"We can set up a data harvester," David said, excitedly. "Given the small geographical areas, we could mine for certain keywords in emails."

"We could use their names," Chyrel said. "That'd be the place to start. Every email starts with 'Hi, So-and-so.' You start creating the data farm, using the keywords I'll send you, and I'll put together a grid map to mine."

David nodded and opened a blank window. His fingers started flying across the keyboard, typing what looked to me like gibberish on the screen. I looked over at Tank and jerked my head aft.

We slid out of the settee and went back to the salon just as Savannah and Flo entered.

"He's a computer hacker, too?" Tank asked.

"They don't like that description," Flo said. "They're IT professionals."

Flo carried what I assumed were two non-alcoholic versions of whatever was in Savannah's pitcher over to where David sat.

"How did you know that could be done?" Tank asked, sitting down on the L-shaped couch at the stern. "All that IP stuff?"

I sat on the port side next to him as Savannah brought glasses from the galley. "I didn't," I replied. "And still don't. They might not be able to do it at all. But if anyone can, it's those two."

"What are they looking for?" Savannah asked, pouring a whitish frozen concoction into our glasses.

"Information about the people we encountered yesterday," I replied. "From their computers. Chyrel told me once that the average person is very sloppy online. Most tend to think their emails and browsing history don't leave a trail once deleted."

"No," Tank said. "You gotta empty the trash bin thing, too. That permanently deletes them."

"Not so," I told him. "What she told me is that permanently deleting a file just marks the space it takes up on the hard drive as available to save new data. But until something is saved there, the information is still available. She even showed me, using just her phone to retrieve a file I thought I'd permanently deleted from my computer." I leaned in close to Tank. "She's probably the best hacker in the world."

I took a sip of the frozen mixture, tasting coconut and banana with a good dose of rum. Probably a silver rum because I couldn't taste anything else.

"Do you like it?" she asked, as Tank placed his glass back down on the table.

"Very good," he said, and I nodded agreement.

"It's our own coconuts and bananas," she said.

"We're in!" David shouted.

I rose and stepped past Savannah. "In where?"

"Moreno's Mac," Chyrel said. "I'm looking through his deleted emails now."

"Won't he know?" Tank asked, stepping up beside me at the settee.

"Chyrel once accessed the CIA's main frame," I whispered, as she and David chattered. "She said getting in was the easy part, getting out undetected was what made it a monumental hack."

"I thought Flo said they didn't like that word."

"We're not hackers," came Chyrel's voice from the speaker. "That's a simplistic noun for simplistic people. Hack is a verb and just a small part of what we do."

"This is all fascinating," Tank said, leaning in close to David and smiling at Chyrel. "I grew up with radio, way before television. You two are to be commended."

I could see Chyrel grin. I knew she could be wild and playful at times but like Savannah, being a Southern girl, she appreciated etiquette.

"Why thank you, sir," she said. "Oo, here's something."

I leaned in to look over Flo's shoulder at the screen, reading what appeared to be an email. It was just two sentences.

She did good, but she didn't come back last night. Will we see her tonight?

It was unsigned, but the email address it came from was marvin.dan@BTGC.com. Benito Moreno was the recipient.

"Who do you think the 'she' is?" Tank asked.

"No idea," I replied.

"There's tons more," Chyrel said. "And we're getting hits on the others, too."

"How late are you working?" I asked.

"Margie is relieving me at midnight," she replied. "The harvester David set up can run by itself and I can dig through the results while keeping the boys awake down in *Manglares*, then email you what I find before dawn."

"Thanks, Chyrel."

"G'nite," she said, touching the shell chain around her neck. "Merry Christmas! And tell Savannah I love the necklace."

"Bye, Miss Chyrel," Tank added.

She winked and the screen went blank.

"Anything else?" David asked.

I shook my head. "No, that's it. Thanks for the help. She'll have a lot of free time to sift through what y'all found. Mostly she's just there to make sure Jerry and DJ don't fall asleep."

David closed the laptop and put it away, and then he and Flo rose and started to leave.

"Um..." I started to say something but stopped.

Flo turned and stood on her toes to kiss me on the cheek. "G'night, Daddy."

She hugged Savannah and then she and David left. I could hear their footfalls going up the steps beside the cabin. I'd wanted to say something like "be careful" but figured that might have a different connotation to them.

"You sure have a lot of sharp knives in your drawer," Tank said. "Just when I think I've seen it all, some new technology tells me I'm a dinosaur."

"You're not *that* old," Savannah said. "I saw how you were flirting with Chyrel at the party. Don't deny it."

"She's fun to talk to," Tank said, his face reddening a little.

"And very pretty," Savannah said. "And single."

"And way too young," Tank said, avoiding eye contact.

"I wouldn't say *way* too young," she countered.

I sipped my drink and watched Tank squirm.

Savannah smiled. She enjoyed the role of matchmaker. "She just turned forty last week."

"Yeah, well..."

"I think we'd best turn in," I interrupted, before Savannah embarrassed him further. I moved to the sink to wash my glass and looked over at Tank. "You feel like going after some bonefish in the morning?"

"I would," he replied, draining his coconut concoction. "Where will we find these fish?"

"I was talking to Dink earlier," I said. "He was the sort of clumsy guy who kept bumping into things at the party. He said he took a client up to Cape Sable yesterday. They hooked quite a few bones and his client caught his limit in pompano."

He and Savannah handed me their glasses and I washed them, leaving them on the drain board to dry. Then we exited the boat and climbed up to the house. Savannah retired to the bedroom and I walked Tank out to the deck.

"Will I need to bring a gun for these bonefish?" he asked quietly.

I held the door to let Finn inside, then closed it.

"That wouldn't be a bad idea," I said.

"I thought as much." His eyes sparkled in the gathering darkness. "I guess you want to rattle Sampson's cage again, then pay that big ape in the truck a visit."

"Naw," I said, with a sideways grin. "We're just a couple of fishermen going out for a day of lip ripping."

He chuckled as he turned and headed for the stairs.

I went back inside and turned off the light in the living room. The bedroom door was slightly ajar, and I could see a flickering glow through the crack. The air smelled of frangipani from one of Savannah's favorite candles.

Pushing the door open, I saw her lying on her side, a thin sheet pulled up to her hips. Her head was propped on an elbow and she was smiling. She wore nothing except for a red bow in her hair.

"Are you ready for your Christmas gift, Jesse?"

CHAPTER EIGHTEEN

I woke well before dawn. A light breeze moved the curtains above my head, their weight directing the cool air down over my face and chest. Without moving, I let my eyes roam the darkened room. Moving would bring pain.

Turning my head, I gazed into the face of the source of my aching muscles. Soft moonlight fell on Savannah's face and hair. She looked so beautiful I was tempted to stay right where I was.

From the angle of the light coming through the sheer curtains, I knew that the nearly full moon, the Cold Moon, was on the horizon. A glance at my watch confirmed it was 0400.

Savannah stirred and stretched as I rose from the bed. "Leaving so early?" she mumbled.

"We want to be on the flats at sunrise," I said. "Go back to sleep. We'll be home before dark."

"If you find the bastard," she said more clearly, "kneecap him for me."

I grinned. There was still a lot about Savannah I didn't know. But she could read me like a book. She knew what I had planned for today and she was okay with it. Some of what I'd learned in the last year had surprised me.

She'd told me of encounters she and Flo had had with the dregs of society and how she'd convinced them of the mistake they'd made. She hadn't elaborated, but having wrestled with her in bed, I knew her strength, and my friend Charity had told me that she'd taken a lot of self-defense classes. Savannah and I had talked about the evils in the world and we were on the same page about that.

Through the window, I could see the light on in the bunkhouse and knew Tank was already up. I closed the bedroom door, went into the galley, and switched on the light, though I didn't need it. Our house was small; there was a place for everything in it and everything was always in its place.

As I was pouring coffee into a Thermos from a pot that had just finished brewing, Tank walked silently past the window. I opened the door to let him in and Finn out. They both paused for just a second, so Finn could get an ear scratch.

"All set?" Tank asked quietly, noting the closed bedroom door.

From the fridge, I took a small cooler, already loaded with fruit, sandwiches, and water, which Savannah had put together before we left for the Anchor.

"Yeah," I replied. "But we're going to make a stop on the way."

"You do this a lot?" he asked, as we walked down the steps to the dock area. "Make a stop on the way?"

"Same place," I replied. "Before we make him bug out, I want to add something to his van."

I stepped down into my Maverick Mirage flats skiff and started the engine. As it burbled, I clicked the fob for the big outside door, then opened the small side console. Pushing on a panel in the top of the storage area, it fell open and I retrieved a holstered Sig Sauer 9mm handgun. I checked the magazine and chamber, then clipped the holster inside my shorts, behind my back. I didn't have to ask if Tank was armed.

He got the lines as if he'd been working around boats all his life, and we soon idled out from under the house. I turned due east, at an angle to Harbor Channel. We talked quietly about what I wanted to do and then I switched on the powerful spotlight mounted to the bow. The water ahead was as flat as a sheet of glass and reflected the light up into the dark sky.

"Hang on," I warned, as I advanced the throttle.

The little skiff launched like a rocket sled on rails, powered by a big 300-horse Mercury outboard.

There were actually three ways to get to the other side of the wide flats to the south of the channel. I mostly used two. In the *Revenge* or *Cazador*, I'd go around the shoal water. In the Grady or *Knot L-8*, I'd follow a twisting, unmarked, natural cut. But in the Mirage, I could just go balls to the wall right across the skinny water.

When we hit the shallows, a little west of the natural cut, only the transom and prop were in the water. There was a wide, sandy shelf where the water was consistent at about a foot of depth.

The light picked up the sandy bottom and I steered toward it, flying across water that most boats couldn't.

Once we were in deeper water, I turned to a heading that would take us to Vaca Cut, about twenty-five miles away. I left the light on and adjusted it with the remote to be able to spot any lobster trap floats ahead of us. Other than those, there wasn't anything in the way to avoid and I brought the speed up to forty knots.

The crossing took a little over half an hour, with both of us hunched behind the console and taking turns leaning into the tiny windshield's slipstream to sip our coffee.

I finally slowed as we neared Vaca Cut. It was still dark, but I turned off the spotlight. Lobstering in the cut wasn't allowed and if anyone were coming the other way, I didn't want to blind them.

"That was damned exciting," Tank said. "You know your way around these waters pretty good."

"Kinda have to," I said. "But cuts and shoals change all the time, so you have to be on your game. What we just crossed is never shallower than five feet, though."

I outlined what I wanted to do, and Tank nodded, asking pointed questions when needed as I navigated the canals to get to Ty Sampson's house.

When we were a few lots from his house, I killed the engine and let the boat drift toward a sandy spot on the bank. Once the hull beached, I scrambled forward, jumped out, and pulled the boat a little higher before Tank got out.

"I'll just be a minute," I said, dousing my head, arms, and legs with a liberal blast of bug spray.

Handing him the can and the bow line, I quickly crossed the lot and moved along the edge of the trees on the wooded lot next to Sampson's house.

From there I'd be in the open. No cars were coming, and I didn't see or hear anything, so I just strolled along like I belonged there.

No lights came from Sampson's, which I'd figured on. Drug dealers kept late hours and I was sure Ty wasn't just a surfboard maker.

At his driveway, I turned and headed to the back of his Volkswagen van. It was built back when bumpers were made of steel, which is why I'd chosen a tracker that was magnetic.

Pulling it out of my pocket, I turned it on and checked it. The small red light came on and a moment later it flicked back off. I took a step closer to the van and the light came on again.

Satisfied that the motion detector was working, I simply reached under the VW's bumper, found a suitable spot for the magnet, and attached it. I checked that it wouldn't move easily, and then retraced my steps to the boat.

Tank and I shoved the Maverick into deeper water, and I restarted the engine.

"Remember," I said, as we approached Sampson's dock, "make enough noise that he hears us, but not so much as to make it seem intentional."

"You're sure you can get in?"

"I was taught by one of the best lock picks there is," I replied. "Sampson's lock's a cakewalk."

"You really think it'll be there?"

"Not a hundred percent," I replied. "But I could tell he was lying about it."

CHAPTER NINETEEN

Ty woke to the sound of something bumping his dock. He'd always been a light sleeper and had a habit of sleeping with the window cracked open a little. He picked up his phone, which activated the screen. It wasn't even six o'clock yet.

There it is again, he thought, hearing a noise in his backyard.

Rising from the bed, he pulled on his jeans, went to the window, and looked out. It was dark as pitch inside his house, so he wasn't worried about anyone seeing in. The nearly full moon had set, but there was enough starlight to see the seawall behind his house.

A boat was out there, and Ty didn't own one.

He still had his phone in his hand and was about to call 911 when he saw two men climb out of the boat onto his dock. It was the same two guys who'd come to his shop asking questions three days earlier. Calling the police would be too risky.

One of them said something, but Ty couldn't make out what it was. They crossed the yard to his shop and the taller one knelt at the door.

Good luck with that, asshole, Ty thought, as the man worked on the door's heavy padlock. It was reputed to be the best lock in the business.

After a moment, the man stood, tossed Ty's expensive lock aside, and opened the door.

"What the hell?" Ty breathed, barely audible. "Who *are* these guys?"

A light came on inside, and Ty could easily hear them moving things around. They were searching his shop and trying to be quiet but weren't succeeding much.

Ty's mind raced, trying to think of anything in there that could get him in trouble. He glanced toward the nightstand, then hurried over to it and opened the drawer. A bag of weed lay on top of a small, tightly wrapped brick of pale blue powder. Beside it sat a .38 caliber revolver.

He picked up the gun and went back to the window, certain that he hadn't left anything in the shop. The two guys were leaving, not even bothering to close the shop's door or turn off the light.

Ty was tempted to burst through the back door, firing away, but then he remembered the cold stare of the old guy when he'd lied and told them he'd sold Cobie Murphy's wakeboard.

That's when he noticed the shorter man, the old guy with the threatening eyes, was carrying something.

A wakeboard.

Suddenly, Ty remembered that Cobie had wanted her name painted on her board.

A moment later, he heard the boat's engine start up and it turned around in the narrow confines of the canal. Ty waited until the two PIs had passed the trees at the back of the next lot, then left his bedroom and went to the back door. He looked out the window first, then opened the door and stepped outside, gun in hand.

He could hear the outboard quietly burbling as the boat motored down the canal. Running across the yard, he peeked into the shop, expecting a mess. Nothing seemed to have been touched or moved. Yet he'd heard what sounded like the place being ransacked.

Stepping inside, he looked around. The only sign that anyone had been there was the closet door standing open. The closet was large, with shelves from floor to ceiling on three sides. It was where he put finished boards to cure.

Cobie's board was gone.

"Fuck!" he shouted in a low voice. *Why didn't I grind that thing into dust?*

In a near panic, Ty next checked the bottom drawer of his desk, where he kept his cash box. It was still there, unopened. He fumbled with the combination and the lid. It looked like it was all there, nearly ten grand. He scooped the cash out and thrust it into the pocket of his jeans.

Without bothering to close the door, Ty sprinted to the house and headed to his room. He pulled out a backpack and quickly stashed his gun in the outside pocket. He took the meth and weed from his nightstand

and stowed them in the bottom. Then, from his closet, he yanked several pairs of jeans and shirts from the hangers, threw in some underwear and stuffed them all into the pack on top of his stash.

He'd rented the house fully furnished, so there wasn't anything else he needed. The boards in his shop waiting for owners amounted to a few hundred bucks. No big loss.

A moment later, he was out the front door with the keys to his van in one hand and the backpack in the other. He tossed the pack onto the passenger seat as he climbed in. It fell to the floor.

Ty started the bus's engine, then backed out of the driveway and drove away. He was living month to month and the rent was paid for five more days. His landlord wouldn't know he was gone for at least a week.

Ty didn't know where he was going, but he felt pretty certain that things were getting too hot in the Keys, so that really left only one direction—north. Maybe Miami.

He turned onto Overseas Highway with the sun lightening the clouds to his right. It'd be up soon. He'd wait and call Moreno a little later, once he was out of the Keys. He knew the Cuban partied and slept late.

The miles ticked by, with little traffic to slow him down. It was a long drive—over a hundred miles—and would take at least two hours. He kept his speed down, not wanting to get pulled over, and only sped up slightly when he got on the long bridge that connected Conch Key to Long Key.

Halfway across, Ty spotted a helicopter. It was flying out over the Atlantic in the same direction he was driving but was silhouetted against the rising sun so he couldn't see any kind of identifying markings. When it turned out over the water, Ty sighed in relief.

His van had windows all the way around and he kept glancing back in the direction the helicopter had disappeared, but it was gone. As he came off the bridge onto Long Key and slowed for the town of Layton, though, he heard a rhythmic thumping sound.

He leaned forward over the wheel, scanning the lightening sky above and all around, as best he could.

Nothing.

Then, when he checked his mirror, he saw the shadow of a helicopter out over Florida Bay. He slowed and turned into a Kwik Stop, got out of the van, and was just in time to see the same helicopter fly over, heading north. It was solid black and had numbers and letters on the back part, but he couldn't tell what it said.

He waited in the parking lot for five minutes, his heart pounding. He had no idea who the two private dicks were or what they were capable of. Could it have been them in the helicopter?

No, he decided. They would've had to go in the boat to the airport first. It wasn't far, but Ty left just minutes after them. Maybe they had others working with them. People in a helicopter waiting to follow him.

Finally, Ty got back on the road, driving slowly, and watching all around. He saw the helicopter again as he made the turn onto Channel #5 Bridge. It was well ahead of him, again flying out over the water to the south. But it wasn't so far away that they couldn't see him with binoculars.

The helicopter disappeared behind trees once he was on Lower Matecumbe Key, but he saw it again as he crossed the bridge to Upper Matecumbe. It was farther away, but still going in the same direction.

Soon, he was passing through Key Largo and onto the long stretch of highway north of there. By then, the sun had fully risen and the sky was bright blue, broken by just a few puffy white clouds. He'd seen the helicopter enough times that he was sure it was following or keeping tabs on him. But it wouldn't be hard to lose it in the city. He was just as sure it wouldn't be allowed to fly between buildings, and he could easily evade it in the concrete jungle.

The road to Homestead was elevated and he occasionally got a glimpse of open water on one side and swamp on the other. He saw the helicopter again about halfway across the long, desolate stretch far to the north.

Had he lost them or had they given up?

Ty figured the best thing to do was go straight through downtown Miami, just to be sure. He pulled his phone out to call Benito. He knew the Cuban would be able to take the kilo of meth off his hands and that'd give him enough cash to go somewhere else. Thirty grand plus the ten in his pocket would go a long way.

CHAPTER TWENTY

By the time we got to East Cape Sable, the sun was above the horizon. We anchored in knee-deep water and waded toward shore, each with a lightweight fly rod in our hands.

Fishing from the boat meant only one line in the water for the most part. I could cast okay from the small poling platform, but with my large size, it wasn't ideal for fighting a powerful fish. I'd been pulled off balance more than once and ended up in the drink. Not the best look for a fishing guide.

"Shuffle your feet," I warned Tank. "You don't want to step on a stingray. And keep a wary eye out for crocodiles."

He looked at me, puzzled. "You mean alligators, right?"

"There are gators father inland," I said. "But Florida Bay and the inland estuaries of the southwest coast are the home of saltwater crocs."

"Is there anything out here that won't eat us?"

"Very little," I said with a chuckle. "This area probably looked the same a hundred thousand years ago. Hang around South Florida long enough and you'll see we have some really big bugs. The state bird is the mosquito. They can suck you dry in an hour out here."

"What makes you think that guy won't call the other guy in Miami?" Tank asked. "I mean, don't you think we should have gone there by car?"

"Cars are slow down here," I said. "To go fifty miles up or down island takes time. On a boat, you can travel full speed, and most of the time, in a perfectly straight line. From here, my house, Deuce's office, and Willy Quick are all within forty-five minutes at wide-open throttle. Deuce has assets close to Miami, and don't forget my daughter and son-in-law. They're both cops and are within minutes of Quick's location. I just know he's behind this somehow."

Tank unhooked his fly from the rod and examined it. "Unusual flies. Bigger than what I remember. You make these on that bench I saw in your living room?"

That was Tank's way of deflecting from a stressful situation. Go through it, around it, or build a wall and go over it. But move on.

"Yeah," I replied. "What's the biggest trout you ever caught?"

"Probably eight or ten pounds," he said. "My dad caught a fifteen-pounder once."

"Bonefish get that big," I said. "They're long and silvery gray—shaped like a torpedo and hard to see. And they have a hard, bony plate in their mouth that a hook

won't pierce. If you hook one, you'll have to keep constant tension, or the hook will just fall out."

We sight-fished for tailing bones in the shallows.
Tank hadn't used a fly rod in many years, but the muscle
memory soon returned and before long, he'd hooked
his first bonefish. Unfortunately, it and the next two
got off the hook.

"You really gotta keep a tight line on these guys," he
shouted from about forty yards down the beach. "And
they're a lot stronger and more agile than any trout I
ever caught, that's for sure."

"You just gotta be ready to zig when they zag," I called
back.

"Well, *duh*," he said with a grin, reeling his line in.
"They just zag a whole lot."

I laughed and he joined me.

"And those other fish you mentioned?"

"Permit can reach thirty or forty pounds," I said, as
we walked around the point. "An average tarpon is as
big as me. And they all have double the fight per pound
over any trout."

"Is that right?"

He'll understand the first time a tarpon bends his rod,
I thought.

"There!" I pointed about a hundred feet down the
beach.

"Those swirls?"

"Yeah, looks like a couple of pompano, tailing around
a rock or something."

We separated and began our casts. I wanted to try to put my fly on the water the same time Tank did his. Maybe we could get a double bite.

"You take the one on the right," I whispered, whipping my line back at the same time he did.

While they didn't hit at exactly the same time, it was close enough, and the water exploded from the double hits.

Some species of pompano could get to colossal proportions—up to nearly four feet in length and fifty pounds for the African pompano. They were usually found in much deeper water. The Florida pompano rarely got over eight pounds and favored the flats and shoals that their big cousins couldn't get to.

I knew right away that the one I had was going to be at least five or six pounds. It took us both a good ten minutes to tire the two big fish and get them close enough to grab.

"Hot damn!" Tank yelled, lifting his from the water with a grin that nearly wrapped around his whole head. "That's a fish!"

"That's dinner," I said, lifting my own out of the water by its forked tail. "Enough for all of us."

Once we'd carried the fish and our rods back to the boat, I opened the live well and switched on the pump. It filled quickly and we dropped the fish in.

"Why do you suppose he stopped?" Tank asked, throwing a leg up onto the gunwale.

"Sampson? That ten-minute stop on Long Key? I don't know. Maybe he needed gas or a bite to eat or something."

"Where is he now?"

I took my phone from the charger and looked at the tracker app. Where he went wasn't as important as why. Taking off after seeing us steal Cobie's board from his workshop gave me all the proof I needed that he was involved in her disappearance. The police couldn't use it, but I damned sure could.

"Downtown Miami," I replied. "Headed north."

I watched the little flashing dot on the phone's screen for a moment. It moved for a few seconds, then stopped again.

"A lot of lights and rush-hour traffic," I said. "I was hoping he'd go to Moreno's, but he should have stayed on the interstate, not drive right through the heart of downtown with all those tall office buildings and condos."

"We should head back," Tank said. "You said earlier that the big swamp ape was sitting tight on the other side of the state, and it's obvious Sampson's not going there. Maybe Chyrel will have some information from any phone calls they make."

"She'd call if there was anything important."

"Your phone gets a signal way out here?" he asked, looking around.

"This one doesn't need a signal for the tracker to work," I replied. "She'd call my satellite phone. We could try for another bonefish if you're game."

"To tell you the truth, Jesse, I'm a bit worn out already. I get tired pretty easy these days."

I studied his eyes. He was stripped down to just his cargo shorts, same as me, and he looked as fit as ever, but there was a sallowness to his eyes. They looked weary and in sharp contrast to the rest of the man. He still looked like he could eat iron and spit nails.

"Okay," I said. "Let's get these home and kick back with a couple of beers."

He swung his other leg over the gunwale and stood up. "Now you're talking."

As I climbed aboard, my sat phone chirped. I picked it up, saw Chyrel's name on the display, and clicked the *Talk* button.

"Sampson is talking to Moreno," she said. "I'll mute both of us and patch you in."

I heard a couple of clicks and put the phone on speaker so Tank could hear.

Sampson's voice came over the speaker. "—black helicopter. But I lost it by going through downtown."

"A helicopter is following you and you're coming here?" a Hispanic man responded, anger rising in his voice. "*Estúpido!*"

"I haven't seen it since Homestead, man. I'm sure I lost them."

"*Maricón*, do not come here!"

"I got a key of some good meth," Sampson said. "I need to unload it and get the fuck out of here. I'll cut you a good price, man—just thirty grand."

There was a moment of silence, then the man I assumed was Moreno said, "Find a place to get outta sight. A parking garage or something. Then meet me at Willy's place out on Alligator Alley at four."

Tank and I both looked up at each other.

"I can't wait that long, man!"

"You can and you will, *hijo de puta*! Or you can try to sell it on the street and hope you don't get busted."

"Okay," Sampson said. "Four o'clock at the shack. But man, we need to get rid of the evidence."

"I'll call him and he can meet us there. He's bringing ten keys later tonight anyway. Let him kill the *putas* and get rid of the bodies. I never liked supplying him anyway."

"You sure?" Sampson said. "The guy's whacked, man. Keeping three of them locked up out there? Totally crazy, man."

"*Si*, Quick is *pervertido*. But he is *un muy peligroso hombre*—extremely dangerous."

"Aight," Sampson agreed. "But I don't want anything more to do with him. Snatching the girl like that wasn't right, man."

The call ended and Chyrel came back on. "Were they talking about what I think they were?"

"Get with Deuce," I said. "See who he has available. I want to get there before fourteen hundred. I'd bet it's the place Willy Quick stopped at on his way home from his east coast drug run. It might be where they have Cobie."

"And it sounds like two others," Tank added.

"You're not even close to a road," Chyrel said. "How do you plan to get there?"

"We're half an hour from Flamingo," I replied. "Any chance someone can pick us up? Or can you get us a car there?"

"Charity was flying some tourists up from Key West. I think she was dropping them this morning at MIA for a flight out. Let me check. If not, Paul's up at Homestead Air Reserve Base and can be in Flamingo in about an hour."

"Charity's back in the States?"

"Since Wednesday," Chyrel replied. "She's been staying with me. Head for Flamingo and I'll see if I can get her there before sending Paul."

CHAPTER TWENTY-ONE

A sliver of light shone through the crack below the door. It was the only indication that it was daylight—the two windows in the room were boarded up tight. The crack under the door was the only *visual* clue. The rising temperature was a good indicator as well.

The second night of Vanessa's captivity went about the same as the first. Throughout each night, she'd heard strange noises from outside, made doubly frightening because she couldn't even see her hand in front of her face. The night sounds seemed to come from all around. Terrible sounds. Branches or birds on the tin roof sounded ominous enough, but the splashing about below, and the calls of wild animals in the distance were even more nightmarish.

The other two women in the room had slept fitfully the last two nights, the younger one sobbing several times. The intervening day hadn't been much different, just hotter. Vanessa could smell the stench coming from her own body but rationalized that it must be from the other two, who had been kept prisoners for much longer.

During the previous day, she'd noticed where a floorboard near each corner was broken, offering a small hole, barely big enough to get her hand through. Mosquitoes used the holes to invade and attack the three women throughout the night.

It wasn't until after darkness fell, when Vanessa needed to relieve her bladder, that she realized what the holes in the floor were for. It made her nauseous that she'd put her hand in.

"Are you awake?" the older woman, Michelle asked quietly.

"I am," Vanessa whispered.

"Me, too," came the younger girl's voice.

"He'll come tonight," Michelle said. "Every other night, right, Cobie?"

The girl mumbled something that sounded affirmative.

"The man who got you into this," Michelle began, in a slightly questioning tone, "you said his name was Benito Moreno and he was a drug dealer?"

Vanessa nodded, though she could barely see the woman in the dim light. "He gets a shipment of coke every other day. Willy Quick, the man who actually brought me here, is his supplier. He probably comes here after—he told me he lives on the west coast."

"If one of us could get loose," Michelle said, "do you think you could remember how to get out of here?"

"What time does he usually come?"

"Just before dark," Michelle replied.

"That's a big if," Vanessa said. "I remember looking up at the shack before Willy choked me out and seeing a big padlock on the door. And all the windows were boarded up, like the ones in here."

Michelle shifted, rattling her chain. "That light under the door is coming from somewhere."

"All I saw was the front," Vanessa said, struggling to her feet. "Maybe there's a window on one of the sides or the back."

She moved over to where her chain was anchored in the corner post, gripped the big eyebolt, and tried to turn it.

"Save your energy," Michelle said. "They won't budge."

Vanessa looped the chain around the bolt, anyway, giving her more to grip. "Save it for what?" she asked, as she strained to turn the bolt.

The chain suddenly slipped in her hands, but she couldn't be sure if it was just the links slipping or the bolt turning. When she removed the chain links, she saw that the bolt had moved, if only a little.

"I turned it," she whispered. "Try wrapping the chain around your bolts for a better grip."

The other two went to their corners, as Vanessa once more wrapped the chain around the bolt.

"I don't know which way it's supposed to turn," Michelle said.

"Righty-tighty, lefty-loosey," Cobie said, her voice straining as she tried to turn her bolt.

"What's that supposed to mean?"

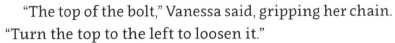

"The top of the bolt," Vanessa said, gripping her chain. "Turn the top to the left to loosen it."

Vanessa twisted the bolt with all she had. It slipped another nearly imperceptible amount, but no matter how hard she tried, it wouldn't go any farther.

Michelle fell against the wall, dropping her chain. A second later, Cobie just slumped to the floor, also defeated.

"We're never getting out of here," the younger woman said. "I'll never see my mom again and she'll never know what happened to me."

Vanessa rose and went to the center of the room, where she sat on the floor. "Don't give up yet," she said. "If we only had something long to put in the eye of the bolt to turn it."

"There's nothing in here," Michelle said. "Just the plastic water bottles he leaves us."

"Mine turned a little both times, but that's it. It's stuck."

Michelle joined her and sat a few feet away, tucking her legs under her. "Is there anything else you remember? Another house nearby? Anything?"

"We only drove a few minutes off the interstate," Vanessa recounted. "There was a small gas station by the exit, but I think that was it. Then he turned left onto a dirt road. I don't remember passing any signs or anything, and once we were on that road, there was nothing but trees and swamp."

"Even if you got the chain off," Cobie whispered from the corner, "the door's locked." Her voice rose slightly. "That light is coming up through a hole or something in the floor of the next room. It's where he'll dump our bodies. Even if you got loose, you'd have to climb down there where the alligators are, carrying your chain, and then swim to shore to get to civilization. It's hopeless!"

She was becoming panicked.

For the first time, Vanessa noticed Michelle was wearing shoes. With heels. She'd left her own pumps in Willy's truck.

"What about your shoes?" Vanessa said. "Maybe the heel can add more leverage to turn one of the bolts."

Michelle looked down at her feet. Her expensive shoes were scuffed and the seam on the back of one was splitting. "I never thought to try."

"Let me have one," Vanessa said. "I budged my bolt. Maybe between the chain and the heel I can turn it enough to get it loose. He won't be here until later, right? It's worth a try."

Michelle reluctantly gave up and tossed the shoe with the nearly broken seam to her. Vanessa picked it up and went back to her corner. In the near darkness, she carefully wrapped the chain around the bolt again, lining the links up with the eye of the bolt. She worked the heel through the links and the eyebolt, then wrapped more chain around the bolt for good measure.

Slowly, she twisted the chain the opposite way, tightening it slightly, thinking that a running start might help. Then she set herself in a position that would allow her to twist as hard as possible.

The bolt moved back to where it had stopped before and Vanessa increased the pressure. Suddenly, it moved. A lot.

"I got a quarter of a turn," she said. "But the shoe's banged up against the wall and in the way now."

Uncoiling the chain, she removed the shoe and did the whole thing over again.

The other two women rose and moved to the middle of the room to watch.

When she was ready, Vanessa put all her strength into it, twisting the ball of chain with one hand and pushing on the sole of the shoe with the other.

Michelle and Cobie urged her on.

The bolt slipped again, then caught. The sudden stop and tremendous pressure Vanessa was putting on the shoe snapped the heel off.

"Dammit!"

"What happened?" Michelle asked.

Vanessa slumped against the wall, panting. "The heel broke. But it moved some more."

There was a scuttling sound and Michelle's other shoe bumped Vanessa's foot.

"You have to keep trying," Michelle pleaded. "Neither of us have the strength and yours is already loose."

Vanessa picked up the shoe, noting for the first time that it was a Louboutin with the red sole. An expensive pair of shoes that were high on her own wish list.

She returned to her corner and went through the process again, this time knowing not to put as much force on the heel.

When she was ready, she twisted the chain mostly, adding just a little force with the shoe.

The bolt turned easier.

She rewound the chain and did it again. Then she dropped the shoe and used just the chain. The bolt continued to turn until finally it fell free.

"You did it!" Michelle said, as if she'd been holding her breath.

Over the next few minutes, Vanessa tried Michelle's chain, then Cobie's, both to no avail. She also broke the heel on the second shoe.

The big eyebolt at the end of her chain was of no use; it wouldn't fit through either the links or the other bolts' eyes.

"It's no use," Vanessa said.

"Maybe there's something in the other room," Michelle suggested.

Vanessa went to the door and tried the knob. "It's locked."

"It's just an inside door," Cobie said, hope in her voice for the first time. "It should have a little hole in the middle. Anything at all shoved in that hole will push the pin and allow it to turn."

Vanessa picked up one of the shoes. The broken heels were way too big to put into the little hole. She was about to drop it when she noticed the steel rod protruding slightly from the heel.

Vanessa sat on the floor and, using the pointed end of the eyebolt, began to scrape and pry at the damaged heel, ripping away the fabric and breaking parts of the inside away from the steel reinforcement rod. Finally, she had enough of it exposed to try the lock.

The rod fit the hole but wasn't long enough. She'd have to expose more of it. She sat down and started working at the heel again. Her hands shook and she gouged her fingers and palms several times, until they became slick with blood. Looking around, she finally just wiped the blood off on the front of her pretty yellow dress and continued prying.

Suddenly, the heel cracked, and the rod fell out.

Struggling to her feet with the thin rod in her hand, Vanessa carefully inserted it into the hole in the door-knob. She felt resistance and pushed. The rod cocked at an angle and slipped past whatever it had hit.

She tried the knob, but it was still locked.

"It's kinda like a pin in there," Cobie said. "It points straight at the hole, and you gotta go in perfectly straight."

Vanessa tried again, using the rod to "feel" around the edges of the pin. It was tiny, smaller than the size of the hole itself. She moved the rod until she thought it was on the center of the pin, then pushed. The pin went in a little but when she tried the knob, the rod slipped, and the door still wouldn't open.

"Keep trying," Cobie said. "You have to push the pin in and turn the knob at the same time."

Vanessa tried once more and finally, the knob turned, and she swung the door open.

"You did it!" Michelle practically shouted. "It looks like there's enough light to see."

Vanessa stepped into the room, dragging the chain, still bolted to her ankle, with every other step. The only light was coming from an opening in the floor, just as Cobie had said. It was about three feet wide and didn't seem to have a door.

There was a bed to the right, just a wooden frame with a bare, stain-covered mattress.

Moving around the hole, she picked up her chain and searched the room. It didn't take long; the bed was the only thing in it. She tried the front door. The knob turned, but the door barely moved inward when she yanked at it.

It was padlocked from the outside.

She went back to the room where the other women were chained.

"There's nothing. Not even a loose nail."

"Go for help," Michelle said suddenly. "It's our only hope."

"Yes," pleaded Cobie. "Bring help."

Vanessa looked from one woman to the other, then nodded. "I'll go see if there's any way out."

She went back to the open hole in the floor and looked down. Judging by the shadows, it was around noon.

Willy wouldn't come for several hours. If she could get out of the house, she knew she could find help before then.

I have to try, she decided, and knelt for a better look at the underside of the shack.

She noted the wooden pilings the structure was built on, with a web of braces to keep them from moving. The water was dark, and she had no way of knowing how deep it was. Directly below, something lighter in color than the surrounding water floated just below the surface.

She leaned over, steadying herself with her hands on either side of the opening. She couldn't make out what it was. The water could be two feet deep and it was a rock, for all she knew.

Then it moved slightly, as if it was drifting in an unseen current. It looked like a small garbage bag, or maybe a fanny pack. It rose slowly.

The face of a young woman broke the surface, blond hair billowing around it.

Just as Vanessa screamed, a large alligator rolled, taking the woman's head in its massive jaws. In one fluid movement, the big bull gator dove deep, barely making a ripple.

"What happened?" Michelle yelled. "Vanessa! Are you okay?"

Vanessa stumbled back from the hole, her hands over her face, until she bumped the door jamb to their cell.

"I...I saw a...a woman's body! Down under the house. She was a blonde."

"Jenny!" Cobie wailed.

"He...he...just fed her...to the alligators." Vanessa whispered, her voice breaking.

"Can you...do you think you can get to shore?"

Vanessa turned toward the two chained women, her hands now clutched below her chin. "I don't know. I'm scared."

"Did you see anything else?" Michelle begged. "Any other way out?"

The sight of the woman's dead face disappearing into the maw of the giant alligator had unnerved her.

"Vanessa!" Michelle shouted. "We don't have much time."

Vanessa lowered her hands to her sides. She had to do something.

"There's like a bridge from the front door," she said. "And some braces and big poles holding up the place. If I can get to the bridge, I can get help."

Vanessa moved slowly back toward the trap door, concentrating, forcing the fear and the vision of what she'd seen from her mind.

At the edge of the opening, she stood and peered down at the dark water once more, half expecting to see the woman's face again. But she saw nothing but the foreboding dark water. Dropping to her knees, she looked around the underside of the shack again, forcing her mind to act. The water was about eight feet below the floor. There were diagonal braces on most of the round pilings, all at forty-five degree angles. From the corner of the house, a brace went down to the next piling, supporting the back wall, then up, down, and up again to the other corner. She was sure she could move from brace to brace to reach the underside of the bridge.

Vanessa hefted the chain in her right hand. It was heavy, but she didn't think it was too heavy to sap her strength carrying it. She would need both hands free, though. She didn't want to let the chain dangle and get caught on something. Or worse, get grabbed by an alligator that would yank her down into the water.

"I think I can get over to the bridge," she shouted back into the darkened room. "I'll let you know when I do."

Taking the end of the chain, she looped it around her neck and tucked the long eyebolt under the thin strap of her dress to hold it in place. Then she sat down with her feet dangling in the opening, like she was sitting at a dock.

The thought of an alligator jumping up and grabbing her feet caused her to pull them back up.

She had to do it. The alternative meant a short life at the hands of a monster. Besides, alligators didn't jump. All she had to do was stay out of the water.

The first brace was just a few feet below her, angling up to another brace that went down to the piling that supported the front of the shack. She scooted forward, until her toes were just inches from the cross brace.

Leaning back, she let her butt slide over the edge and felt the rough wood on her feet. Slowly, she worked her way down the brace, until her body hung precariously in space.

With a surge of adrenaline, she reached out with her left hand and grabbed the brace, slipping a little and nearly falling.

Steadying herself, Vanessa twisted and swung her lower body over the brace, while moving her right hand to the corner of the opening. After centering her weight on the beam, she let go of the opening and grabbed the rail, straddling it, thighs pressed tight against the rough wood to keep from sliding down.

Still terrified, but gaining confidence, she looked around, tossing her long dark hair out of her eyes.

She was on the brace angling up from the piling supporting the back wall. The piling in the middle of the shack was just in front of her. She scooted higher on the brace to reach for the other one that went down to the piling supporting the front.

She could see the bridge right next to it.

Both braces were bolted to the middle piling, one on each side. Getting around the telephone-pole-sized support column would be difficult. No matter which way she went, it meant going around the full girth.

Sweat streamed down her face as she got up close to the floor beams. Spider webs caught on her slippery skin and in her hair, but she ignored them. Slowly, she reached around the piling to grab the other diagonal brace.

Once she had a firm grip, she stretched her right leg around the piling and looped it over the brace. Quickly, she moved her body around the pole and was straddling the next cross brace.

She smiled in the darkness, confidence building. She was going to make it.

Vanessa looked around again. She saw no sign of the alligator.

She'd have to work her way down the brace to where it was bolted to the exterior piling about a foot above the water. Then, somehow, she would have to climb that thick pole to the rickety bridge.

She moved slowly, trying to be as quiet as possible. She didn't know if alligators could hear, but she didn't want to take the chance. The rough wood drove splinters into the insides of her thighs and belly.

The pain was excruciating. For every three inches she slid down, she had to pull herself back up an inch to pull a sliver of wood out of her skin.

Finally, Vanessa stood on the crook between the angled brace and the upright piling. It was bigger around than she'd thought.

She could get her arms around it to the point she could touch both forearms with her fingers, but it was slick with damp, spongy moss on the shaded side.

Vanessa moved her left arm under the chain, moving it from in front of her to behind her back. Then she wrapped one leg around the pole.

Her bright yellow dress was now filthy and ripped to tatters. She was bleeding from several open wounds on her left thigh and belly.

"So help me, God," she muttered breathlessly, "when I get back to the Upper East Side, I'm going to kill Benny for this."

She threw her other leg around the pole, locking her ankles like some crazed john was pile-driving into her. She knew the strength in her inner thighs.

Reaching up, the chain now dangling below her butt, she moved higher. The length of the chain was shorter, now wrapped one and a half times around her neck. It stopped her from going too high.

From her neck, the chain curved down and back up again to where it was shackled to her leg, raised high on the other side of the pole.

She let go with her left hand to remove the chain from her neck and slipped down almost as much as she'd gained.

Her breath came in rasps as she held tightly to the pole again. If she fell in, even if an alligator didn't eat her, the weight of the chain would pull her under. Vanessa wasn't tall, and the water could easily be over her head.

Clinging desperately to the pole, she looked around, her eyes filled with terror at what she might see below her. The water looked impenetrable—dark brown, almost black.

She couldn't see the bottom.

Beyond the pole, the high ground where the bridge ended, where the big man had stopped and nearly choked her to death, was only twenty or thirty feet away.

She decided not to remove the chain and just work her way up the pole, like an inchworm.

Squeezing her thighs together, she stretched her body until the chain tugged at her neck, then moved her arms up to get a higher grip.

Just as she eased up with her thighs, she heard a splash from below and something grabbed at the thin fabric of her dress.

The alligator!

And it had the chain in its jaws as well.

Vanessa held on for dear life, surprised that the weight on the chain was so little. The alligator wasn't pulling her off, but the chain was tight around her throat, cutting off her windpipe.

What she didn't know was that the big bull gator was only barely moving its giant tail, lifting itself slightly to get an idea of what was on the pole.

There was another louder thrashing of water and Vanessa's left leg was violently bent up against her shoulder as the alligator tried to pull her from the pole.

The terrible jaws opened wider and engulfed the left side of her butt and her thigh. Clamping down, the sharp teeth pierced the skin of her back and thigh. The pain in her hip was excruciating as the alligator squeezed her leg against her torso at an impossible angle until there was a loud pop.

She screamed and tried desperately to keep hold of the pole, but the animal's weight and power were far more than she could withstand.

The last thing Vanessa heard as she hit the water was Michelle screaming her name from above.

CHAPTER TWENTY-TWO

Asoft morning rain fell on the old house as Willy finished weighing the fourth brick and sealed it up. He was making another east coast run later in the evening, with deliveries to four night clubs.

Jo and Sue Roy, his late wife Marley's younger sisters, had been watching him like a hawk. But he'd worked hard at getting the sisters to trust him. Marley's daughter, Kurt, was in prison. He'd explained to Jo and Sue Roy that until Kurt was home with them again, he was going to hold fast to his late wife's dying wish as she lay gasping in his arms. He would keep the operation running and the fortune intact until the family could decide on who would lead the clan.

Another week was all he needed to put up with them. Then the timing would be right. Moving forty million dollars in gold bars from the underground vault in the backyard would take some time.

Willy stared out the window at the rain falling down. Then he looked around the room. He'd accepted living in squalor for the last fifteen years, but it would soon come to an end.

Jo and Sue Roy were driving up to Raiford to visit Kurt next weekend, so he knew they wouldn't be around. That was when he planned to load the bars into his pickup and head for South America.

Willy heard the bong of the sensor he'd placed in the dirt track leading to the house. He rolled his eyes, wondering which of the Blancs was stopping by this time. It seemed that someone was visiting every three hours or so. It'd been going on for months, throughout each day. At first, he thought the family was genuinely concerned about him since Marley's death.

He was fairly certain that the highway was being watched at night.

Just the same, Willy was a cautious man and quickly put the cocaine and scale away. Then he went to the door and took his rifle from a rack just above it. He opened the door and stepped out, waiting under the cover of the small porch.

A white Ford Expedition pulled into the yard, splashed through a puddle, and drove toward the barn. It was Sue Roy, the youngest of the Blanc sisters.

Willy stepped back inside and put the rifle in its rack, then trotted to the barn to open it.

Sue Roy stopped just short of the barn door and waited. When Willy swung the doors open, she drove inside and shut off the engine.

As a rule, Willy made sure that all vehicles were out of sight, giving the house and barn an abandoned look.

"I wasn't expecting you for a coupla more hours," Willy said. "Your product ain't ready yet."

"This rain's got me antsy," she replied, stepping down from the cab.

Aside from being the youngest, Sue Roy was also the best-looking of the sisters. And unlike her sisters, she was small. Standing at just five-foot-four, she was rail thin and Willy didn't think she weighed much over a hundred pounds. Meth does that to a person.

But between the two still living, Sue Roy was the most dangerous and unpredictable. Another by-product of meth use.

But neither held a candle to Marley's daughter, Kurt. *That woman was just pure mean*, Willy thought.

He knew Sue Roy always had a gun on her and today was no exception. It was stuffed into the front of her tight jeans.

"You gonna shoot your cooter off with that thing one day," he said, pointing at her crotch.

"That cooter's highly trained," she fired right back. "It can pull the trigger without me even taking my gun out."

"What the hell are you doing here?" he asked.

"Figured I'd come and help ya weigh out the deliveries," Sue Roy said, stepping toward him. "Are you doin' okay?"

More like it's your turn to keep an eye on me, Willy thought. They had a rotation, he realized. With so many in the clan, and with the loss of his wife over three months earlier, at first it didn't seem strange.

Willy lowered his gaze, feigning the distraught widower. "Good days and bad," he grumbled. "I do miss Marley come nighttime, though."

Together, they ran through the rain to the house and Willy held the door open for his sister-in-law, noting with some glee that the cold rain had soaked her tank top and turned her nipples into little rocks.

The woman's got some pretty titties, he thought, remembering seeing her dance in a topless joint one time.

Over by the couch, Willy lifted the hinged top of the coffee table, took the scale out and set it aside. "I got the coke ready. Was just about to start on your meth."

He sat down and pulled out a large, plastic container holding ten pounds of light blue crystals. "Three keys, right?"

"Two keys and two half-key bags," she said, sitting next to him and eyeing the meth with a look that bordered on ravenous. "And an ounce for me."

He took a glass pipe from inside the table. It was about six inches long and had a rounded bowl at the end with an air hole in the top.

He placed the pipe beside the container and looked at her. "Knock yourself out."

Sue Roy picked up the glass pipe and anxiously peeled the top off the plastic container, reveling in the scent as if it were an aphrodisiac.

The chemical stench hit Willy's nostrils like a tenth-grade chemistry lab. He didn't like meth. It smelled nasty and he knew it was highly addictive. Willy preferred beer, then maybe whiskey. He smoked a little weed now and then, and on occasion would snort a line of coke if it were offered. Those all came from natural things.

Meth was made in a lab.

Selecting two small rocks, Sue Roy dropped them into the pipe and flicked a lighter beneath it, waiting for the drug to start vaporizing.

When it did, she drew deeply on the pipe, then fell back on the couch, arching her back to hold the smoke in. The outline of her ribs and breasts didn't leave a lot to his imagination and Willy felt an urge to pinch those two little rocks. He also felt a stirring in his loins.

Slowly, her body relaxed as she released her breath and slumped into the cushions. She looked over at him and caught him staring at her chest. With a dreamy expression on her face, she extended the pipe to Willy.

"You know I don't use that stuff," Willy said.

"Don't knock it till ya try it," she mumbled.

She was lit now. Pupils dilated and breathing shallow.

But the effect meth had was short-lived and Willy knew she'd start tweaking again within fifteen minutes, as the drug wore off. The ounce she was getting wouldn't last the rest of the weekend. And she'd probably screw half a dozen men before it ran out.

Sue Roy put another smaller crystal in the pipe and again offered it to him. Willy looked past the offered pipe at her face. She was still pretty for her age, but her teeth were stained and rotting, and she was missing a few. She looked hungry. For the meth or for something else, he wasn't sure. But he knew she was as horny as a goat when she was high. The five kids she'd had before she was twenty-five attested to that. Carrying those babies hadn't done anything to her body, though.

"What the hell," he said, taking the pipe from her hand.

He held it out and she flicked the lighter again. When he hit it, he felt a wave of euphoria wash over him. He'd smoked meth a few times but was always cautious about not doing too much or doing it too often, due to its addictiveness. Though he didn't like it, there were times when it helped smooth things over with a new buyer.

They both leaned back on the couch. With his greater weight, he sank deeper. Gravity, combined with her relaxed body, pulled her into him, their shoulders touching.

He felt the fire of her skin against his and looked over at his late wife's sister. The truth was, Willy had always hated his wife. He'd wanted Sue Roy for years, but Marley had always held the power.

And the key to the gold.

Willy was a very patient man. He knew he'd outlive his fat wife. He was five years younger than her and in much better health. He'd been an athlete while she was getting high on pain pills and anything else she could find. So, for the last two decades, he played the part of the devoted, big-woman-loving husband.

Sue Roy turned toward him, their faces just a few inches apart. "Tell me that don't put lead in your pencil," she said, trying her best to be seductive.

They'd played this game many times, back before Marley died. Sue Roy knew he'd wanted her, and she was a constant tease. Toying with her brother-in-law had always been a game to her. He let his breath out slowly, feeling the stirring in his pants.

"Yeah," he sighed, as she loaded the pipe and flicked the lighter again. "It sure does."

Sue Roy did another hit, again falling back onto the couch against him, her hip now pressing against his leg. When she emptied her lungs, she looked straight into his eyes. "Are you as big down there as you are everywhere else?"

When he reached for her, she flinched slightly. That should have warned him. But he grabbed one of her little breasts in his big hand and kneaded it like dough.

"What the hell!" she said and started to resist him, but he easily held her in place.

She began to struggle against him, reaching for the gun in her pants, but was too high to do anything more than let it fall from her waistband and clatter to the floor.

Willy didn't notice it and reached for her jeans with his other hand. She struggled harder and he forced her back on the couch.

"You know you been wantin' it," he slurred, pinning her to the couch with one mighty hand at her throat.

She couldn't speak but beat on his arm as he forcefully yanked at her jeans with his free hand.

It was over in seconds. Sue Roy tried to lunge for his eyes, and he pressed down on her throat with his full body weight, snapping her neck like a dry twig.

Sue Roy fell limp, eyes staring blankly at the ceiling.

Willy hadn't meant to hurt her. He'd genuinely thought she wanted it. But she was dead, and he was screwed. As soon as one of the others found out, they'd all come gunning for him.

Shaking the cobwebs from his head, he stood and looked down at her lifeless body.

"Dammit," he growled, then kicked her foot.

There was no response.

Willy looked at the clock on the wall. It was almost noon and Jo would be arriving to pick up her delivery in two hours.

His phone rang, and Willy practically jumped out of his skin. He looked at it and saw that it was one of his clients on the east coast. He quickly calmed himself and touched the *Talk* button.

"Yeah," he snarled, almost afraid to say anything more for fear of being found out.

"It's Benito, *amigo*. We have a problem."

"What problem?" Willy asked, his head starting to clear.

He looked out the back window toward the wood pile, which concealed the entry to the underground bunker.

"My man in the Keys flew the coop," Benito said. "He says the private investigator the Murphy woman hired is on to him. I think we better meet at the shack and get rid of the evidence."

A part of Willy's mind was aghast at the thought of getting rid of what he considered his personal property. Having been so close to satisfying his urges with Sue Roy, he now needed to get to his shack for his own reasons.

"What do you mean?" Willy asked. "What's a punk in the Keys got to do with me?"

"The girl I brought you last month?" Benito said. "The young one? She's not from my stable. She's a friend of my guy in the Keys and some hotshot PI is looking for her, *hermano*."

"Fuck!" Willy bellowed, his mind racing. "Okay, okay. I was planning to head your way later. I can leave in about an hour and be there by three or four."

"*Es Bueno*," Benito said. "My man thinks a helicopter was following him. So, I told him to find a parking garage and stay outta sight until the afternoon. We'll meet you there and help you get rid of everything, including him."

Willy agreed, then ended the call.

He could do hard time for running drugs. But his shack out in the Everglades was the scene of four murders. He'd planned on killing the young one later that night, anyway, having found a suitable replacement.

He quickly stuffed the four bricks of coke and the ten-pound bag of meth into his backpack, then opened the table again. There were several bundles of cash, which he also put in the pack. He also pulled out a large bag of weed, which went into his pocket.

Going back to the living room, he stared at the body.

"From now on, I'll stick to weed," he said to Sue Roy's corpse. "Meth kills."

Then, without another thought to his dead sister-in-law, he went out the door and to the barn. Sue Roy's Expedition was parked behind his truck. He opened the driver's door and saw the keys were still in the ignition.

He tossed the pack in the backseat and went out the rear door of the barn to the wood pile. By putting his weight against the stack of firewood, he toppled most of it, then began throwing the rest out of the way.

Once the steel door was exposed, he took the key that hung from his neck and unlocked it, throwing the door open.

Stepping down into the musty confines of the long-buried cargo container, Willy let his eyes adjust for a moment. The gold was stored in small metal boxes, two little bars in each box, each weighing twelve and a half kilos, a little over fifty-five pounds per box. There were thirty of them.

He carried two of the heavy boxes at a time over to the steps and hefted them up onto the wet ground, then climbed up and carried them to Sue Roy's truck.

Repeating this process over and over, Willy was soon exhausted. Even with his strength, it was a lot of weight to move. But he finally had them all in the truck, slid as far forward in the back as he could get them. He didn't want the rear suspension to squat too much.

It was time to fly.

But first, he had some business to take care of at the shack. If Benito and his street dealer in the Keys were going to meet him there, he could kill them both and make it look like they'd killed the women, then shot each other. The gators could only eat so much and if the PI was onto them, they'd eventually find the shack,

Once he'd opened the barn doors, Willy went back to the truck and reached in with one hand on the brake pedal to start it. Then he used the electric seat controls to move the seat all the way back. Five minutes later, he was on Highway 41, headed toward Carnestown. There, he'd go north on 29 to get to the interstate.

The problem with getting three-quarters of a ton of gold to South America was a big one, and he'd already decided how to do it. He couldn't very well carry it onto a plane. But with the cash in the backpack, he could hire someone to fly him and the gold to South America.

"Brazil," he said aloud, grinning. "Land of hot little *chiquitas.*"

CHAPTER TWENTY-THREE

T ank and I idled into the little marina in Flamingo. There were slips for at least a dozen boats the size of my Maverick, with a boat ramp to the left, fuel dock to the right, and the marina store at the center. I headed straight toward the empty fairway in front of the store.

Charity had called and I told her to hang on, while we docked, then slipped the phone in my shirt pocket.

The dockmaster came out and greeted us. "Planning to stay long?"

"Probably all day," I replied, turning into an empty slip, and reversing the engine. "Maybe till tomorrow."

I killed the motor and we climbed out and secured the boat. Digging my wallet out, I handed the man my credit card. "Is there a place to land a helicopter nearby?"

"A heli...say, what the heck's going on here? Who are you guys?"

"No time to explain," I said, showing him my old Homeland Security ID. "I have a helo inbound. It'll be here in just a few minutes. Where can it land?"

"Over in front of the Information Center, I guess," he replied, pointing to the southwest. "By the flagpole. They sometimes land them there when someone gets hurt."

"Thanks," I said, pulling my phone out. "Hang onto my card till we get back for the boat."

Tank and I started around the west side of the slips. I could see the flag flying above and far in front of a large building ahead of us.

I put the phone to my ear and heard the noise from Charity's chopper. "Look for a flagpole, Charity," I said, already hearing the heavy whump-whump of her helo's rotors in the distance.

Tank paused and listened. "Your pilot's in a Huey?"

"Yeah," I replied. "Be like old times."

We walked around the Information Center building, not seeing anyone around. Flamingo didn't get a lot of visitors. I noted the direction of the wind from the flag. Out of the southeast, in line with a long, grassy area beyond the flagpole.

"Easy LZ," I said into the phone. "Wind's southeast, you have an area not quite as big as a football field, tapered at the approach end and fifty yards wide at the center."

The black helo came into view, flying low out of the east and turning toward us. With a main rotor diameter of less than fifty feet, she had more than enough room and the wind on her nose.

Tank and I crossed the road and walked out to the flagpole as Charity made her downwind turn and swooped in toward us.

We both kept watch to make sure nobody got near the field, but the campground, marina, and Information Center all looked abandoned.

A couple of minutes later, Charity touched down softly in the grass and the heavy whump of the blades changed to a whir as she moved the pitch angle to neutral.

We bent low and ran toward the bird.

"You get in the front," I yelled to Tank.

I went around to Charity's side and opened the rear door behind her as Tank climbed in the copilot's side.

Taking one of the jump seats, I pulled on a headset that was hanging on the bulkhead, adjusted the boom mic in front of my mouth, and turned it on. "Charity, meet Owen Tankersley. His friends call him Tank."

I looked forward and saw Tank pause, looking at Charity. She was dressed in her usual snug-fitting, black flight suit and aviator sunglasses. Her blond hair was pulled back tight in a ponytail at the back of her head.

The interior of Charity's bird was still the same basic setup Marines flew in Vietnam.

When Tank got his headset on and connected, I said, "Tank, this is Charity Styles, our pilot."

"Pilot?" Tank asked. "Wish they all looked like you, Miss Charity."

They shook hands and Charity grinned. "Flattery will get you anything, Tank. Strap up."

He quickly got into his harness and fastened it up, no stranger to the inside of a Huey.

Charity looked back at me. "Good to see you again, Jesse. How're Savannah and Flo?"

With that, she simultaneously twisted the throttle, pulled the collective up, and eased the cyclic forward, causing the Huey to leap into the air, nose down and climbing. She turned to the left as we rose, just enough to avoid the flagpole, then circled around the rows of trees that bordered the field. In seconds, we were a hundred feet high, nose down and accelerating toward the northeast.

"They're doing great," I replied, once my stomach caught up to us.

Tank sat there grinning.

"Will you be around for the wedding?" I asked her.

"Wouldn't miss it for anything," she replied, then turned toward Tank. "I was being flippant earlier. I'm sorry. That's just the way I am sometimes. It's a real honor having you aboard my aircraft, sir."

Tank's notoriety was strong among Army helicopter pilots. He'd been a door gunner in his early years as a Marine, in a bird exactly like the one we were in. He'd earned his Medal of Honor by ignoring his pilots orders not to get out.

"Now, why'd you want to go and get all formal and ruin the mood?" Tank asked with a wink. "I was gonna butter you up a little more."

Charity laughed.

"You have the coordinates where we're going?" I asked.

"Plotted," she replied. "ETA is thirty minutes. Paul, Tony, and Andrew will get there about the same time."

"From what Chyrel said, you might not be able to land. Lean on it and get to the area ahead of the guys. We'll land somewhere and join up with them."

"Roger that," Charity replied. "My long gun's in the safe. Once I drop you, I'll have to go back up. Chyrel told me to tell you that the guy on the west coast is heading east on I-75."

"Willy Quick? What's his ETA?"

"If he goes straight to where we're going, about fifteen minutes behind us."

"That's cutting it close," I said, opening the storage compartment in the floor.

In a tray below the lid were several cameras, lenses, tripods, and other photography equipment, all nestled in form-fitting foam inserts. At the other end lay some kind of nylon harness and rope. I picked it up. It was a rappelling rig and there were two of them.

"You been doing some rock climbing?" I asked.

Charity looked back and smiled. "A friend got me into it recently. He and I climbed Love Shack on Brac last week."

"Love Shack?" Tank asked.

"It's a seventy-three-foot, nearly vertical rock wall on Cayman Brac," she replied. "It gets its name from a little shack built up on top."

"Whatta ya think, Master Guns?" I said, holding up the rappelling harnesses. "Wanna jump out of a per-fectly good aircraft again? We'll gain a few minutes."

"There's two pairs of gloves in that top bin," Charity said. "Sorry, but one pair is small. You can belay to the bulkhead, then run your lines through those D-rings in front of each door. That way, I can reach back and retrieve them myself."

After separating the two lines and harnesses and laying one of each on either side of the cabin, I reached behind one of the uprights of an equipment rack and pressed the hidden release mechanism. The tray with the camera gear popped up slightly and I lifted it out.

Tank looked back as I removed Charity's M40 sniper rifle from its case. Hers was a newer variant of my A3, which she'd given me for my birthday earlier in the year. This one had a longer picatinny rail to mount various optics, and where mine had a five-round integral magazine, her A6 variant had a removable ten-round mag.

"That weapon looks like it's right at home in your hands," Tank said.

I looked up at him and grinned as I opened the bolt. Nothing came out. Not that I expected anything to, but I always checked. I flipped the weapon onto its side, muzzle down, and checked the chamber before I closed the bolt. There were two loaded magazines in the case. I inserted one and checked that it was locked in place.

"Go directly to the location Chyrel gave you, Charity," I instructed. "Tank and I will rappel in and Andrew and the guys can meet us there."

"If they can get to it," she replied. "I checked it as I was coming in—it's in the middle of a swamp."

"I know," I replied. "But Quick got there. There are bound to be tracks they can follow."

After I put the case back into its hiding place and reinserted the tray, I closed the lid and sat sideways in my seat. Once I'd folded the butt stock, I looped the strap over my head and shoulder, adjusting it so it was comfortable and at the ready against my chest.

Turning, I could see through the windshield. We were low, just fifty feet above the sawgrass. Bare spots revealed the dark, tannin-stained water below. Wading birds took flight below and ahead of us, but their efforts were wasted—we were past them before the third or fourth beat of their wings.

Ahead was a cypress stand and, rather than maintain altitude and fly around it, Charity pulled up just enough to clear the tops of the branches without losing much speed.

The airspeed indicator showed we were flying just under 124 knots, which was a little more than what the helo's maximum speed was back in the day.

I knew the engine was original, rebuilt several times during the last fifty years, but Charity took great care of her bird and had done a lot to lighten its weight and increase both its range and speed.

The miles to destination readout ticked down slowly. We didn't talk much. Tank removed the magazine from his Beretta, locked the slide, and inspected the chamber carefully. Not once, but three times. I remember him telling me that keeping your hands busy at familiar tasks calmed the mind and brought clarity.

Was he nervous?

How long had it been since Tank was in a combat situation? By Desert Shield, he'd been promoted to master gunnery sergeant and was primarily a marksmanship trainer. He *did* go to Saudi Arabia when we shifted gears to Operation Desert Storm, but he never crossed the border into Iraq or Kuwait. By then, I'd already been in Kuwait for over a month, hiding by day and moving by night to identify targets.

It was probably that Christmas in Panama, more than thirty years ago. That would have been the last time he'd been shot at. Not that it was anything a person ever got real used to.

Whenever he glanced back, or over at Charity, I could see the same resolve in his features I remembered. That sheer determination to not let his fellow Marines down had made him a man for all Marines to look up to. A hero.

People today have sports and TV heroes. Most would wet their pants going into places Tank had. They'd run from the sound of death and destruction. But a real hero moved toward it.

He shouldn't be here, I thought. The man was seventy years old and retired. He should be on a beach somewhere, enjoying the time he had left.

"You don't have to go with me, Tank."

His head snapped around like the arm of a rat trap, his eyes locking on mine. "I know that, Gunny. I *want* to go and I am, in fact, going in there. So, you just get any notion you might have of protecting the old man stowed in that grape on your shoulders. You read me?"

What was I thinking?

I grinned at him as Charity began to slow the chopper. "Five by five, Master Guns. Loud and clear."

"Three minutes," Charity said.

Tank removed his harness and joined me in the rear, taking a seat on the opposite side. We both got into the rappelling rigs, then looped our lines through the D-rings by the doors and belayed them to two more rings on either side of the bulkheads that separated the cockpit from the cabin.

"Two minutes," Charity said, looking back. "I see a shack dead ahead."

Tank and I busied ourselves readying the lines by looping them through round Petzl rings, clipping the loop to carabiners on our rigs. We both snapped on about the same time, ready.

"Won't work," Tank said, trying on one of Charity's gloves. "Too small."

I handed him one of the other pair, which were larger, and he put it on. I kept the right one, remembering that Tank had natural ambidexterity, and never considered which hand he felt comfortable using.

"One minute," Charity yelled back. "We're slow enough to open the doors."

When we slid the doors back on either side, the wind began to buffet the inside of the chopper. It was an oddly comforting feeling. I moved to the middle of the door with my line in hand, ready to throw it out. Tank did the same on his side.

"Line of departure," Charity ordered. "Lock and load."

"Saturday night, Gunny," came Tank's voice over the com, his back toward me.

I ratcheted the rifle's bolt, sending a Lapua .308 cartridge into the chamber. "Rock and roll!" I replied.

"Don't forget to take off your headsets," Charity reminded us. "We're coming up on the target."

I scooted forward, extending my legs to the chopper's skids, knowing that every movement I made was being mirrored by Tank, sitting behind me.

I was braced in the door opening as Charity came in hot, flaring at the last moment to a hover. We were about a hundred yards from a decrepit-looking shack, sitting above the water on stilts.

Forty feet below was a crude trail on high ground. The rotor wash lashed at palm trees and sawgrass, sending white water spray away in a circle.

I tossed my line down. It uncoiled as it fell, the bitter end landing in the water next to the trail. Then I removed my headset and stepped out onto the skid, facing inboard. Looking down, I saw Tank's line on the ground right next to mine.

The two of us looked at each other, then he nodded, falling away from the bird and down as I did the same.

I fell backwards, head turned toward the ground, while holding the line below the carabiner with just enough tension to slow my fall.

The ground came up fast and I increased the pressure, slowing me further.

Suddenly, I was on the ground.

Tank was already removing his rig, clipping it to the rappel line for Charity to haul back up.

I stripped out of mine and did the same, then we both stepped away from the buffeting rotor wash and toward the house.

Charity flew off, the lines dangling below her bird. One was getting shorter and shorter as she pulled it in.

"You feel that?" Tank asked, his Beretta in his hand.

"Feel what?"

"The jazz, man!"

I grinned at him. "Yeah, I feel it."

He meant the adrenaline rush, and I *did* feel it. But lately, I felt it in a different way. There was an element of danger in some of the things I did, and it's only been in the last few years that I've come to realize what the consequences of making a mistake might be.

Hell, two gray-haired boomers jumping out of a helicopter wasn't something that happened every day.

I pulled an energy bar from my cargo pocket and tapped Tank's shoulder with it as I surveyed the area. The shack and the rutted trail were the only signs of progress, and neither looked all that civilized.

Tank held his Barretta at low ready, muzzle pointed to the ground, as he also scanned the area. He took the bar

I handed him and ripped the paper off with his teeth. He bit off half before putting the rest in his pocket.

I left the rifle slung on my chest, ready to bring to bear in a heartbeat if needed. But like Tank, I had my Sig in my right hand and my head on a swivel. A rifle's better at longer distances, but I could get fifteen rounds at least on target before I could rack the bolt on the rifle to load a round after the first shot.

We were alone, about a hundred yards from the shack.

With the sound of Charity's chopper receding in the distance, I pulled up Tony's number, figuring Andrew would be driving. Tony answered on the first ring.

"We're on the ground, Tony. There's an old shack here and a trail leading off to the east."

"We just turned off the paved road a few minutes ago," Tony said. "We could hear Charity hovering. Good thing, too. We almost passed the trail. Be there in two minutes."

"I'll stay on, with my phone in my shirt pocket."

Tank and I advanced toward the shack, guns now raised, as we scanned both sides of the trail.

Just as a pleading sound reached my ears, Tank froze.

"You hear that?" he asked.

"Coming from the house," I said, taking the lead and jogging up the trail toward it.

I heard the sound again, more distinct. It was a woman's voice, crying mournfully.

Breaking into a headlong run, I sprinted up an unstable-looking wooden bridge connected to the house.

The imploring cries for help were clear in my head. Two women, maybe three. The thought of one of my daughters or my soon-to-be wife being held captive urged me faster.

Time seemed to slow, as everything came into clear, sharp focus. I saw the padlock on the door, but it meant little—I wasn't stopping to pick it, like I had Ty Sampson's. I heard the women pounding on the wall on either side of a boarded-up window to my left, wailing for help. I heard the creaks and groans of the rickety bridge with each footfall.

I measured each step, so I would arrive at the door pushing off with my right foot. My body was low, as I put everything into my pumping legs. I could see the weak center of the old wooden door. Below came a thrashing sound, maybe a startled gator.

All these things, and more, flashed through my mind as I took the last step, launching my body like a missile, shoulder low.

Two hundred and twenty pounds moving at high speed is hard to stop. I hit the center of the door and it exploded in pieces. My momentum was slowed, but not stopped, as I rolled on through the opening.

Instantly, I came up to one knee, my right leg extended to stop my slide. I was a little groggy, but my Sig was up and moving around the small room. I'd almost slid right into a hole in the floor.

Through an open door, I saw two women huddled in the corners of a bare room. Looking down, I saw a patch of yellow fabric floating on the surface of the water just below the house.

Rising, I moved slowly toward the open door, angling to see the part of the room hidden from my sight.

Tank came through the mangled doorway, quickly assessed the situation, and moved to my right to cover the part of the room where the two women were.

"He's not here," the nearer woman said hopefully.

"We're here to help," I reassured her.

She looked rough, wearing a torn, light-blue blouse and a checked navy skirt, also worn and tattered. She'd recently had a black left eye. It was nearly healed, leaving a pale purpling discoloration to the area around it. Her left eye was deeply bloodshot. Tiny capillaries in the eye had burst from taking a hard right fist to the side of the head.

I looked past her to the other woman, kneeling, her face buried in her hands. She wore cutoff jeans and a pink and gray flannel shirt, both nearly torn off and badly stained. There were bruises on both arms, just above her elbow. A part of my mind recognized the injuries caused by being forcefully pinned down.

These women had been held captive and abused repeatedly.

Slowly, the second woman looked up at me, an expression of hope on her gaunt features. She had a swollen lip that was healing and a scar over her left eye that had mended poorly. Her eyes were blue but somewhat vacant.

I breathed a sigh of relief, certain it was her. "Cobie Murphy?"

Tears welled in her eyes. "You...know my...my name."

I heard the sound of a car outside and pulled my phone out. It was still working. "All clear inside, Tony. We need some tools—wrenches or pliers. Whatever you have to remove bolts."

Tank moved toward the woman nearest the door while I crossed the room. I put my phone away and holstered my Sig as I knelt next to the frail-looking girl.

"My name's Jesse," I said softly. "You know my daughter, Flo Richmond, and I'm a friend of Manny Martinez. He and your mom sent me to find you and bring you home to her. Would you like that?"

Tank was talking to the other woman, but I was concentrating on Cobie, on how she'd react. She'd been held captive for over a month, starved, beaten, and probably raped. Charity had spoken to me openly about the shock of being abused. I remember her telling me it took a long time before she was comfortable with physical contact, even with a trusted friend. The girl before me was going to need a lot of help.

"My friends outside are bringing something to get that chain off," I said quietly, hearing rushed steps on the bridge. "Will it be okay with you for them to come in here and help us?"

I could hear movement in the other room, and without taking my eyes from hers, I raised my right hand in a halt command. All movement and sound in the other room ceased.

247

Her eyes went to the door in fear.

"Those are my friends, Cobie," I said quietly.

Her eyes came back to mine.

I sensed that she needed more reassurance than the other woman—reassurance that came from familiar words that carried great authority, even if she didn't know what they meant.

I raised one corner of my mouth in a half grin. "The big guy with the mustache is Master Chief Petty Officer Andrew Bourke. With him are Chief Petty Officer Tony Jacobs and Secret Service Agent Paul Bender."

Her eyes cut to the men I knew were huddled at the door, then they dropped to Tank. "Who's he?"

"That's Master Gunnery Sergeant Owen Tankersley and I'm Gunnery Sergeant Jesse McDermitt. You're going to be okay, Cobie. Nobody's gonna hurt you anymore. You have my word on that."

Like an uncoiling spring, her hands reached toward me, and she fell into my arms, sobbing quietly.

I sat next to her and let her cry on my shoulder as Tony entered the room cautiously, a toolbox in one hand.

"Tony's going to take that chain off now," I said. "Will it be okay if he touches your ankle?"

She moved her head gently against my chest and I gave Tony a nod to go ahead.

Andrew knelt by the other woman and he and Tony went to work removing the women's shackles.

Paul stood in the doorway, his psychoanalytic mind taking in everything.

CHAPTER TWENTY-FOUR

We only had a few minutes. Using Quick's phone's GPS, Charity had found him on the interstate and was pacing him from behind and out over the Glades, out of view from his mirrors and out of earshot. She reported that he was in a big, white SUV but couldn't confirm he was driving or even get a positive ID on the make of the vehicle.

I walked Cobie out to the car. She and the other woman, who we now knew as Michelle Tate, squinted in the bright sunshine.

"Cobie, I want you to go with Andrew," I said at the back door of the sedan. "He and Paul will take you and Michelle to the hospital in Weston, on the outskirts of Miami. It's a short ride."

"No," she said forcefully. "That's too far away from home."

I looked over at Paul for guidance.

"They both seem to be physically okay," he said. "Dehydrated and malnourished, but we can take care of that in the car. Missus Tate lives in Miami. I can take her into Weston, then Andrew can take Cobie on down to Fishermen's Hospital in Marathon."

Looking into Cobie's eyes, I asked, "Will that be all right? We just need to get you out of here before the man who abducted you gets here."

"You're not coming?"

"No," I replied, searching for words. "I'm going to stay here with Tank and Tony to meet the man."

Her blue eyes bounced from one of my eyes to the other, as if searching for something. "You're going to kill him."

She said it as a statement, not a question.

"Kill him for me, too," Michelle said, sliding into the front passenger seat. "And for the other women here before us."

"And Vanessa," Cobie said, looking back toward the shack.

"Vanessa?" I asked. "Vanessa Ramos?"

"Yes," Michelle said. "She got loose and went for help just before you arrived. We heard her scream, then there was a lot of splashing. I think the alligators got her."

Andrew helped Cobie into the car, then went around and got in the other side as Paul climbed in the driver's seat and started the engine.

"Here," Andrew said, removing his earwig and tossing it across the roof of the car. "Beats a cell phone."

I caught it, wiped it clean and put it in my own ear, adjusting the bone mic around it.

Paul turned the car around and headed in the right direction, and as they drove away, Cobie looked at me through the back window.

Then they were gone.

"We're standing in the middle of the street," Tank said. "And the kid is safe from traffic. What now?"

"Um, I don't see any traffic," Tony said. "And this hardly qualifies as a street, man."

I faced my mentor. "Now we make it safe for other kids, so they don't get drawn into traffic."

Tank looked at the busted door. "He's gonna know someone's been here as soon as he pulls up."

Paul's voice came over my earwig. "You have an inbound bogey. A Volkswagen van, of all things."

"Ty Sampson," I said, looking around, then pointing to a fallen palm across the trail from the shack. "Tony, take cover there. Tank, you go inside."

"What are you gonna do?" Tony asked.

I looked past them, toward the end of the road. "I'm going to stand right over there and greet him."

Charity's voice came over my comm. "The SUV is five minutes out," she said. "What do you want me to do, Jesse?"

"Be ready to exfiltrate," I said. "There's room to land just beyond the shack. I'll tell you when."

We split up and I headed to a large clump of sawgrass at the water's edge and waited. It was a good fifty yards past the shack and the sun was low and behind me. I holstered my Sig and folded the rifle's butt stock out, locking it in position. I was good with a handgun, but better with a rifle at that distance.

I could hear the van's air-cooled engine chugging and wheezing as it came up the trail toward us. Finally, it rounded a turn and came into the open, rolling to a stop between Tony and Tank, oblivious to the fact that he was caught in a deadly crossfire between three highly trained marksmen.

Ty Sampson was driving, but he had a passenger. I couldn't tell who it was, but knew they were unable to see me, silhouetted against the sun. They both got out at the same time.

The second man was Benito Moreno, the man I'd seen selling drugs behind the Rusty Anchor. He stepped around the passenger door and met Sampson in front of the bus.

Neither man seemed to notice the broken door.

"Let me handle them," I whispered.

Knowing that only Tony could hear me, I looked toward the shack. Tank was behind the door opening, out of their line of sight, but he could see me. I signaled him to stay where he was, and he nodded back.

Stepping out into the open, I called out, "That's far enough, Moreno."

Both men turned at the sound of my voice, recognition registering in both expressions.

Paul's voice came over the comm. "The girl's talking," he said in a whisper. "She said it was a guy named Ty who abducted her with help from a Cuban man with slicked-back hair driving a black sportscar. She also said the big man sometimes came with an older man."

Moreno's hand moved quickly to his pocket. I didn't hesitate. As his handgun started to come out, I brought the rifle to my shoulder and fired.

A pink mist splattered against the van's open passenger door. The impact of the round in the middle of his chest took Moreno off his feet, smashing him to the ground.

As my barrel came back down, my hand instinctively ratcheted the bolt, extracting the spent cartridge and chambering a fresh one.

When the scope came back into my line of sight, Sampson's surprised face appeared in the crosshairs. Whether he was armed or not, I didn't care.

I pulled the trigger and sent his soul chasing after Moreno's, straight to the fiery depths of hell where they belonged.

It was over in two seconds, but I racked the bolt just the same, chambering another round, then quickly policed my brass, dropping the two empty cartridges in my pocket.

Both men lay dead on the ground. I felt no more remorse than if I'd stepped on a palmetto bug. As I walked toward the van, I drew my Sig, just in case.

There was a gaping exit wound in Moreno's back. Sampson's face was still intact, save for a hole in the middle of his forehead, but the rest of his skull had exploded, covering the windshield with brain tissue and blood.

"The SUV is leaving the interstate," Charity said.

"What do you want to do?" Tony asked, rising from cover.

"Tank," I called to the shack. "You and Tony go up the trail and block him if he tries to leave."

Coming quickly down the steps, Tank ignored the bodies on the ground and joined Tony. The two of them hustled to where the trail came out of the overhanging mangroves.

I went up the bridge to the house, entered through the splintered door, then went into the captives' room. There, I pulled the rifle off my shoulder and removed the magazine, dropping it in my pocket. When I racked the bolt on the rifle, the cartridge flew out, and I caught it in midair. Dropping the Lapua round in my pocket, I then stood the rifle in the corner.

I did the same with the Sig, cleared the chamber, and placed it on the floor by the rifle, just as I heard the sound of a vehicle outside.

Moving intentionally, I closed the door to the room, stepped to the far corner, and stood waiting.

I had every intention of killing Willy Quick, but it wasn't going to be merciful, like it had been with Moreno and Sampson.

The room he'd used to torture and abuse who-knew-how-many women suited my sense of karma perfectly. It was about fifteen-feet square. Not as big as a boxing ring, but I had no intention of adhering to the Marquess of Queensberry Rules.

"What the hell?" I heard the big man bellow from outside.

He'd found the bodies.

A moment later, I heard heavy footfalls on the bridge, then cautious footsteps as he stepped past the busted door.

I stood watching the closed door to the room. The knob slowly turned, then the door flew open.

Willy Quick stood beyond the doorway, filling it almost completely.

He was a giant.

And he held a revolver in his hand, pointed in my direction.

"You again!" he growled, stepping through the door.

He had to lead with one huge shoulder, ducking his head slightly to clear the top of the door.

What the hell was I thinking? This guy wasn't another Quint Robbins, gone soft around the middle. He was at least four or five inches taller than me and more than a hundred pounds heavier. And little of it was fat.

Still, in my experience, big guys rarely had to fight, so few ever learned how. They went through life either intimidating opponents or winning with a single blow or body slam.

If Quick had a weakness it would be his size, which, unfortunately, also happened to be his second greatest asset—the first being the gun in his hand.

"How've you been, Willy?" I asked, stepping away from the shadowy corner. "It's been a long time. Last we met, you said if I put down my gun, I'd be no threat at all."

I nodded to the corner. "Both magazines removed and chambers empty."

His giant chest heaved, just a little more than I thought would be normal. The adrenaline and climb up the bridge had done that. His heart couldn't beat fast enough to get oxygen to such a massive body when exerted.

He pointed outside. "Did you—?"

"Yes, I did," I interrupted him. "And the women are safe."

He took a step toward me, his head lowered, eyes glaring from behind his long, stringy hair.

"I'm gonna start with your eyes," he growled. "That way you won't have to look at what I do to the rest of you."

"Many have tried," I said. "Most recently, those two men outside."

He stopped his advance, considering his options. I knew he could kill me any second, but I was betting on his inner bully taking over. He glanced over at my guns.

"They're unloaded," I told him again.

"What are you doing, Jesse?" Tony's voice came over my earwig.

"It's just you and me, Willy," I said, more for Tony's benefit than Quick's. "Two men. No guns."

An evil smile spread across his face.

"You're certifiable, you know that?" Tony said in my ear.

"That was a dumb decision," he said, tossing his gun aside and lunging for me.

I easily stepped under his ape-like arms, hammered him hard in the left kidney, then stepped back just in time to elude a wicked backhand. The swing brought him around to face me, his arms spread wide. I stepped in with an overhand right to the heart. A lesser man would have gone down from the powerful blow, but he just staggered back.

Quick roared in anger as he turned and came at me as before, arms wide, to try to grab me. Those tree-branch arms spanned half the room and I had little doubt of the outcome if he got hold of me. I feinted the previous move and then ducked under his arms the other way. This time, I slammed his other kidney with a quick left and right.

Stepping away, I whip-kicked him in the back of his left knee.

Quick went down, and I followed with another whip kick to the base of his skull, then danced away once more.

I wasn't about to jump on him. That'd be a deadly mistake. I'd slowed him down, but not enough to where he couldn't tear me in half if he got his hands on me.

Willy pivoted and faced me, down on one knee and a hand but definitely not out. There was some serious rage in those eyes. It was probably the first time he'd been on the receiving end of an ass-whooping in decades, if ever. There was something else there, too.

Realization?

Quick rose to his feet and assumed sort of a fighting stance, though his feet were squared under his shoulders.

"So, you know how to fight, huh?" he growled, still only barely breathing hard.

This was a new problem. I have an unusually long reach for my height. The average man's arm span from fingertip to fingertip was usually very close to his height. But at 6-3, my reach was 6-5, a decided advantage in a straight up, bare-knuckles brawl against most opponents. But not when he's 6-8, with shoulders wider than a door. With any skill at all, he could strike from a greater distance than I could reach.

Going toe-to-toe was also out of the question.

Instead, I rolled forward in a somersault, shooting both legs out as I finished the roll and catching him square in the *cojones*.

His hands went to his groin as he doubled over in pain,

I whipped my right leg up, catching him on the chin, straightening him back to his full height.

Spinning on my shoulder, I scissored his legs, bringing all of what I was guessing to be 350 pounds down hard onto his kneecaps.

Scrambling to my feet, just out of his reach, I shot a front stomping kick at his chest, my heel striking just to the right of center with all the force behind it I had in me.

There was a loud cracking sound, as if stepping on dry twigs.

Quick slowly fell backward onto his heels, then slumped against the wall, both hands going to his chest.

I stood there, my breathing a little raspy, and watched the realization come to his eyes.

The ribcage is an extraordinary thing. It protects the internal organs and creates a platform anchoring the major muscles of the upper body. Curved bones run from the sternum to the backbone, an engineering marvel, really. The curved shape of the ribs means they can withstand great outside forces for such small bones.

My guess was that at least one of those ribs had broken from the relatively small impact area of my heel. And a part of that bone had torn through his heart.

The color was draining from Quick's face. He was bleeding internally.

His eyes darted around and finally came to rest on his gun, lying on the other side of the room. He got one knee up, but when he attempted to stand, the knee wouldn't hold his weight and he fell forward, unable to move an arm up to break his fall. His face hit the deck with a sickening thud.

I moved wide around him and kicked his gun through the open doorway to the outer room.

Quick's head was turned, eyes open and unfocused, staring vacantly in the direction I'd sent the gun.

I got a hand under each of his shins, but it took all I had to drag him, facedown, into the other room. I continued to pull him toward the opening in the floor, unsure if he would even fit.

As I dropped his legs over the hole, one bent at the knee, slipped through the opening, and dangled below. I moved the other leg over the hole and it too, hung there in the open.

Straddling the opening, I grabbed his belt loop and pulled, then let gravity do the rest. There was a loud splash below the house, followed by several more. When I looked down, a big gator had Quick's torso in its massive jaws, trying to swim away with it. But a second, smaller one had a knee firmly in its bite and was doing a death roll to tear the limb from Quick's body.

Tony and Tank came through the front door and looked down at the macabre scene. Another gator had arrived and was trying to tear off an arm.

Tony looked up at me. "Are you okay?"

I picked up Quick's revolver, moved over, and dropped it through the opening. "Yeah. I'm fine."

He looked me up and down. "That guy was huge, Jesse. And you don't have a mark on you."

"Of course, he doesn't," Tank said. "It's called LINE training."

"Let's get out of here," I grumbled, then headed for the back room.

I picked up my Sig, slid the mag in, and holstered it behind my back. Slinging the rifle over my shoulder, I stepped past Tony and followed Tank outside.

In the distance, I heard the familiar, heavy whump of an approaching Huey.

"What do we do with this?" Tony asked, opening the back of Quick's vehicle.

Tank stepped up beside Tony. "We should drive it into the swamp under the house and torch it. What's with all the boxes?"

"I don't know," Tony replied, reaching for one of them.

When he tried to pull it to the rear, I could tell the box was heavy.

"What the hell's in this?" Tony said, lugging the box closer. "Dive weights?"

He opened the box and we looked down at the contents.

"Is that real?" Tank asked, trying to pick up one of the bars that lay inside the box. It was a little bigger than a dollar bill and less than two inches thick. "Damned thing weighs at least twenty pounds."

I hefted the other one and looked at it in the fading light. It was stamped *12.5KG*. "Over twenty-five," I corrected him.

"What is it?" Charity's voice came over my earwig.

I counted the boxes; there were thirty of them. "Can you lift off with the four of us and sixteen hundred pounds of cargo?"

"Yeah," she replied. "What's the cargo?"

"Gold."

CHAPTER TWENTY-FIVE

An hour later, after Tony and I checked the water around the shack for Vanessa Ramos's body and not finding anything but the remnants of her yellow dress, we left the shack.

Paul called and reported that Andrew had dropped him and Michelle Tate at the hospital, explaining that her husband was there waiting.

"I told them that when the police asked, they were to just say that she'd escaped her abductor and made her way to the highway, where I just happened to find her."

"Think they will?" I asked.

"I believe so," he replied. "I gave the husband my card and told him to call me tomorrow, once he got his wife home."

"Good thinking," I told him. "How are you getting home?"

"I have an Uber on the way. Wait...I think he just pulled up."

Ending the call, I sat in the back of the chopper and stared out the window at the passing skyline of Miami off to the left.

I tapped Charity on the arm. "Head for Tavernaero Park."

She nodded without comment, pulled up the small, private airport on her navigation system and then turned slightly more westerly.

I called Andrew and kept it short, telling him that he'd see me and Tank on the side of the road in Tavernier.

"Me, too," Tony said. "I want to see this through to the end."

"Tony, too," I added.

They were ahead of us on the Sawgrass Expressway but wouldn't be for long. We'd have to wait a few minutes when we got to the airstrip.

Fifteen minutes later, Charity touched down at the west end of a single runway, situated between rows of houses. The three of us climbed out with our gear and I closed the cargo door. When I opened the pilot's side, Charity pulled her headset down around her neck.

"Thanks," I shouted over the turbine, extending my hand. "I owe you one. You know what to do from here, right?"

She nodded as she took my hand, then pulled me into a tight embrace and kissed my neck. "Don't you ever do anything stupid like that again, Jesse McDermitt. Ever!"

I pulled away and could only nod.

Charity closed the door and put her headset back on.

Before we could move to get out of her rotor wash, she twisted the throttle and pulled up on the collective, causing the three of us to squat and cover our eyes as the heavily loaded chopper lifted off the ground.

When the rotor wash subsided, we stood and picked up our bags, then headed toward the main road. From there, it was only a hundred yards to the Overseas Highway, where we walked south a little way and stopped in front of a boat dealership.

I dropped my pack. "They won't be long."

Tank and Tony stood on either side of me. "You should call your fiancée," Tank said. "She'll be worried."

I looked at the tracking app on my phone. Andrew was still fifteen minutes away. I had another call to make first.

Removing Manny's card from my wallet, I punched in the numbers. He answered on the third ring.

"We found her," I said, without waiting. "We'll be at Fishermen's Hospital in about an hour."

"Is she all right?" Manny asked, his voice cracking a little at the news.

"She will be," I replied. "But it's going to take a while."

Next, I called Savannah and told her what happened. She started to ask a question, but I cut her off. "Andrew's arriving to pick us up," I said. "We'll be at Fishermen's in an hour."

I ended the call and put my phone away. I didn't want to talk to her about the details. Not now. Maybe not ever.

"This is what you do," Tank said. He wasn't asking. "You dart through traffic to save someone's kid. That's no easy job."

"When you stood on that wall," I said, without looking at him, "when you faced down that tribal leader and his mob, did you think about how it might have changed everything if you'd pulled the trigger? Changed who you are?"

He was silent for a moment. "Those thoughts go through a man's mind in an instant," he said somberly.

"I killed three men tonight. One might not even have been armed."

"There's rarely time to debate your instinct," Tony said. "You did right, Jesse. That's all."

Tank nodded. "I don't know you well, Tony. But I've been around long enough to know a thing or two. We've all had those thoughts *and* pulled the trigger. We do what needs to be done and there just isn't enough time to dwell on it."

I looked at him, understanding exactly what he meant.

The big sedan turned into the boat dealership. Cobie was in the backseat alone. Andrew climbed out and then got in the backseat with her.

"One of you drive," I said, getting in on her other side.

Cobie's arms went around my neck and she held on as if her life depended on it. She was sobbing.

"Did you—"

"It's over, Cobie," I said, stroking her tangled hair. "You're safe."

Tony turned the car around and we got back onto Overseas Highway.

Pushing her away a little, I said, "Nothing's going to happen to you now. I talked to Manny a minute ago. He and your mom are going to meet us at the hospital."

She looked at each of us in turn, took Andrew's hand in hers and settled in on my shoulder. She continued to sob quietly.

By the time we got to the makeshift hospital, everyone who knew about Cobie's rescue was there waiting for us. Fishermen's Hospital had been damaged so badly during Hurricane Irma three years ago that it had to be almost completely rebuilt. They'd set up an emergency room to the right of the old building, sort of a modular unit to handle emergencies only.

Tank and I were the first to get out.

An orderly stood by the entrance with a wheelchair. Tank marched straight up to him.

"I'll take that," he said. "Get me a warm blanket. Do it now."

Without waiting for a response, Tank pushed the man aside and wheeled the chair to the back door, where I was helping Cobie out of the car. The orderly appeared with a blanket, which I wrapped around her shoulders.

Her clothes barely hid her body.

Manny and Donna came out to us and she rushed to her daughter's side, crying.

"She's going to be okay," I reassured Donna, as Tank pushed the wheelchair to the open door.

Once inside, the ER staff took Cobie away. She wanted me to go with her, but only one person was allowed, so

Cobie and her mom were whisked off through the security door.

Savannah and Flo were there, too. And sitting quietly beside Flo were Finn and Woden.

I looked from the dogs to Savannah, questioningly.

"They wouldn't get out of the boat," she said, quietly. "When we got to the Rusty Anchor, they both jumped into the back of Rusty's pickup and wouldn't get out."

"And when you got to the hospital, where dogs aren't allowed?"

She shrugged. "They can be stubborn sometimes." She paused. "Jesse, Deuce called and told us everything that happened. I wish it hadn't happened, but you did the right thing. I've come to accept over the years that there is evil present in this world. I just wish it wasn't drawn to you."

"What's three more to the nightmare?" I said with false bravado, holding her tightly.

She squeezed me back. "I won't let them come for you," she said. "I'll watch over you when you sleep."

I conjured a mental image of a mythical blond guardian standing over me.

The orderly who'd held the wheelchair approached, looking over at Finn and Woden. "Dogs aren't permitted in the ER."

"They're service dogs," Tank lied.

"They don't have vests."

"I'm a Marine, son. Am I any less a Marine because I'm not wearing a uniform? Is a police officer any less a cop when he's not wearing his badge?"

Just then, Detective Clark Andersen strolled in and looked around. He spotted Manny and headed straight to him.

"Who found her?" he asked.

Manny's eyes flashed to mine and the detective followed his gaze.

"I did," I replied, stepping away from Savannah. "She was being held captive in the Everglades."

Once he heard my voice, I saw a sudden spark of recognition in his eyes. "You're the anonymous caller."

"Jesse McDermitt," I said.

"You and I," he said, pointing toward the door, "we need to talk."

I followed the detective outside, where he turned and strode down the sidewalk, away from the emergency room entrance. When he stopped, he looked all around before turning to face me.

"How did you know about the pictures?" he asked.

"What did you learn?"

"I'm asking the questions, Mister McDermitt."

I just stood there and looked at him, waiting. It really doesn't matter the position of authority; when two people are facing one another and one is silent, the other will talk.

Finally, he threw his hands up in exasperation. "Whoever drove Miss Murphy's car was a lot taller than her," he finally conceded. "She didn't run away. Now, how did you get access to my files?"

"I'm afraid I'll have to invoke my fifth amendment rights, Detective. Suffice it to say that the internet, just like the real world, isn't as secure as it should be, and there are both bad and *good* people who know how to thwart the best security."

"Yeah, well, that evidence is now inadmissible."

"It'll never be needed," I said.

"What's that supposed to mean?"

"I told you where she was being held," I said, hearing rhythmic footfalls behind me. "The Glades cover a million and a half acres. They can hide a lot."

Tank joined us. "You better come inside, Jesse."

"We're not through here," Andersen said. "Hide a lot of what?"

"It's over, Detective," I said, more venomously than I'd intended. "The men responsible won't kidnap any more girls, and two of at least five women they abducted are safe. My only wish is that I'd learned of it in time to save the others."

"You've said your piece. Now it's my turn," Tank said, turning to face the cop. He handed the man a coin in a sleeve and waited until Andersen looked at it and grasped its meaning. "I keep these handy to give to people who *I* think are deserving. Jesse has one and now you do. He also has one from the President of these United States. People are safe in this world because of folks like you, Detective. And like Jesse, here. You two are two sides of the same coin, but *you* have rules to follow. Now, if it comes up in court, everyone involved, including myself, will all say the same thing. The women got away and were found by a passing Samaritan. Nobody knows what happened to their abductors."

"Arrest me or walk away," I said.

When he did neither, Tank and I turned on our heels and marched back toward the entrance.

"You think you can be judge, jury, *and* executioner?"

I stopped and slowly turned to face him. "You and I both know there are elected officials—prosecutors, judges, even cops—who will turn a blind eye to a victim if they can line their own pockets. I can't be bought."

Then Tank and I went back inside.

An older man, wearing a black suit and sporting a neatly trimmed white beard, was talking to Andrew, who was clearly irritated. An attractive, dark-haired woman was with him. She was slim and wore a black skirt and jacket. My first thought was that they were ambulance chasers, lawyers who prowled hospitals looking for wrongful injury cases.

"I demand to know who you people are!" the grey-haired man said.

"And who are you?" I asked.

I recognized the man instantly when he and the woman turned to face me. Senator Jubal Blanc.

What the hell's he doing here? I wondered.

I saw recognition in both their eyes, too. I'd never seen the woman before and had no idea how either of them might know me.

"You again," the senator said.

I grinned. "That's funny. Your late brother-in-law said the exact same thing just an hour ago."

He stepped closer. "You saw Willy?"

"And a couple of his friends," I replied. "I'm afraid we had a bit of a disagreement."

He eyed me suspiciously. "You're probably not aware, but he's wanted in connection with the murder of one of my sisters."

"You're right," I said. "Not aware and don't care."

He stepped even closer, lowering his voice. "He took something that didn't belong to him."

So, that was it, I thought. He knew about the gold.

"What your family does is no concern of mine, Senator. Except when it comes to abducting innocent young girls."

I could see the hatred seething in his eyes.

The woman stepped forward, as if she were going to come between us. Savannah grabbed her arm and the woman wheeled, aiming a fist at Savannah's face.

Savannah raised an arm, trapping the woman's forearm in an arm bar, exerting backward pressure on the elbow joint as she stepped in and delivered two vicious elbow strikes to the woman's face.

It happened so quickly, I'd barely registered it when the woman dropped to the deck in a very undignified position, skirt askew and blood staining the front of her crisp, white blouse.

The senator stepped back, shouting vehemently at Savannah. When he took a step toward her, Finn and

Woden suddenly blocked his path, teeth bared, ears back, and hackles up.

I raised a hand to the dogs. "*Bleibe*," I commanded. They stood their ground but were ready for anything.

I turned my attention back to Blanc. "I think you'd better take your girlfriend and get out of here while you still can, Senator."

The woman slowly struggled to her feet, glaring at Savannah.

"This isn't over," Blanc said, taking the woman's arm and helping her to her feet. "Are you all right, Chloe?"

As they started toward the door, Tank stepped in front of him. "Yes, it is over," he boomed. "I don't care who or what you are, Mister. If you show your ass around here again, you'll join that scumbag brother-in-law of yours. Do I make myself perfectly clear?"

Blanc looked at him with an incredulous expression. "Are you *threatening a public official*?"

When Tank leaned in closer, the woman moved to intervene again.

Once more, Savannah spun her around. "Bless your heart, sweetie," she said, gripping the woman's blouse with one hand, while the other was poised to strike. "You *don't* want to do this again."

"Mister," Tank sneered, "I have less than a year to live. So, I'm disinclined to waste time by repeating myself. Take your public official ass back to where you belong and forget you ever came down to these islands."

Just then, the door opened. Tony and Andrew were returning from parking the car, and they had Rusty, Sid, Jimmy, and Naomi with them.

The two former special operators reacted instantly to what they correctly interpreted as a tense situation. Rusty and Sid did as well. The three men separated, forming a semi-circle around Tank as Sid moved instantly to Savannah and helped restrain the Chloe woman.

"You knew!" I said vehemently, finally figuring out why Blanc was there.

He'd said Quick was wanted for the murder of his sister—which one, I didn't know—but nothing had been mentioned on the news, or Chyrel would have let us know instantly. The senator must have gone to the shack after finding his sister dead and the Blanc gold missing. That was why he'd shown no surprise when I'd called Quick his "late brother-in-law." He must have known Quick was taking off with the family gold. So, the stories Billy had told about them hoarding money were true.

I spun Blanc around. "You knew about the girls Willy Quick had chained up out there in the Glades. You went there tonight, didn't you? And it wasn't the first time you'd been to that shack, was it?"

I turned my head and looked at the door Cobie and Donna had gone through. Turning back to him, I pointed at the door. "There's a girl in there who is going to identify you, Senator."

The man's face drained of color and his eyes instinctively followed my pointing finger. "I don't know what you're—"

"Save it," I said, stepping closer to him. "I killed that big swamp ape with my bare hands," I hissed, barely able to control the anger boiling in my veins. "I could have done it from a distance, but I wanted him to see it coming and know who it was. People like you and him disgust me. Pure evil with no place in human society. Roaches to be squashed under my foot. Watch your back, Senator. I'm coming for you next."

"He forced—"

"I said save it," I warned. "Look around. You're complicit in holding a girl from this community captive, *and* you took part in her torture and rape. Do you think anyone in this room gives a rat's ass about you or your family?"

Finn barked, as if accentuating my words. Woden just snarled.

Blanc looked around, then took off out the door.

The woman struggled against Savannah and Sid. With a glance in my direction, they released her, and she bolted through the door after her master like an obedient lapdog.

"How did you know?" Tank asked, as the door closed.

"Paul told me something," I replied. "While he was driving Michelle to the hospital, he and Andrew coaxed some information out of her and Cobie."

Andrew nodded. "Cobie told me it was Ty Sampson and a Cuban man who'd abducted her," he added. "She learned through another woman, who was killed just before we arrived, that his name was Benito Moreno and the man holding them was Willy Quick."

"The most recent captive got loose," I said, "but was killed by an alligator just minutes before we arrived. It was the girl we saw with Moreno and Quick, Vanessa Ramos."

"Cobie also told me," Andrew began, "that there were at least two others before her, and they'd talked of others before them. She also said that Quick sometimes brought an *older man* with him."

The security door on the other side of the room opened and a doctor appeared. He looked around nervously. "Is anyone here with Cobie Murphy?" he asked.

"Yes, Doctor," Savannah said, stepping toward him. "We all are. How is she?"

He looked around again. "She's going to be fine. She can have one more visitor. Are you Flo Richmond?"

Flo had been sitting there the whole time, quietly taking everything in from the moment they wheeled Cobie through the door.

"I'm Flo," she said, standing up. "But I hardly know her."

"Miss Murphy said she saw you when she was brought in and has asked if she could talk to you."

Flo looked at me and Savannah.

"Go see her," Savannah said. "She asked for you."

CHAPTER TWENTY-SIX

Cobie was released from the hospital after four days. I was at the Anchor and had just finished meeting with a friend from the local bank and was in the midst of a discussion with Tank when Donna called, looking for me. She wanted to thank me again and to tell me that Cobie was physically okay, but the doctor had referred her to a psychologist. She'd lost a good bit of weight, and the scar over her eye would be permanent, but she was otherwise healing well.

"The scar doesn't have to be permanent," I told her. "And I agree, she needs help dealing with the mental trauma she's been through."

"Be that as it may—"

"Do you know Pam, over at Keys Bank?" I asked, cutting her off.

"First State? Yeah, everyone knows Pam."

"Good," I said. "Give her a call. She's waiting to hear from you."

I ended the call and looked over at Tank, shaking my head. "You're out of your mind, Master Guns."

"How many years are between you and your intended?"

"Less than ten," I replied.

"There you go," he said. Tank paused. "Look," he said. "She likes me and I like her. It won't be long before I won't be able to do a lot of the things that I take for granted now."

"So...hire a nurse."

He drained his coffee and signaled Amy for a refill.

"What do you think Donna's going to do when your friend at the bank gives her the news? She strikes me as a prideful woman."

With the agreement of everyone involved, two of the gold bars from Willy Quick's SUV had been converted to cash and deposited in a trust fund for Cobie. A third bar was liquidated for Michelle Tate. Over the next few years, the rest of the gold would be quietly sold off and the money split into three funds, two of which I'd had set up for years—one to help kids of local watermen and another to help kids of fallen or disabled service members from the area. Tank had suggested the third fund. He'd even added half of the ten million he'd set aside. A trust fund to help women and children of abuse.

"The girl needs help Donna can't provide," I replied. "She'll use the money for that and to further her education. She's prideful, but she strikes me as a practical woman, too."

The door opened and Chyrel came into the bar, pausing to take her sunglasses off and look around. She spotted us and came toward the table, smiling.

"Hey, Jesse," she said with a wave. Then she hugged Tank. "How you doing, old man?"

He laughed and returned the hug. "I'll show you *old* one of these days."

She plopped down on the bench next to Tank. "So, what was so important you had me drive all the way down here?"

"I decided I'm staying here in the Keys," Tank said. "My pension can go a long way here."

"That's great news!" Chyrel said, as Amy brought the coffee pot over with another mug.

"Yeah," he said. "I talked to a real estate agent. She's meeting me here any minute. Want to help me look for a house?"

The door swung open and an attractive, well-dressed woman came in. She held a thick notebook in her arm. If there was a "look" for a real estate agent, she had it.

Since we were the only ones in the place, she came toward us. "Is one of you Mister Tankersley?"

Tank rose and offered his hand. "You must be Connie. Have a seat."

Connie sat next to me and introduced herself, shaking hands.

"So, you're looking to retire here?" Connie asked. "It's a great location. What kind of home would you consider?"

"Nothing big," he replied. "Three bedrooms, a couple thousand square feet. With a pool. Oh, and it has to be on deep water."

Connie's eyebrow arched slightly, whether in doubt of Tank's ability to afford such a house or at the prospect of a huge commission, I couldn't tell.

"Okay," she said, opening her notebook and flipping to a tabbed spot. "What's your price range?"

"Four million," he replied. "It will be a cash deal, but we have to close right away."

Connie gulped and the pupils in her eyes constricted a little as she digested the information.

Then she closed her notebook. "I know the perfect house," she announced. "It just came on the market, so I don't even have the listing in my book. In fact, I just came from closing the deal. The homeowner is anxious to sell."

"Let's go look at it," Tank said, then grinned at me. "But let me finish my coffee, while you call my friend Pam at First State Bank of the Florida Keys—the branch here in Marathon. I told her you might be calling. She can verify the availability of the funds."

Connie smiled. "Then I'll meet you outside, and you can follow me over there."

"I don't have a car," Tank said.

"You don't—"

"I'll drive you," Chyrel said.

With that, Connie went outside.

I shook my head. "You're going to buy a four-million-dollar house and you don't even own a car?"

"I have a couple of cars," he retorted. "Up in Jacksonville. I didn't drive down for the same reason I'm in a

hurry to buy a house. There just isn't a lot of time left."
He took a sip of his coffee. "I've done my duty for most
of my life. Now it's time to indulge myself."

He rose and offered his hand to Chyrel, and they disappeared through the door after Connie.

"What was that all about?" Rusty asked, coming over
and taking a seat across from me.

"Tank wants to settle down."

"Good for him," Rusty said. "There are worse places
to spend your last days."

"He wants to marry Chyrel."

"He *what*?" Rusty spluttered. "He just met her, fer
cryin' out loud!"

"You heard me," I said. "They went house hunting."

"She said yes?"

"He hasn't asked her yet."

"Wait," Rusty said, leaning forward conspiratorially.
"She knows he's dying of cancer, right?"

I nodded. "He wants someone he likes to look after
him when the time comes."

"He don't have to get married for that," Rusty said,
shaking his head.

"If he's married," I explained, using Tank's own rea-
soning, "his wife would receive a survivor's pension.
He figures since he's only going to collect his veteran's
pension for a year or two at best, he should leave it to
someone much younger, and Chyrel has no desire to
get married."

"So, she'll tell him no."

"He made it sound more like a business deal," I said. "If the survivor of a retired veteran remarries, the pension is ended. Tank figures it's the best way to keep funding his endowment. Plus, she gets the house."

"The house she's going to help him pick out, not knowing any of this?"

I shrugged. "Pretty much."

"What's Savannah think of all this?"

"She's all for it," I said. "She even urged him."

"Where's she at now? Tomorrow's the big day."

"Over on *Sea Biscuit*. Flo and Sid are helping her try on her dress. They just picked it up from the seamstress."

"And y'all are staying on different boats tonight?" he asked.

"Yeah," I replied, less than enthusiastic about the idea. "We won't see each other again until the ceremony."

"Hey," Amy called over. "There's something on the news about that senator up in Marco."

Rusty and I walked over closer to the bar as she turned up the TV.

"An anonymous source close to the senator said he was despondent over two recent deaths in his family and allegations of their wrongdoing. He was found early this morning at his residence, with a single gunshot wound to the head. We'll have more on this breaking story this evening. This is Sonia Morris, Action 6 News, reporting."

"Whatta ya think of that?" Rusty asked, as the mid-morning news cut to a commercial.

"Coward's way out," I replied. "But it saves the taxpayers' money. I bet the anonymous source was his aide. What'd you say her name was?"

"Chloe Devlin," Rusty replied. "I heard she killed a man up in Miami some years back."

I placed my mug on the bar. "Well, I have some chores to do on the boat."

The truth was, I just hadn't been in much of a talkative mood since getting Cobie out of that shack. I left the bar and walked along the dock toward *Salty Dog*, thinking.

Peter Tate, Michelle's husband, had called Paul two days after the rescue and invited him to lunch and to help convince his wife to see a psychologist.

For an hour over lunch, Michelle had recounted her ordeal to Paul in a detached, analytical manner. She'd told her husband and he'd suggested going to the police. But Michelle had been reticent to do that, because of what Paul had told them to say.

Paul had openly explained to them that the man who'd held them, along with the two men who'd kidnapped Cobie, were dead and there was nothing to go to the police about.

Climbing aboard *Salty Dog*, I went below, then down to the engine room. I needed to busy my hands. I closed the valve to the air conditioner's raw water intake and removed the strainer, cleaning it in a small bucket of water.

Paul had related to me the story Michelle told him of the violence and depravity of Willy Quick's visits to the shack.

"A classic psychopath, I'd guess," he'd told me over the phone. "And given the man's size, what he did to those women was no different than what he likely did to small animals as a child. He treated his captives as things—toys to be played with when it suited him—and when one was used up or broken, he raped and beat them one last time, then dumped them through the hole in the floor to the waiting alligators."

I knew I shouldn't feel remorse about killing the three men, but I did. Willy Quick probably didn't feel an ounce of remorse, but I wasn't him. I had a conscience, a soul.

It wasn't the first time I'd struggled with these thoughts. In the heat of the moment, I didn't have the luxury of dwelling on them. But afterward, I did. I knew I'd get past it. I knew I did what was right, even if it wasn't legal. Andersen had called me an executioner, but that wasn't quite right. I'd simply put down three rabid animals.

That was pretty much what Cobie had told Flo that night in the ER, when she'd asked to see her. Flo told Savannah the next day but had remained mostly distant from me throughout the day.

She'd finally come to me and apologized for the thoughts she'd had about me. She said that Cobie had told her not to think bad of me for doing what I did the way I did it. Then she'd warned me, as Charity had, to never do anything so foolish again.

I worked for several hours, changing the oil and filters, cleaning and scrubbing the engine, generator, water maker, and deck. Soon I noticed there was no light coming through the overhead hatch.

It was dark out.

I finished up and went to my cabin to get a shower. Ten minutes later, I was stretched out on the bunk, alone. Through an open hatch, I could hear the sounds of the Rusty Anchor.

Small waves lapped at the shoreline and rock jetty. In the trees across the canal, a whippoorwill sang its mournful tune. Music and laughter from the bar at the far end of the dock reached my ears. I occasionally heard people along the dock talking and caught Savannah's laugh from just across the canal.

Then, though the night was still young, I drifted off to sleep.

The nightmare came. I hadn't had it in some time. The darkness, the swirling vortex of specters trying to grab me. The images of people I'd killed began to appear before me, one at a time, then vanish in a puff of dust.

Suddenly, Savannah's face appeared.

I shrieked in horror, sitting up quickly and banging my head.

It took a moment to get my breathing under control as I rubbed my forehead.

What did it mean? Why would Savannah appear in my dream?

I'd dreamed of her many times over the years, but not *that* dream. Was it my subconscious somehow telling me that marrying me put her in danger?

I rose and got dressed, then headed to the galley. I was about to pour a healthy dose of Pusser's into a glass when someone knocked on the hull.

"Dad?"

It was Flo.

I switched on the interior lights and went up the companionway.

"Are you okay?" she asked, stepping up to the side deck, then down into the cockpit. "I heard a yell."

"I just bumped my head," I lied.

She pulled my head down and looked at it. "You have a huge knot on your forehead. What'd you bang it on?"

I sat on the starboard bench and she sat down beside me.

"The nightmare came," I said.

"It's just a dream," Flo said.

"Your mom was in it."

"What?"

I'd told both Savannah and Flo about the recurring nightmare I sometimes had, how the faces appeared in order, starting with those I'd killed in Lebanon and continuing through to the present. Through a rifle scope, a person could see into the lives of their targets, see their faces up close, and now the images of the last second of their lives haunted me.

"It was a warning," I said, rubbing my head again.

"What's that supposed to mean?"

"Being around me puts you and her in danger."

"Don't be ridiculous, Dad. Besides, Mom can take care of herself. Ask Charity."

I glanced over at my daughter. "What's that supposed to mean?"

She looked over toward *Sea Biscuit*, then, after a moment, she turned her gaze toward the rising moon. It was bright and just a day past full—the Cold Moon.

"It happened a long time ago," Flo began. "In the Berry Islands. I was about eight or nine. We ran into Charity at Hoffman's Cay and were just having fun at the blue hole when these men suddenly arrived."

"What happened?"

Flo looked down at the deck. "One had a gun and another, a knife. I'm not supposed to know, but Mom and Charity killed all four of those men."

"*What?*"

"Please don't tell her I told you," she said, looking at me with tear-filled eyes. "She doesn't know that I know."

I pulled her to me. I knew that Savannah had some martial arts training and, like the other night with Blanc's aide, I'd seen her fight before. Charity killing four men was believable. But I couldn't see Savannah being a part of it.

"You mean Charity killed them," I said.

She shook her head. "Charity killed two, Mom killed one, and Woden killed the other one."

"You saw this happen?"

"Woden killed the first man by knocking him off the cliff. He was the one with the gun. Then Mom kicked one to the ground and beat him to death. Her knuckles were cracked and bleeding for days. Charity took out the other two with her bare hands and one of them had a knife. Then she shot all three for good measure. They used an anchor and put their bodies in the blue hole."

I'd had no idea.

"When did Mom appear in your dream?" she asked, looking up at me.

"Near the beginning," I said, somewhat confused.

Flo smiled. "We're not in danger being around you, Dad. Remember at the hospital the other night? She said she wouldn't let them get you in your dreams."

CHAPTER TWENTY-SEVEN

I didn't sleep well. I was both worried the nightmare would return and nervous about the wedding. Not the typical groom's trepidation, but more concerned whether I was doing the right thing or not.

A friend once told me, "the heart wants what the heart wants," and it was true. But the emotional side had to be tempered by the conscious mind, especially where others were concerned.

Regardless of what Flo had said, being close to me meant they were close to danger. I'd already given up on the idea of "hanging up my guns," like John Wayne in *The Shootist*. Each time I tried, something came up, like what happened to Cobie Murphy, and I was sucked back into it. I couldn't ignore the pain and suffering of others, and many of my friends and I had certain skills that could alleviate some of that hurt.

It was already light out when I finally woke. I lay there staring at the overhead for a moment, then went to the galley for coffee.

I was startled by what sounded like several hands slapping the hull.

"Rise and shine!" a familiar voice called from outside.

I went up the companionway to find Charity and Chyrel standing beside my boat.

"What a catch," Charity said sarcastically. "Savannah's sure one lucky woman."

Chyrel laughed. "You look like shit, Jesse. Too much bachelor party?"

"There's coffee if you want," I said, going back down to the galley.

The two women boarded and came down the companionway.

"What's wrong?" Chyrel asked, noting my sour disposition. "You're drinking coffee, so you should be almost human."

I sat at the dinette and she sat across from me, while Charity leaned against the bulkhead beside her.

"I'm having second thoughts."

"That makes you certifiably nuts," Chyrel said, then looked up at Charity. "We might need a straitjacket."

"I can't stop what I do," I said. "And having Savannah at my side puts her in danger."

Charity looked down at the deck, avoiding my eyes.

"Last night, Flo told me what happened when you were with them at Hoffman's Cay ten years ago."

"You needn't worry," Charity said. "She might be every bit as capable as you; maybe not as strong or as good with a rifle, but she can take care of herself. Hoffman's Cay wasn't the first encounter she's had."

"What do you mean?" I asked, almost afraid to know the answer.

"She told me there had been others," Charity said. "Men who wouldn't take no for an answer. She's not a delicate little flower, Jesse."

"How do I not know this?"

"Because she chose not to tell you," Chyrel said.

"You know how she is," Charity added. "She doesn't brag on anything except Flo." She paused. "There's something else you should know."

"What's that?"

"We've gotten together again several times over the years. While I was teaching Flo to swim, I was also training Savannah to fight and shoot. She was already a black belt, but taekwondo is defensive. She wanted to take it to the next level. The first time we got together after Hoffman's, Flo was abducted and—"

"What?" I shouted. "Abducted? By who?"

"Men working for Savannah's ex," Charity said. "She was a mess at first, but when we found out it was him, she became as enraged as a mother lioness. If she'd found out on her own, she would have killed him."

Why had she never told me this? I wondered.

"See?" Chyrel said. "She's a strong woman, Jesse. You don't have to watch over her all the time. She can take care of herself."

"Rusty sent us down here to get you," Charity said. "You need to go up to the house and get dressed. The ceremony starts in an hour and Savannah can't leave her boat until you're at the altar."

"So, come on," Chyrel said, pushing my mug toward me. "Down the hatch and all that. We gotta get you married."

I locked up the *Dog* and we went to the bar first. I needed something to eat and I didn't need an hour to get dressed. I was still conflicted, possibly because I hadn't slept well and partly because I knew that unless she carried a gun everywhere she went, Savannah would one day be in danger.

At the appointed time, Tank and I went out to the deck behind the bar. David was already at the altar with Rusty. He was the only groomsman.

"You clean up good," Rusty said, when Tank and I reached them.

He, too, was wearing a coat and tie. Sidney had insisted, after shopping with Savannah for a dress. Like me, he had to buy one, since neither of us owned anything dressier than a fishing shirt, unless you counted old dress blue uniforms.

The scene was eerily similar to the morning fifteen years ago when I'd married Alex. The thought of how she'd been murdered on our wedding night weighed heavily on my mind.

"I know what you're thinkin'," Rusty said, as the four of us stood in front of a crowd of about thirty people.

Giant butterflies were doing aerobatics in my gut. "Oh yeah?"

Rusty looked me in the eye. "You're worried for Savannah. Scared that your violent life could rub off on her."

"It's a valid fear," I said. "But I've learned a few things, and come spring, I'll be aboard *Ambrosia*, directing other snake-eaters."

"What's *Ambrosia*?" Tank asked.

"Armstrong Research's primary excursion vessel," I replied. "A two-hundred-foot converted yacht."

There were a few gasps and whispers from the crowd. They were all looking across the canal.

Rusty grinned. "Last chance. Here she comes."

I looked across the canal but didn't see anyone. Then Flo came from behind the boat docked next to *Sea Biscuit*. She wore a flowing pink dress, which the wind caused to billow in front of her.

"Wow," David breathed.

Behind her came Finn and Woden. The two big dogs marched with their heads up, looking around, and occasionally taking a quick glance behind them.

Then Savannah came from behind the boat and my mouth fell open. I hadn't seen the dress she'd chosen, and she hadn't told me anything about it. I'd only been told that I had to wear a jacket and a tie.

And shoes.

Savannah's dress was white, with long sleeves and a somewhat revealing neckline. It hugged her body tighter than I ever could, all the way to her narrow waist. From there, the dress flared out to the sides, exposing her long legs in front. Behind her, Charity was holding a moderate train up off the dock. She wore nothing on her head and her hair was pulled up, but then cascaded down in long, dangly curls at her shoulders. In her hands, she carried a small bouquet of white flowers.

I saw a flash of white on a tanned thigh and was instantly struck dumb. If I had to form words, I was done for.

With each step she took, I could see it. On Savannah's upper left thigh, instead of the traditional garter, she wore a small white holster, holding a pearl-handled Derringer.

I felt the press of the holstered Sig behind my back and smiled.

There wasn't going to be a repeat of fifteen years ago.

The trio came around the end of the dock as a string quartet played "The Wedding March" in muted tones.

Smiling at me, Flo led the procession between the rows of chairs.

I noticed the dogs checking each row of guests, looking for an unfamiliar face. They saw none.

Then Savannah joined me at the altar. Flo and Charity took their places by her side.

As if they'd rehearsed it, Finn came and stood between me and Tank, while Woden took a spot between his charges.

"I've never seen any woman look as beautiful as you do right now," I said softly, looking down into eyes as blue as the Caribbean.

"Aw, that's sweet," she said, smiling mischievously. "But I think you're just turned on by the gun."

I smiled back and we turned to face Rusty.

"Friends and family," he began, "we're gathered here today to witness the union of Jesse and Savannah in marriage. If anyone here knows of any reason these two shouldn't be married, I'd advise you to keep your pie-hole shut. She ain't fooling around."

Everyone had seen the Derringer. There was nervous laughter from some of the assembled crowd.

"Do you have the rings?"

Tank produced a small box and opened it. My fingers shook as I removed the gold band and turned to Savannah.

"Place the ring on her left hand," Rusty instructed.

I did, and then Savannah took a ring from Flo and put it on my hand.

"The giving of rings symbolizes love," Rusty said. "It has no beginning, no middle, and no end. It just is. Jesse, do you take this woman to be your wife, forever and ever?"

"I do," I replied.

"And Savannah, do you take this man to be your husband for all time?"

"I do." Savannah smiled at me, as bright as the morning sun.

"That's all I need to hear," Rusty said. "By the power vested in me by the great state of Florida, I say you are husband and wife. Jesse, you may kiss your bride."

Savannah turned and handed her bouquet to Flo, then melted into my arms, kissing me with a passion she'd never shown in public.

"Ladies and gentlemen," Rusty shouted over the cheers, "I present to you, the McDermitts; Jesse, Savannah, and Florence."

We didn't want to make a big deal about it but the day before, Flo had gone to the courthouse and changed her name, taking the one she should have had since birth.

Tables were quickly covered with food as Rufus directed a work force of fishing guides.

The party was starting.

Later, as Savannah and I were talking to my daughters, Eve and Kim, and their spouses, Nick and Marty, Rufus made his way over to us. He smiled, clasping his hands in front.

"Dis is a great day, Cap'n Jesse and Miss Savannah. I and I thought dat it would nevah come. Di start of a new *adventuh*."

"Thank you, Rufus," Savannah said, hugging the slight old man. "It's very sweet of you."

"Yes," I added, "and thanks for all the work you put into this."

"Di work have only begun," he said. "You will have many happy years; di gods have told me dis. But it will take work. Remember dat not all storms come to disrupt yuh life. Some come to clear di path."

EPILOGUE

We partied with our family at the Anchor throughout the day. Then, as the sun began to dip toward the western horizon and the Cold Moon rose to the east, Savannah and I slipped away.

That night, the new year arrived as we made love on the Grady's padded foredeck under the stars. We spent most of the night in each other's arms, anchored in the Gulf half a mile north of the Contents, watching the stars and drinking a vintage wine.

We spent the next two days alone on the island. Our island. Cut off from everyone but each other. We walked hand-in-hand from island to sandbar to island, splashing through the shallows and collapsing on the sand.

Flo stayed on *Sea Biscuit* with Tank and the dogs. We checked in with her each day and the first morning, she reported that Chyrel had come and picked Tank up.

The house the real estate agent took him and Chyrel to see was on Grassy Key and was exactly what Tank was looking for. The price was under his budget and he didn't bother to negotiate it lower.

"Offers and counter-offers take weeks," he explained to us when we'd returned from our brief honeymoon.

While we were gone, Chyrel and Charity helped him pick out new furniture, and as soon as the couch was delivered, he sat Chyrel on it and asked her to be his wife.

What the terms of the marriage were to be and how far it extended, I didn't know and didn't ask. But I could tell Chyrel cared for him and she made him laugh. In the end, that's all that really mattered. They went to the courthouse the following day and had the judge marry them.

Returning to that shack, deep in the Glades, wasn't something any of us relished. But four days after the wedding, that's exactly what we did.

Chyrel had dug into Vanessa Ramos's past and found that she had no living relatives and only a small handful of friends. We invited the friends, but only two agreed to go with us. Cobie, Donna, and Manny, along with Michelle Tate and her husband joined us.

Out there in the marsh, we doused the interior of Willy Quick's SUV with gas and pushed it under the shack before torching them both.

None of us knew Vanessa, except the two friends who'd agreed to come. One of them said a few words about the kind of friend she'd been and then Tony, whose father had been a preacher, said a prayer for the girl's soul, that she might find peace.

The following weekend, just a week after Savannah's and my wedding, I took the *Revenge* up to Singer Island, just north of Palm Beach, for the big sailfish tournament. The evening before the start, while Jimmy, Rusty, Tank and I prepped our gear, I got a call from Buck Reilly.

"You find what you were looking for yet?" Buck asked.

I leaned on the gunwale and looked to the south. "Nothing to my liking," I replied.

The truth was, I hadn't even looked for another plane yet. But Reilly was a shrewd businessman. If he knew his was the only game in town, the price would be higher.

"I have something for you," he said.

"Details? Price?"

"It's complicated."

"I remember it being complicated last time," I replied. "Is it always that way, Reilly?"

"I need your help. Here's the deal…"

He outlined what he needed done and, as luck would have it, my long-range trawler, *Floridablanca*, was only a day's sail away and was well equipped to handle the job. If things worked out well, I'd have a flying boat very soon.

We didn't do well in the tournament, at least not well enough to make the top four. But we had a great time just the same. Out of forty-two boats in the tournament and over a hundred anglers, nearly everyone hooked and released at least one sailfish. We only released three between us and Tank's was by far the biggest.

I went to see Cobie just after we'd returned from Singer Island. I'd taken her wakeboard with me to the tournament, dropping it off to a guy in Miami who built such things. I'd arranged for him to do a rush job and paid him a thousand dollars to make a board to the exact dimensions as the one Ty Sampson had made, only better, and with one small detail added.

When I brought it to her at their trailer on Grassy Key, she had a bandage over her left eye. I ignored it and handed her the board.

At first, she thought it was the same one.

"No," I assured her. "This one's almost like it, but better."

She examined the board, which was lying on the hood of her little blue car. She picked it up. "It's lighter."

"And more rigid," I said. "Balsa core with carbon fiber mat."

"What's this?" she asked, looking sideways at the board's nose.

I held it up, so the image painted on the tip was upright. "It's said that if you save a life, you're responsible for it."

When I moved the board in front of my face, covering one eye, she gasped. "It's a picture of your eye."

I moved the board to the side and winked. "I'll be watching you, Cobie."

She flung her arms around me and the tears began to flow. Finally, she broke free and picked up her new board. "The kids are gonna freak."

Then she turned to Donna and asked, "Can I take it over to Cable Park and try it out?"

I could see the fear in Donna's eyes. She'd almost lost her child and I knew she never wanted to let Cobie out of her sight again. Donna looked at me and I nodded.

"Be back in time for dinner," she said.

Cobie ran into the trailer to change.

"I took her to a cosmetic surgeon in Orlando," Donna said, explaining the bandage. "When I explained the circumstances, he agreed to perform the surgery immediately. It's almost healed, but she doesn't want to see it till it's gone. Thank you for that and for everything else. The scar would have been a constant reminder."

"She'll be okay," I said. "Give her time. I have a friend she should talk to and get to know."

"Oh?"

"Her name's Charity Styles. She was on the swim team in the Sydney Olympics and won a medal."

"I've heard of her."

"After 9/11, Charity became an Army helicopter pilot and flew missions in Afghanistan. She was shot down and captured by the Taliban."

Donna's hand went to her mouth.

I nodded somberly. "She endured the same thing Cobie went through. We work together sometimes."

"Work together?"

"After the Army, she became a cop in Miami, then worked for a while with Homeland Security. She's a martial arts expert in many disciplines and now works with my agency from time to time."

"She lives here in the Keys?" Donna asked, as Cobie came running out of the house.

"I won't be long," she said, giving her mother a hug. Then she turned to me. She'd removed the bandage and the scar was healing very well. "Thank you, Mister Mc-Dermitt."

Then, like a flash, she'd hopped in the little Ford and was driving away.

I looked beyond the flats just to the north, where an old sailboat rode at anchor about a hundred yards out.

"Charity doesn't exactly live anywhere," I said, in reply to Donna's question. "That's her boat out there, *Wind Dancer*. I've asked her to be Cobie's storm."

Donna looked puzzled. "Storm?"

"Something a wise old man told me," I replied mystically.

"Where is she?"

I shrugged. "Probably over at Cable Park."

The End

Don't miss the next exciting Jesse McDermitt novel, Rising Tide, to be released on April 26, 2021.

If you'd like to receive my newsletter, please sign up on my website:

WWW.WAYNESTINNETT.COM.

Every two weeks, I'll bring you insights into my private life and writing habits, with updates on what I'm working on, special deals I hear about, and new books by other authors that I'm reading.

The Charity Styles Caribbean Thriller Series

Merciless Charity
Ruthless Charity
Reckless Charity
Enduring Charity
Vigilant Charity

The Jesse McDermitt Caribbean Adventure Series

Fallen Out	*Rising Storm*
Fallen Palm	*Rising Fury*
Fallen Hunter	*Rising Force*
Fallen Pride	*Rising Charity*
Fallen Mangrove	*Rising Water*
Fallen King	*Rising Spirit*
Fallen Honor	*Rising Thunder*
Fallen Tide	*Rising Warrior*
Fallen Angel	*Rising Moon*
Fallen Hero	*Rising Tide*

THE GASPAR'S REVENGE SHIP'S STORE IS OPEN.

There, you can purchase all kinds of swag related to my books. You can find it at

WWW.GASPARS-REVENGE.COM

AFTERWORD

As I write these closing remarks, it is the morning of October 23, 2020. On this day in 1983, Islamic extremists detonated two truck bombs, which rocked the Marine barracks in Beirut, Lebanon, killing 307, including 220 of my fellow Marines. I think of them often; on a mission of peace, they were mostly young men with a full life ahead of them, cut short by Hezbollah cowards. I will never forget.

Knowing that I would finish this book some time around this day, I brought back an older character, Owen "Tank" Tankersley, who was with Jesse on that fateful day in 1983. This allowed me to explore Jesse's emotions more fully and try to explain why he is the way he is, what drives him to "stand up" when needed. I'm quite pleased with the result and hope you were too.

A special thanks to the people at Aurora Publicity who have made it possible for my books to now be purchased just about anywhere books are sold. Since earlier this year, they have slowly been introducing my books to a much wider audience.

Thanks also to Lala Projects for the seamless integration of my website and for the beard-o-meter. If you haven't seen it yet, check it out at www.waynestinnett.com. It's a hoot. When they learned I tend to let my beard grow between releases, they came up with this crazy idea to use my 'man-hair' growth as a progress bar of sorts.

As always, I give thanks to my wife and family for their support. Sometimes, even without knowing it, they contribute directly to the story. Greta is and always will be my anchor, holding me fast in turbulent waters.

I'll be sending the second draft to my beta team shortly, which is made up of long-time friends, fellow Marines, pilots, doctors, lawyers, fishermen, divers, and locals in the Fabulous Florida Keys. Without their knowledge and insight, this story would be kinda drab. We can thank Jason Hebert, Mike Ramsey, Glenn Hibbert, Dana Vihlen, Debbie Kocol, Alan Fader, Tom Crisp, John Trainer, Katy McKnight, Charles Hofbauer, Drew Mutch, Charles Hanner, Deg Priest, Rick Iossi, and Debbie Cross, for this not being so boring.

After my beta team, the manuscript goes to the desk of Marsha Zinberg with The Write Touch editing service. The two weeks she spends polishing my manuscripts is one of the most important steps to turn a story into a novel. Thanks also to my final proofreader, Donna Rich, who always has the last critical eye on my work.

Then the manuscript goes into the studio for audio-book recording. While Nick Sullivan doesn't read it with a critical eye to prose or grammar, he does find things that might be changed to make the overall listening experience, and by default, reading experience, even better.

The interior look of this book came from the formatting skills of Colleen Sheehan of Ampersand Book Interiors. Thanks also to my cover designer Shayne Rutherford, of Wicked Good Book Covers, who makes sure the outside look of the book catches the readers' eye.

As you can see, there are a lot of people involved in bringing you this story, but it all started with a story. A lot of my story ideas come straight from TV shows like Forensic Files, which Greta and I watch every evening. This novel is no exception. What happened to Cobie Murphy happens more often than you know and not usually with the same outcome.

Lastly, I owe a heart-felt thanks to you, my readers. Without your continued support of my work, none of this would have happened. You've made it possible for a 62-year old man to realize the dream of his 12-year old former self. Thank you.

Made in the USA
Coppell, TX
23 December 2020